AMONG THE DEAD

ALEX GRECO
ADA SERIES BOOK 1

BY
ROGER CANAFF

TITLE: Among The Dead

ISBN: 978-1-952991-00-4 (e-book)
ISBN: 978-1-7345724-9-0 (paperback)

Library of Congress Catalog Card Number: 2020910146

2nd Edition

*To Judge Robert K. Holdman, retired, without whom
I would have never discovered the Bronx,
its heartache and its magnificence.*

"My job as a prosecutor is to do justice, and justice is served
when a guilty man is convicted and an innocent man is not."
**-The Honorable Sonia Maria Sotomayor
Associate Justice, United States Supreme Court,
and Bronx native**

"We are all in a race for dear life:
that is to say, we are fugitives from death."
-Theodor Reik

ALSO BY ROGER CANAFF

BLEED THROUGH
Alex Greco Series Book 2

COPPERHEAD ROAD

PART I: SPRING

PROLOGUE: HECTOR

Thursday, April 7
E. 178th Street
44th Precinct
Bronx, New York
3:25 p.m.

The smell of blood drove the reality home. She could almost deny her own eyes, but not that smell. It was wet and tinny, like the rusty metal of her fire escape after a rain. It emanated from the young boy's body, crumpled in the bathtub, face up with his throat cleaved open.

Joseliz Perez, not quite twenty years old, was standing in the doorway of the little bathroom, stunned into an unbelieving silence. Her dark eyes were feeding her brain a vision it could scarcely absorb— the act of doing so felt like tiny razors cutting into her consciousness, sending her thoughts scattered and bleeding.

Bleeding. But it looked like Hector was no longer bleeding. It looked more like he had bled out, his vital fluid pooled around him and already congealing, creating a sickening, scarlet line around the tub.

The grip of her right hand, the knuckles growing white,

tightened on the side of the doorjamb. In her left hand was a lollipop she had brought for him. It fell and shattered on the tile floor, but she scarcely heard it.

Oh, God, no. Please.

Joseliz had a family, school and friends, but the truth was Hector had been her life. He was severely autistic, profound by any measure on the spectrum to the extent he could even be measured. She was a volunteer at the center where he received care, and for the most part his principal attendant and only companion.

And she had been *reaching* him. Almost anyone else would have given up on that, but Joseliz had pushed through with patience and skill she hadn't known she possessed. She understood this boy like no one else, their connection as deep and real as anything she had ever experienced. She had unlocked a part of this beautiful, helpless child no one thought possible. He had been trapped, but she was opening up the world to him, watching it awaken in his eyes like a new miracle, day after day.

But now those eyes were blank. His head lolled to the side, exposing a gaping wound across his neck. A cut so vicious white cartilage and yellowish ligaments showed through. He seemed impossibly still, like a doll in a pool of blood.

Joseliz felt her breath catch, the need to retch crawling up her throat. When she threw up, eyes clenched shut, she heard the vomit splattering on the tile. A few seconds later she was staring down onto what remained of her lunch. It was easier to view than what was in the tub. With a fortifying breath, she walked her gaze forward to where the clawfoot tub casted a shadow over the uneven surface of the old floor. She covered her mouth, turned, and ran, fleeing the little row-house, the front door banging wide open.

CHAPTER 1

The pain, framed with cruel precision around his late son Jordan, hit Alex like a brick. With a clenched fist, he waited for the wave of grief to pass. He collected himself quickly, burying the emotion the same way he did as an ADA when a juror's response, a detective's report, or even a witness' hollow look triggered something similar.

But in this case it wasn't about work. Instead it was a view of his former father-in-law, Jonah, at the bar of the steakhouse, frowning through reading glasses at a drink menu. He had forgotten about their meeting, mostly because he wanted to forget it, but that wasn't about Jonah. It was about the ache that, for Alex, Jonah was forever associated with.

It was undeniable, the resemblance between Jonah and Alex's son. Dara, Jordan's mother, had said so all the time; Jordan was Papa Jonah's reflection. He had the same frown line, the same look of consternation. Alex could almost hear Jordan himself saying "Daddy, don't be a crybaby." But that was just imagination, not memory. Jordan had never really spoken. That, like so many other things, had been denied him.

Giving himself a mental shake, Alex pasted a smile on his face and strode over to the bar. The older man rose to greet him with a hug. As always, Jonah looked impeccable in perfectly tailored clothes, this time a powder blue dress shirt and tan slacks. Jonah was kind looking and handsome, and at sixty-eight still enjoyed a full head of silver hair and a slim but appreciable build. He was rich, and he looked it.

"*Boychic*," Jonah said, smiling and using the Yiddish nickname for a beloved boy, usually a son or grandson. He looked Alex up and down as if he really were Jonah's son and not a man who had once, tragically, been married to his daughter. Alex was a big man, broad shouldered and handsome, with an old-school haircut that gave him a little bit of a Robert F. Kennedy look. Usually he tried to sweep it back, but a little shock of it nevertheless tended to flop down in a half-moon shape over his forehead.

"It's good to see you, Jonah," he said, and meant it. Theirs was an odd friendship, forged largely in horror and secrecy. But it had become quickly hard and fast. "Busy day, I forgot we were meeting." Up close now, Alex could see the age creeping into Jonah's face, the sad lines along his brow, a drooping of the lips. Jordan's death had let that in, he figured. They were both pretty much in the same boat that way.

"Don't worry, I had to be here anyway. So how are you?" Jonah stared at Alex with sharp, piercing eyes as his second martini arrived. They were at NYY Steak, the upscale restaurant inside Yankee Stadium. A game crowd would arrive within the hour, ready to be liquored up for the first pitch, but this steakhouse would lure less beer-bellied guys in jerseys and more hedge fund types in suits.

"It's his birthday," Alex said with a sigh. "How can I be?"

"Stupid question," he said, looking away. "I'm sorry."

"It's okay. How's Dara?"

"She's had a bad few weeks. Happens every year."

"I got a weird text from her the other day," Alex said. "Wasn't sure if it was a meds issue, or just the time of year."

"It is what it is," Jonah said with a shrug. "She's a survivor. Listen, let me buy you a drink."

"I'm on homicide duty," Alex said, patting the phone in his breast pocket. "Gotta stay dry."

"Feh, we've got to get you out of that office."

"I like it up here," Alex said, a grin finally appearing on his face. "The Bronx suits me." And it was true. Alex Greco had been at the District Attorney's Office, just up the hill from where he was meeting his ex's father, for a little over two years. In his previous life he had been a prosecutor in Alexandria, Virginia, just outside of Washington, D.C., where he had grown up with and married Jonah's daughter, despite the protests of everyone involved. New York was a move he had made after all of that had fallen apart. After Jordan was dead, and Dara and he were dissolving. It was a move Jonah had brokered for him because he desperately needed it. In particular, he needed a place that would swallow everything he had been before, leaving him blank, like a beach at dawn.

"The Bronx? Please. I grew up in the Marble Hill projects. Don't tell me about the Bronx."

"And look at you now," Alex said, patting his arm. "No need to worry, I'm doing okay."

"You're doing more than okay," Jonah said. "You're becoming a superstar very quickly. The Prince case was all over the press." *People v. Prince* was a brutal homicide Alex had tried successfully a few months earlier, and it had won him city-wide acclaim. "With that kind of momentum, I can get you something better. Look, the Bronx makes for an interesting experience, I'm sure. But it's a dead end, kid. Lousy conviction rate. Impossible juries. You're thirty-nine. That's exactly the place where the world is judging whether you're heading up the ladder or rounding a curve to head back down. Let me help you take another step forward. A federal office, maybe."

"I owe you too much already."

"We're even. At best," Jonah said, dead serious. The older man's eyes searched Alex's for a moment, wanting that to sink in. Before Alex could respond, his phone buzzed in his pocket. He looked and saw it was an office extension. Jonah excused himself to the men's room as Alex took the call.

"ADA. Greco."

"It's Raquel Silva," he heard. "Do you have the bag still?" The 'bag' meant the satchel senior ADA.'s carried when on homicide duty, still called "beeper duty" for the centrality of the beeper that used to summon them to crime scenes back in the day.

"I do, and I'm sober," he said half-jokingly. Raquel was the Chief of Special Victims, and not someone he worked with regularly, but he liked and respected her.

"Listen," she said. "Something came in. But it's really not your style, so I'm not sure I want to stick you with it."

"What is it?" She paused and he could hear her breathe out on the other end.

"Child homicide. It's bad. An autistic kid I think, eleven or twelve. Someone cut his throat ear-to-ear. Damn near took his head off." *Autistic.* The word sank into him with cold, mean familiarity. He shook it off.

"Where?"

"A row-house in the Four-Four." When cops and prosecutors referred to one of the eleven Bronx police precincts, they expressed them as two numbers side by side, so that the 44th was the "Four-Four," and so on. "I can ask Frank to go out on this, Alex."

"Rock, I'm fine. It's my job." Raquel, Alex knew, was more aware of his circumstances than most. He had shared with her that he'd lost a son, albeit without many details. Raquel had three children, and one of them, Alicia, had died of leukemia right around the time Alex joined the office. They had commiserated on it more than once.

"I lost a kid, too," she said quietly. "I get it." Alex felt his gut tighten and a wave of emotion rose through him. But this was work, and he choked it back.

"I know you do," he said. "But it's okay, I'll handle it. And I'm in the Four-Four, at Yankee Stadium. I can be there in ten."

"Okay," she said, and sounded relieved. He knew her unit had been busy lately, and she was probably short-handed. "Are you driving?"

"No, my car's in the city. I'll cab it."

"Hang on," she said. He heard her speak into another phone, probably her cell. Then she was back. "Danny Lopez will pick you up in front of gate six in ten minutes. He's in the Four-Four squad now, and he's catching it. Tip will want a briefing tonight, but take your time there." Tip Healy was the Chief of Homicide. If you caught a homicide on beeper duty, you talked to Tip before anyone else. If no one was dead, or at least not yet, you talked to Gerald Jackson, who was the Chief for Non-Fatal Major Assaults. Gerald dealt in the living, Tip in the dead.

"I'll call you later also," he said. "I'll brief you before you assign it to one of your people."

"I'd appreciate that," she said, and Alex could hear the smile in her voice. "I'll be here late. Thanks, Alex."

Jonah returned and seemed to read the look on the younger man's face.

"You gotta go, right?"

"I've got ten minutes," Alex said. "I'm sorry."

"It's okay. I'm meeting a couple guys here for the game anyway. So, who shot whom?"

"It wasn't that."

"Do I want to know what it was?"

"No," Alex said with a sad smile. "You really don't. So, what's this about, Jonah? What's troubling you?" Jonah sighed, and stirred his drink.

"I just want you to be happy up here. You deserve that."

"Thank you. But what else is going on? Tell me."

"You know there's an election for Commonwealth's Attorney next year," he said at low volume, even though that didn't seem to matter in the environment they were in. "Back home."

"Of course, I know," Alex said. The Commonwealth Attorney was the chief prosecutor in Alexandria. It was the job Alex was seen as the heir-apparent for when he had Dara and Jordan by his side and a much different life in front of him. "I'm not going back there, believe me."

"You could if you wanted to," Jonah said. "There are a few people down there who'd like to recruit you to come back and run. You still have friends, and they remember how it was supposed to happen."

"That was another life. It's gone now. Anyway, don't you

know I'd come to you first if I was considering something like that?"

"I know," he said. He seemed almost ashamed. "And I'm sorry for what this looks like. Like I'm trying to keep you in New York."

"You're looking out for me. You know I'm better off up here. I know it too."

"I worry about the past, that's all," Jonah said. "About some asshole down there digging it up if you ever did go back." Alex tensed. *The past. Again.* It was amazing, after nearly three years and a string of successes, how close he could still feel to old hurts. And threats.

Then Jonah leaned in, waiting until Alex's eyes were on his before he spoke again. "But listen to me. If you did want to return? I'd back you as hard as I did when you were my son-in-law. It's you I worry about, not me. I know they don't scare you. But I know they can't touch me." A smile at that point, a sardonic grin even, would have been inappropriate, but Alex hid one just below the surface regardless. Jonah Schwartz was, in street terms, 'a swingin' dick.' He was wildly successful, powerful, and philanthropic. He was also controversial.

"I'm where I belong, Jonah. But thank you. Listen, I've gotta run. How long are you in the city for?" Jonah still lived most of the time in Alexandria, but he had a lavish apartment in Manhattan.

"Just until tomorrow. But keep in touch, okay? We'll talk more. I'm still moving you up when the time is right."

They said their goodbyes, and Alex made his way through the still quiet, echoing stadium down to the street. The air outside was cool but fresh and spring-like, even in the South Bronx. He molded himself into work mode as the steps receded behind him, pushing out the cares of the day and even the burden of memory that Jonah had brought back. He was practiced at this, shutting out distractions and opening his mind to the task at hand. Usually, that task was a homicide. This was, he told himself, just another one. But it was also a child case, and he didn't like those. Deeper still was one word that kept punching up through his thoughts, a word he loathed and knew intimately at the same time. A word that, like the past itself, wouldn't seem to let him be.

Autistic.

CHAPTER 2

4:11 p.m.

"It's fucked up man," Danny, the Four-Four squad detective, said over the squawking police radio as they sped north on Jerome Avenue, away from the stadium. "You're catchin' it, right?"

"No," Alex said, a little more forcefully then he intended. "I'm just on homicide duty. Not sure who it'll be assigned to."

"We could use a good D.A. on it," Danny said, giving Alex a sideways grin. The two didn't know each other well but had worked on a sex assault case when Alex had first arrived at the office and Danny was in the Bronx Special Victims squad. Although they came from very different backgrounds, they clicked instantly and had stayed in touch ever since.

"Plenty of good people over there," Alex said, returning the grin. Danny shrugged.

"We'd rather have you. Sean was happy when I told him you were going out on it. But he said you probably wouldn't want to keep it."

"Sean?"

"Yeah, Sean Regan. He's coming in from homicide."

"Oh yeah," Alex said, nodding in recognition. Alex worked in a newly formed, elite unit in the office that prosecuted homicides exclusively. He had worked with Sean on several cases. "Good guy. Quiet. And no ego."

"Correct. Sean wouldn't say 'shit' if he had a mouthful of it."

"But he said I wouldn't want it?" Alex asked, his brow knitted. The truth was, Alex avoided child cases for very private reasons, but he assumed that fact was unknown, at least to anyone but Raquel. And even she didn't know the real reason.

"Yeah, he said you don't like kid cases. That was his take, anyway."

"Huh. Okay." It could have been more unsettling, but ultimately it didn't bother Alex that Sean might have seen something in him and gotten that impression. The guy was a detective, after all. "Where's he now?"

"He's with the kid's father at the precinct. They'll meet with a victim-witness rep from your office. We'll meet them at the Four-Four after you see the place."

Homicides in the Bronx were usually responded to by squad detectives in the precinct where they occurred. The squad guys were supported by one or more detectives from Bronx Homicide, a specialized detective group that worked borough-wide.

At thirty-three, Danny was young for a full squad detective. His rise through the ranks had been swift, due mostly to hard work and a little luck. He was great with victims, especially kids, funny, and dangerously charming. Alex's female friends in the office seemed to view him as not classically handsome exactly, but with remarkable sex appeal. He had a well-shaped face, but with small eyes that seemed perpetually squinting, and he was usually a few days away from a decent shave–a look the ladies in Danny's life seemed to appreciate. Italian-American on his mother's side and Dominican on his father's, he was not tall, but blessed with a muscular and angular build. He was also covered in tattoos, the two most prominent being the rosary beads that went around his neck meeting above a large crucifix in the middle of his chest, and his first name spelled out in a gothic font down his right forearm.

"Where did Sean find the father?" Alex asked.

"A hardware store a few blocks away. A neighbor had his cell number and called him."

"Where's the mother?"

"Dead, I think. The father is a, whaddayacallit? Widower. I'm still putting it together, but I don't think she's in the picture."

"So who found the kid?"

"A volunteer from a community center up on the concourse where he goes. She had a key to the place. Came in to read to him or feed him or something. Found him in the tub."

"No signs of forced entry?"

"No. Everything looked undisturbed."

"The victim. Raquel said he was eleven or twelve."

"Yeah, eleven I think, but like... I don't know. Autistic or something."

"Autism, I heard," Alex said. "I'm familiar with the condition, if that's what it was."

"He was pretty low functioning, whatever it was." As he spoke, Danny navigated Jerome Avenue like a NASCAR driver during casual practice. Above them, the elevated tracks of the "four" subway line shaded the sun and occasionally provided the racket of a passing train they had to shout over. In front of them kids, mothers pushing strollers, vendors pushing carts, and countless others crossed the streets and avoided the cars–like Danny's–weaving in and out of the lanes and around the stout iron and concrete posts of the subway. Alex had gotten used to driving with NYPD detectives in his first few weeks on the job.

"So is the volunteer a suspect?" Alex asked. He was beginning to sort the facts he was hearing, organizing them in his mind. Danny waived him off.

"Nah, I don't think so," he said, shaking his head. "*Pobrecita*, she's just a kid. She's completely freaked out. The father should've been there when the girl came over, too. He wasn't supposed to be left alone at all." Danny cursed quietly in Spanish as he narrowly avoided a couple of teenagers strutting across the avenue. He took a right and they began down another, less crowded block.

"OK. So the father's a suspect. For now, anyway."

"Oh yeah," Danny said. "My guess is, he's the guy. That's one shitty thing I've learned."

"What is?"

"When a kid's murdered, it's usually family." Alex felt a mental slap, almost recoiling with it. He absorbed it silently and stared straight ahead. They were almost there.

The row-house where Hector Ruiz spent the last months of his difficult life was fairly typical for the Bronx. Somewhere between fifty and eighty years old, the outside was wood paneled and painted a dull, peeling white. Three red-painted concrete stairs led from just inside a rusty chain-link gate to a small porch. The front door was a faded brown with a diamond shaped window at chest level. The Ruiz house was the last in a motley, tightly-pressed row of seven. On the open side was a narrow alley that ran back to a small parking area and a side door.

Danny parked after weaving through the various vehicles—fire trucks, an ambulance, and several Four-Four patrol cars—while holding his detective shield out the window. In front of the house, officers waited on the sidewalks and jawed with each other.

The scene, to Alex, was impressive. Even in a place like the Bronx where violent death was sometimes sadly common, there was no lack of a public service response to it. There were a handful of firefighters as well as the police, and EMTs from nearby Lincoln Hospital. The boy in the tub, though, most surely wouldn't make a stop at Lincoln. Instead the EMTs would "call death" on the scene, and he'd go directly to the Office of the Chief Medical Examiner for processing and autopsy. OCME would respond after the EMTs cleared the scene and the detectives and the Crime Scene Unit had done their work.

Inside, a police lieutenant was in a neat but sterile-looking living area, the part of the house Alex's grandmother would have called the "front room." There was a sofa and a couple of stiff-looking padded chairs surrounding a coffee table with a yellowing doily on it, all seemingly untouched for God-knew-how-long. This was where, maybe, you brought company, but it wasn't where kids were allowed to play. Beyond it was the entrance to the kitchen, straight ahead from the front door. To the left was a narrow hallway that led to the bedrooms and the bathroom. Alex could hear crime scene guys milling around and snapping pictures back there.

The lieutenant was talking to a young, red-haired, stout patrol officer. As Alex would soon find out, he was the first responder, a rookie named Murphy, whom Joseliz found at the corner.

"You doing okay?" Alex asked the officer. The cop looked at him quizzically, as if it was an odd first question.

"Sir? Yeah. Just a bad scene."

"I'm sure. Anyone else been inside?"

"No. From the time I found him until investigations got here, it was just me. The door was open while the girl was looking for a cop though."

"Open like wide open?"

"Yeah. She just… panicked I guess. Ran out."

"I don't blame her," Alex said glancing toward the door. "Where is she now?"

"She's in an ambulance," the lieutenant answered. "EMTs are looking at her, she was kind of in shock." He nodded in Danny's direction. "Lopez, you want to show him the body?"

"Yeah let's do that before OCME gets here," Danny said, looking back at Alex. "Ready for this?" Danny, of course, had no idea how loaded the question was for Alex, let alone on Jordan's goddam birthday. But Alex had been steeling himself for what was coming next during the whole, white-knuckle car ride over. At the end of the day, this was his job, he loved it and was good at it. It was time to work, and that was a good thing.

Yes, but the kid is autistic. Scratch that: Was.

"Lead the way."

The boy had been a beautiful child, although small for his age. Alex could tell that much as he knelt carefully beside the tub, once the crime scene photographer gave him room. His body was slender and well-proportioned, the skin smooth. Around it, there was no water in the tub, only a quickly congealing pool of blood. Dressed in loose-fitting khaki trousers and a soccer T-shirt, his eyes, still open, were a chestnut color, deep-set beneath a strong brow and thick black eyebrows. He had the kind of eyelashes most women covet, naturally and luxuriously long and arching. His mouth was parted and his tongue rested against his lower lip.

The tub, Alex noticed, wasn't a standard one that ran the length of the wall. Instead it was a porcelain clawfoot model, the kind a person would expect to see in an old home, although this particular one looked relatively new. Hector's head rested against the slanted surface opposite the hot and cold spigots. An opaque shower curtain hung from a track attached to the ceiling and was bunched up on the spigot side. About eighteen inches of space separated the end of the tub where the boy's head rested and the radiator and wall behind it.

"There're pieces of candy on the floor," Alex said. "You see it? That yellow stuff."

"Yeah that was a lollipop," Danny said. He was standing in the bathroom doorway. "The stick slid under the tub. She brought it for him. Dropped it when she saw him."

"Ah. OK." Alex moved his eyes slowly across the scene, left to right. "No sign of a struggle, right? Nothing to indicate he was pushed into the tub? No defensive wounds?"

"No, nothing," Danny said. "It's more like he was dozing in an empty tub when the perp came up on him. Never saw it coming. Could be the guy pulled his hair back, then brought a blade across. He's got a thick head of hair. Looks like a bit of it was grabbed. You see that?" Alex looked;

sure enough, there was a tuft of hair somewhat out of place, as if it had been pulled together in a clump.

"Shit. Yeah. Like a quick, one-two motion?"

"Possibly. Pull the head back, draw the blade across. At this point, I'd say it was a razor or a box cutter. Went through him like butter."

"From here, maybe?" Alex asked, pointing to the space behind the tub.

"Yeah, exactly. Perp could've stepped behind him, just like that. It would have been tight for a man, but not impossible."

Alex stood up, relieving the strain on his hamstrings. The smell of blood was in his nostrils, metallic and rusty, and it mixed with the girl's puke. "I think you're right. Looks like a fucking assassination."

"It's the only thing that makes sense, so far at least. For his sake I hope he went quick, but I don't know. I saw a guy once who'd just gotten his throat slit. It was a gang thing when I was on patrol. We came up just as the perp took off. There wasn't a goddam thing we could do for him, but his eyes were going back and forth between me and my partner. Like begging."

"Remind me to get you to read bedtime stories to my niece and nephew," Alex said. Then Danny's phone went off. It was Sean Regan, calling from the precinct's squad room.

"Sean says the father will talk to us," Danny said after hanging up.

"Any vibe from him so far?"

"Sean says he seems like he's in shock, but not hysterical. We'll see. What's up, you with us on this?"

"Yeah, for the evening anyway. You'll do the initial interview of him, right?"

"Looks like it."

"Okay, I'll observe. Gimme a minute, I'll be right out."

In the small, drab kitchen where the dead boy's meals had presumably been prepared, Alex felt the assault of memory all around him. The home he had shared with Dara and Jordan had been bigger and neater than this one, but not dissimilar in structure. Jonah would have set them up anywhere, but Alex had insisted on making his own way with his wife and child. That could have driven them apart, him and Jonah, and it might have, except for what happened later.

Out of the corner of his eye, he caught sight of a bright-red toy fire truck pushed half-way under the old refrigerator. He pulled it out and inspected it. It was die-cast metal and had the FDNY insignia on it. Jordan had played with police and fire vehicles also; they were some of the only things he didn't smash together in a rage. He had been enraptured with toy cars more than anything, and sometimes handled them with surprising care and dexterity. It was love, maybe. The only kind Jordan could express. Alex squeezed his eyes shut and breathed deeply. He sat again on his haunches, his tie almost touching the kitchen floor, and waited for the grief to pass. Then he looked at the fire truck again, turning it slowly in his right hand. He stood and looked back at the small crowd of men and women attending to the horror behind him, talking on phones and radios. Snapping pictures. Scribbling on pads. This is what they did. And they were brothers and sisters to him. This thought led to another one, not entirely unexpected but intrusive nonetheless.

I should ask Raquel for this case.

His pulse thrummed in his throat. The thought of

taking the case felt like lead slipping down into his gut. There were many prosecutors who didn't like kid cases, but he had more of a reason than most.

It wasn't that he gravitated toward easy cases. Far from it, he loved the challenge of getting juries—especially in the Bronx—to value things like gang homicides, which often involved interchangeable parties of who was shooting or stabbing whom. But Alex could work them, finding empathy and substance in the witnesses, the families, even the suspects. He did so as a technician, though, through a cold professional lens and from a healthy emotional distance. This case, with a dead little boy at its center, could close that distance quickly.

Still, he had a good working relationship with Danny already. If the boy was, in fact, autistic, then he understood the mental and medical issues better than most. And, he was right there. On the ground floor.

So you're right for it. But you'll run from it anyway. It was a familiar, scolding, internal voice.

No, you're being ridiculous, another voice spoke up. *Raquel will have competition for it from her own senior people. It's not an option anyway, so it's not worth beating yourself up about.*

But it didn't feel that way. He knew Special Victims was slammed with cases lately. If Raquel had had a senior ADA ready to take a case like this, she probably would have sent that person out even though Alex was technically on homicide duty. Eventually he stopped arguing with himself. Better to do the job that was before him. And right now, that job was to observe Danny Lopez and the boy's father at the precinct. What the man said, if anything, would set the stage for what was to come.

CHAPTER 3

44th Precinct House, NYPD
2 E. 169st Street
5:07 p.m.

The murdered boy's father was a graying, compact-look-ing man of average height. He sat slumped forward in the chair of the main Four-Four interview room as if he was out of breath. From behind one-way glass, Alex watched with his arms folded as Danny conducted an as-of-yet informal interview, just off of the detective's squad room on the second floor. The room was bare except for sound-proofing panels, and painted an uninspiring pale green, which matched the squad room itself. A speaker in the interview room allowed Alex to hear the conversation in an artificial and boxed tone.

Norman Ruiz looked older than he was and had proba-bly put on a few pounds in recent years, but he had strong, fine features, not unlike the graceful ones his son had possessed. He had been handsome when he was young, Alex figured. He had one muscular forearm resting on the table, the other on his thigh. He shook his head from time to time and shrugged to quite a few of Danny's questions.

He definitely wasn't hysterical and didn't seem grief stricken, but Alex had been in the business long enough to know that trauma, and its psycho-physiological companion shock, could create misleading appearances. More than anything, Norman looked bewildered.

So far, they had mostly clarified timelines. Norman told Danny he had gotten off work early, picked Hector up from school and gotten home around 2:00 p.m. Thursdays, he said, were early days for him, so he often picked Hector up from school. His story was that he made lunch for Hector and then left again on some brief errands after the boy had fallen asleep, apparently in the bathtub. He was pretty sure he had left a little after 3:00 p.m.

"Is there anything you can remember, or we can check, that would indicate exactly when you left, Mr. Ruiz?" Danny asked. "Like a text you sent, or the clock in the car you noticed?"

He paused, and then said, "No, I can't think of nothing. I had an errand. I went out. Around three o'clock, like I said."

"What was the errand?" At this, Ruiz squinted at Danny.

"What does that matter?"

"Sir, it all matters. All the facts. What was it you went out to do?"

"I had some money to pick up. From a guy who owed it to me. I picked it up where he told me to pick it up. Then I went to the hardware store, a few blocks from my house. That's where they found me, the police."

"Okay. Let me ask you about the tub where your son was found. Do you know your son was fully dressed when he was found there?"

"Yeah, so?"

"Well, we need to know why. Why would he just be

lying in a bathtub in the middle of the day with all of his clothes on?"

"I wish I could tell you. Why did he go there? He liked it. Felt safe, maybe. I have no idea. When I first brought him here, he'd go in one of the closets. Wouldn't come out. So now it's the tub. Next month, maybe a closet again. What do I know?"

"Okay, so what would he do when he was lying there?"

"Nothing. He didn't say much. He didn't do much. But sometimes he fell asleep there. Lately, more and more, he was going to the tub and just climbing in. That's what happened today. Then he fell asleep. After that I left."

"Why did you leave him alone?"

"Well, he was asleep. You don't know my son. When he's asleep, a bomb could go off. Nothing wakes him. He fell asleep in the tub. He was happy and he was fine. So I left. I was coming right back. What, that makes me a murderer?"

"Of course not. But my understanding is that Hector wasn't supposed to be left alone at all."

"You try to raise my son," Ruiz said, looking up at Danny, and then beyond him to the one-way glass where Alex stood. "You be there one-hundred-percent of the time. You can't so much as go to the bathroom. You can't go out to get the papers."

"I'm not judging you, Mr. Ruiz, I'm just trying to understand what happened."

"What happened is I left my son. Safe and sleeping. In my own house for a few minutes to run two errands. Then someone comes in behind me and cuts his throat. That's what happened."

"Is there anyone you can think of who might want to hurt your son?" Danny asked. "For any reason?" At this,

Norman became very still, staring in front of him. Then, slowly, he shook his head.

"I've made mistakes," he said. "I've gotten mixed up with some bad people. But I can't think of anyone who would do this."

"Do you have enemies?"

"I have people who don't like me," he said with a tired shrug. "My wife's family, they hate me. But someone who would do this? I don't know. I just...don't know."

Alex and Sean chased down some other details while Danny finished that first interview. Danny also secured Ruiz's consent to a search of his house, his car, and his boat, and also to collect his clothing for analysis. Ruiz was a truck driver for an ice company in Westchester, and confirmed he had no plans to leave the area. There was a co-worker he could stay with until he could arrange for the cleaning of the scene and move back into the house he had shared with Hector.

Alex and Sean stood a few feet away as Danny gave him some details about accessing services and claiming his son's body, eventually, from the morgue. Like many crime victims Alex had seen over time, trapped in the confines of an environment they never imagined seeing outside of a television show, he looked overwhelmed and a little spacy.

"We're sorry we have to keep the car for now," Danny said to Ruiz. "I'll be in touch when it's released. Do you have transportation in the meantime?"

"I got a friend with a car I can use," he said. "He's coming with clothes for me to change into, then you can have mine. They're just work clothes."

"Please tell the desk sergeant when your friend gets here," Danny said. "We'll get you out of here as soon as we can." Ruiz nodded, and his eyes roamed over his surroundings. Finally, they settled on Alex, who had turned back to his phone to check messages.

"I didn't do this thing," he said, taking a step toward Alex, eyes wide and searching.

"I'm an assistant district attorney, Mr. Ruiz," Alex said. He glanced over toward Danny and Sean to make sure at least one of them was alert to the conversation and properly witnessing it. "I'm very sorry for your loss, but it's best you don't talk to me."

"But they think I killed him. Do you?"

"I don't think anything, Mr. Ruiz. And I'm sorry, but I really can't speak with you." With that, Alex walked past the two detectives and gave them a minute eye-roll. "Please write that up," he said. Danny nodded.

Alex turned to his phone again, this time to call Raquel and give her an update. Then he paused, his thumb shadowing the call button. He had felt a pang of concern when Ruiz started speaking to him, but it wasn't any reaction to the man himself or the circumstances. Instead, he had been concerned because he knew if Ruiz got him alone and started making statements to him, he'd be completely ineligible to prosecute the case. No prosecutor can keep a case if he or she becomes a witness to a relevant event, like a defendant blurting out something no one else was around to hear. So that meant he wanted it on some level. Or probably more to the point, he felt he should take it. At least ask for it.

Oh really? You think asking for this shit-show is a good idea?

The argument in his head threatened to begin again, but this time Alex cut it short. The decision, in his mind at least, was made. Raquel answered on the first ring.

"Raquel, it's Alex."

"Hey, Alex. How does it look? You guys like the father for it?" Like a lot of ADA.'s, Raquel had picked up cop jargon over the years.

"He's a suspect, but we're keeping our minds open. Listen, have you assigned this one yet?"

"No. Frankly I'm not sure what I'm going to do. Normally I'd have at least one or two people competing for it, but everyone is crazy busy right now." She paused. "Why?"

"I want it," he said. "If you'll give it to me."

"Are you sure? If the father ends up being charged, it'll be tough for a top count conviction. It's more likely to end up in a disappointing plea. And that's assuming we ever make an arrest."

"I have a handle on some of the background issues," he said. "And I'm getting a feel for it already. Completely up to you, but I'm willing to take it on, and I'm up for it." Alex listened as Raquel seemed to mull it over on the other end. He knew he was probably the best trial attorney in the office for his level of experience, and he knew Raquel knew it also. If he wanted the case, it was good for everyone involved. Except maybe him.

"Okay," she said finally. "I'll call Gregg." Gregg Rosenthal was the chief of Alex's homicide bureau. "As long as he okay's it, it's yours. Good luck. And Alex? Take care of yourself. Take inventory from time to time. Okay?"

"I will."

10:35 p.m.

"The mother never made it here," Danny said as he, Sean, and Alex sat in a tiny and excellent Italian restaurant in an area of the Bronx called Morris Park, in the Four-Nine. No one had eaten for most of the day, and they were all famished. Danny and Sean were still on duty, but that didn't stop most detectives from having a glass of wine or a beer with dinner. And sometimes more than that.

"Never made it? From where?"

"The D.R. That's where the kid was born. It's where Norman got her pregnant."

"Dominican Republic? But Norman's a U.S. citizen."

"Sure," Danny said. "He was naturalized. But these guys, it's what they do if they can afford it. They go back. They bring money, see family, whatever. Norman, it looks like he went back once, maybe twice a year. One of those times he hooked up with the kid's mother, Bianca Garcia. The families know each other. Then he came back, once or twice. Then she was pregnant."

"And he didn't bring her back," Sean said, not really a question.

"No. Looks like he never legally acknowledged paternity. I think he heard about it, or she reached out to him. He says he sent money though."

"The ASD," Alex said, "sorry, the autism. It's called Autism Spectrum Disorder sometimes. That was determined over there?"

"Sort of. He said it was discovered when the kid was around two. She—the mother, Bianca—worked at a T-shirt plant outside of Santo Domingo. The kid was in daycare. One day the daycare lady said he was... what's the word? Losing language. Not paying attention to stuff anymore. Not looking at her. Or anyone."

"Regressing," Alex said, taking a big gulp of red wine. "That happens sometimes. The kid seems normal, and then..."

"Shit," Sean said, shaking his head. "My sons can be thick-headed, but I can't even imagine."

"It's bad yeah," Alex said. "So then what?"

"So there's a doctor she went to in Santo Domingo. He lives in New York, but he has an office there. He told her it was probably autism, but Norman says he never heard about a formal diagnosis."

"It's a team diagnosis, sometimes," Alex said. "I don't know where she would have gone over there."

"Nowhere," Danny said, shaking his head. "There are a few services you can get for a disabled kid over there, but not many. As far as Norman knows, she just took him home. She had to pay extra for the daycare people to deal with him. There wasn't anything left after that. No school, nothing.

"Then she got sick. Cancer. She was diagnosed over there when Hector was about eight. She got worse, so finally he went over around Thanksgiving, year before last. The plan was to bring them both back, and maybe get her some better care here. He married her over there, but she died like a month later. He came back here with Hector around New Year's, going into last year. Since then he's been raising him alone." Danny paused, and pulled out a notepad. "He says Bianca has a brother here, Rolando, who's been around from time to time, although they don't get along. I'll find him. And there's this community center, or something, that's been involved with the family for a while. HCC, he called it. That's where the volunteer came from. Joseliz."

"There's services in place on this side, right?" Alex asked. "There has to be." He was mentally adjusting as the task at hand was once again prying open the door of his mind, ushering in the dark things. The whisperings. He swallowed the distracting memories, for now, with more wine. Danny was answering him, saying something about services he got through the city schools.

"There's someone who comes every morning, gets him ready, and takes him to school," Danny continued. "Someone else takes him back. His father picked him from school today though. He got off work early, so he picked him up and they got home around two o'clock."

"And this girl who found him, Joseliz?" Alex said.

"She's a student. Bronx Community College. She wants to study special education, work with kids like him. She met him as a volunteer, but she's there a few times a week. She reads to him, cleans him up, stuff like that." Alex was vaguely aware of how Danny was talking about Hector, the dead boy, as if he was still alive. A few detectives he knew did that, spoke in a sort of historical present tense. Maybe it helped them piece things together.

"I'll start looking into the services tomorrow," Alex said. "Anything else stand out about today?"

"One thing I thought smelled funny," Danny said. He opened his notebook and flipped to a page. "Before I ended the interview I asked about the money Ruiz went to pick up, the thing he said he did before the hardware store. He wasn't happy talking about it, but he said he got a text around two o'clock from some guy who owed him a few bucks. He said he didn't recognize the number, but that he does side jobs for different people, so he figured it was one of those. He couldn't give me any names, though. Said he wasn't sure who it was. Maybe it was shock, whatever. Anyway, he showed me the text. It was from a seven-one-eight number, and it was two lines. One was the name of a used tire place near the Mt. Eden subway station, and the amount waiting for him. The other was a time, three-fifteen. He said he figured that was the pick-up time, so he went, and there it was. The guy at the tire place had an envelope with his name on it. He took it and left. I asked to see it, and he showed me a white envelope with his first and last name on it. I didn't ask to count it, but it had maybe two hundred bucks in it."

"You got the phone number, right?" Alex asked.

"Yeah, I took a picture of his screen and wrote it down. I'll run it tomorrow, but I wouldn't be surprised if it comes back to a burner."

"You think he's mobbed up?" Sean asked.

"Maybe. It could be nothing, but I wouldn't be surprised if he's got something going on he'd rather us not know about."

"I've only been here a couple of years," Alex said. "But it seems like there's a lot of that going on around here." At this, both Danny and Sean chuckled in agreement. "We'll keep it in mind, I guess. What about the searches?"

"The house and boat we'll get to tomorrow," Danny said. "We've got guys on both places for now."

"Terrific." Alex downed the last of his wine. The emotional ache that had been pulsing through him all day was now being eclipsed by simple fatigue. All other things aside, it had been a hell of a long day. "We should consider other suspects, too. Anyone even on the radar?"

"Not at the moment," Danny said. "But there's this Rolando guy, who's the brother-in-law. We'll see what the searches produce also. Come on, Alex, we'll run you back to the city. You've got to be beat."

Sean and Danny sped Alex back to Manhattan in Sean's city car just before 11:00 p.m., slipping through the occasional red light and then barreling down the West Side Highway at a breakneck but somehow relaxed pace. Cool air rushed in through open windows, damp with the Hudson River sliding by to the right and reflecting the lights on the Jersey side. To the left were the towering electronic billboards and brick structures of the west side. The two cops gossiped along the way and bitched about the usual things, NYPD politics and the so far dismally performing Yankees. They were very different, but both likable and bright. Danny was young, energetic, and reliably irreverent. Sean, a fourth generation Irish-American cop, was in his early forties but looked like an older man with sad gray eyes and a drawn quality to an otherwise pleasant and kind face. Alex thanked them as he climbed out of the backseat, happy about the hand he had been dealt with these two as his primary detectives.

"You got someone up there, waitin' for ya?" Danny asked with a wink as Alex stretched to his full height. They were in front of his apartment building, a late nineteenth century, five floor, tenement walk-up, classic to the neighborhood. It was the kind of place that, not three years before, Alex would have never imagined himself living.

"No such luck. You guys be careful. And thanks."

They peeled off down the block and Alex lit a cigarette, his first since waking and one he could have used much earlier, although he was trying with some success to cut back. He stood in scuffed dress shoes that now pinched his feet, enjoying the smoke and the happily mild April weather. Two older men Alex had seen before strolled past him hand in hand, walking a tiny black dog. They were staples of his Hell's Kitchen neighborhood and he was pretty sure they were both retired actors. They nodded in his direction, and he nodded back and smiled.

"Someone had a very long day," the taller of the two said. "Put that out and get some rest, honey."

"That's good advice. Have a great night guys."

They walked on and he was alone on the street again, his block shadowy and yellow-lit with sodium street lamps. There was an edge to his thoughts as he considered his new circumstances. In an almost disciplined fashion, he waited for something else shitty to float to the surface—fresh worry about what Jonah had said earlier, or dull hurt as Jordan's latest non-birthday slipped into yesterday. But nothing stepped forward. The dark things were, for now, at bay. He looked around with quiet contentment. The buzzing, groaning city around him, the city he had fled to for cover and solace, was doing its job. He crushed out the cigarette and climbed his stoop.

In retrospect, he should have known it wouldn't pass that easily. Jordan somehow wouldn't allow it. And Dara certainly wouldn't. Her call woke him out of a sound sleep at 2:12 a.m., occurring to him first as pounding on a thick wooden door in a dream. In the darkness of his small bedroom he fished around for the phone and knocked it off the nightstand. He cursed and followed it to the floor, slumping to a seated position in his boxers between the bed and the wall, just below a narrow window. The window looked out into the alley between his building and the one next to it, but there was a thin slice of sky that reached through. In it, he saw a couple of dim, hazy stars.

"Dara," he breathed into the phone, "Jesus. Are you okay?"

"I... saw Marnie Solomon's son yesterday," she said,

panting into the phone. She sounded like she might hyperventilate. "He's s-s-s-s..."

"Six," Alex whispered, wiping his nose with his other hand. The same age Jordan would have been on April 7th, the day that had just passed.

"I'm so sorry, Alex. I just... don't have anyone to talk to."

"It's okay."

"What did you do today? Well, yesterday I mean."

"I worked," he said. "Just worked. I saw your father, for a few minutes. He looks good."

"He's up there for some meeting," she said, and then paused to blow her nose. "Is work okay?"

"Work? Uh, yeah. It's fine."

"Any exciting cases?"

"Not... not really, no." Flipping things around was a common pattern with Dara. A crisis, then a few mundane, almost cheerful queries. He expected a renewed dark turn though, and sure enough one came.

"Did you talk about him?" she asked. "With Dad?"

"About Jordan? A little. There isn't much to say."

"When we stop talking about him," she said, her voice starting to rise. "When we really stop? Then we stop thinking about him. And then he truly dies, Alex."

"Dara."

"I can't p-picture him, sometimes," she said, her voice now taking on the familiar panicked tone he had heard so often. "It's happening more and more I swear!"

"You will never forget him," Alex said, punctuating each word. "I will never forget him. Take a breath, Dara. Now. Do it. Breathe." There was a long pause, and then another nose-blowing.

"I'm so sorry. I'm so sorry, Alex."

"There's nothing to be sorry about," he said, and she made a guttural, choking sound.

"Oh God, you know there is," she breathed. "Oh God." This cut Alex to the core, and he felt his own composure coming unglued.

"Not now, Dara. Please. Just Relax, okay? Try to go back to sleep. This was...like a dream or something."

"I have no one to talk to. I'm so sorry. I'm just so...lonely." He opened his mouth to say something, but nothing came out. He reached for something comforting, something calming, the kind of thing he could reliably come up with to offer her going back to when they were kids. But nothing swam up. He craned his neck toward the sliver of sky through the little window and wished he could fly.

"Don't be sorry," he managed finally. "Okay Dara? Please. Don't be sorry. For anything. Not anymore." She breathed out something like 'thank you' after some seconds had passed, and then the call clicked off. *The line went dead*, he thought for some reason, although that's not really what telephones did anymore.

Dead.

Then, alone in the dark, he rested his head against the wall and squeezed his eyes shut.

Mt. Eden Subway Station
Friday, April 8
2:45 a.m.

Her name was Paula, pronounced *Pah-O-lah*. She had high cheekbones, chiseled features and meticulously groomed, black eyebrows. They lifted when she saw Norman pull up.

"Where you taking me, *Papi*?" she asked, standing back

from the car window and crossing her arms. She was where she had been told to be, under the elevated tracks not a half-block from the tire shop and the steep, worn steps to the Mt. Eden subway station. Norman was her escort to the party she was going to work, one involving probably four or five guys. "And why you even working after what happened today?"

"What does it matter?" he said, tilting his head toward her, his gaze sleepy and mean. "Get in."

"This ain't right, though," she said, her brow knitted. "I got concerns, you know?" She wore a black, Bebe rhinestone tank-top with a leather jacket and low-rise, stylishly torn jeans.

"Fuck your concerns and get in. I'm on a clock, just like you."

"Whose car is this?"

"Friend."

"Yeah, 'cause they impounded yours, huh?" Norman quietly fumed, his nostrils flaring.

"One more fucking question, and I'll drive away and tell Juan you were a no-show. There's two grand easy you'll earn tonight. You want to explain to him why you didn't?" After a reluctant pause, Paula gathered her purse over her shoulder, walked around to the passenger's side and climbed into the vehicle.

"Folks saying you cut your own little boy. It's scary, okay?"

"Yeah, yeah." He seemed to have not even registered the accusation as he scanned the street and pulled away from the curb.

"I've seen you with a knife," she said, like it was just a tiresome detail. She dug in her purse for a cigarette. "I hope you didn't do that shit. That's all." She lit up and took a deep drag, then handed it to him. Norman grunted in reply. He drew on the cigarette, deeply as she had, and then made a point of flashing her a grin and flicking it out the window. The point to be made by both gestures, she knew, was that her mouth would be occupied for the rest of the ride over to where she'd be working. Everyone paid to play. Her favors *en route* to a job were a part of Norman's compensation.

"Shut up and get to work," he said. "Or we'll both have something to cry about."

CHAPTER 4

Friday, April 8, 2:30 p.m.
Office of the Chief Medical Examiner
160-15 82nd Drive
Jamaica, Queens, New York

Hector's body lay stretched out on a steel cart in one of the four "cold rooms" across the hall from where autopsies were performed. Around him, the bodies of 10 or 12 other deceased New Yorkers reposed under stark fluorescents. The old-style body fridges that held individual cadavers like filing cabinets made for great movie sets, but for the most part they were gone. They weren't nearly as efficient in terms of space and the trays were constantly breaking or catching on the roller machinery.

"See anything unusual?" Dr. Hettinger asked, her arms crossed against the chill as Alex looked him over. "Look past the obvious." Margaret Hettinger was in her mid 50's but looked surprisingly youthful with smiling, blue eyes and straw-yellow hair she arranged every single morning in a long, beautifully intricate braid. The hair was dyed and she didn't deny it; in her opinion, anything that brightened up a morgue was a good thing. She was chief of the

Queens division of the city's Office of the Chief Medical Examiner (OCME), and a 25-year veteran of working with the dead. She was also a natural educator who loved to share the occasional lesson with cops and DA's who cared enough to learn. Alex was one of her favorites.

"Other than a child with his head nearly cut off?" he asked, staring down at the boy and letting his eyes move slowly from one end to the other. The eyes were sunken, the lids like dark pools in the shadow of his brow. The mouth was closed, set and peaceful. It was really only the terrible spilt across his neck, that and a profound paleness, that indicated for sure he was dead.

"Yes. That would be the obvious. What else?" Alex cocked his head. There were a few healed scars he could see, in typical places for a child, like the knees and forearms, but nothing stood out.

"I give up, Doc."

"Left wrist," she said. "Compare it to the right one."

"Ah. Looks a little bigger, maybe."

"Correct," she said. "I think it's also slightly malformed. Could be an old injury that didn't heal correctly. The wrist is a complicated joint. Eight bones in there. If he fell and broke something and it didn't heal correctly? This could be the result. I ordered a full set of X-rays. I'll send them over to my guy at QG. Will let you know." QG was Queens General, the city hospital on the same grounds.

"Good to know," Alex said. "Anything on the knives?" Sean Regan had brought her three of them earlier that day, all seized from Norman's home.

"In comparison to the cut, not really," she said, shaking her head. "I don't like slashings and stabbings, to be honest. Gunshot wounds talk to me a lot more."

"Ruiz is the father. He says the knives are for fishing. Apparently he takes good care of them, too. Sean said he's got a pretty nice electric sharpener in the house, and they all looked recently sharpened and oiled."

"Oh yeah, they were all very sharp. Not serrated either, just straight blades. Two were folding knives, one was for fileting. Any one of them could have done it, but there are a million more out there that could have also."

"Yeah but look at the depth. It damn near took his head off. Doesn't that tell you anything about how sharp the blade must have been?"

"The toughest organ to get through is actually the skin. After that, even a kitchen knife will sail through most tissue."

"The skin?"

"That's by design," she said, smiling and lightly pinching his arm. "For my money, it's the most important organ you've got. It's tough. Other stuff- even muscle, ligaments- they cleave easier than most people think. Even a short blade, like a box cutter, could have made the cut and then just been dug in there to go deeper. I can say the cut was clean, meaning how it went across his throat."

"Probably not a serrated blade, then," he said, his eyes brightening a little. "So the knives we found can't be excluded."

"True, the knives Sean found can't be *excluded*. But that doesn't mean some serrated blade couldn't be *included* as a possibility. This is skin we're talking about, not wood." Alex nodded, appearing to accept this without protest. Another thing Margaret liked about him was that, unlike a lot of prosecutors, he didn't treat her like a dispenser for favorable opinions. There were limits to what a body could tell her as a crime scene. Alex didn't push her on them. "Here's what's more interesting to me. Usually with throat cuts the victim is struggling, whipping his head back and forth, that kind of thing. That can cause some zig-zagging you can sometimes make out. But this was straight across. If I had to guess I'd say the kid was unconscious when the killer came up on him. Either that or taken completely by surprise. No time to react. But it's possible the disability could have impacted his ability to react. I'll go through the medical records, but you should talk to his providers also."

Alex left Margaret's facility around 3:30. He had just started his car when a call came in from Danny.

"Just checkin' in," he said. "We're at the twenty-four hour mark."

"Yeah, I guess we are. I'm leaving the M.E.'s office." Alex's eyes drifted over to the busy sally port to the rear of the facility. With the nearly constant flow of ambulances and hearses, it was like a turnstile in a parade of the dead. The OCME accepted human bodies seven days a week. After autopsy, they were released to funeral homes or back to the city for burial in the potter's field if no family could be located or there was no one who could assume burial expenses. There was a rhythm to it that, in an odd way, always seemed to Alex to mimic breathing or a heartbeat. *Dead in. Dead out. Dead in. Dead out.*

"What's Margaret say?"

"Kid got his throat cut."

"By the knives we found?"

"No telling yet. They can't be excluded, at least. Anything on your end?"

"Couple o' things. First, I can't find Rolando Garcia. He

left work early yesterday and hasn't been in today. He's got an apartment near Fordham Road. Not there either."

"So, no clear alibi for the time of death?"

"Not yet. He was just…missing. I'm on it, don't worry."

"Thanks. What's the second thing?"

"Well, it turns out Norman Ruiz is a scary guy. Sean and I interviewed a few people today. We'll have them at the office for you on Monday."

"Scary how?"

"Didn't treat his kid very well," Danny said. "Talked some mean shit, too."

"Huh. What about the errand he was on? The phone number you got. Anything?"

"Burner. No permanent number."

"Like you suspected," Alex said. "Good instincts. So he probably *is* doing something on the side he doesn't want us knowing about."

"Could be. We'll look into it. Oh, we got out to his boat today also. It's a nice one."

"It's a fishing boat, right?"

"Yeah, a Grady White cabin cruiser. Had to have cost low six figures. Sean says he owns it free and clear, too. No loan. That's a nice boat for a guy who drives an ice truck."

"Gotcha. Anything on the hardware store, like what he was shopping for when police found him?"

"Sean's running that down," Danny said. "There are two brothers who own the store. We've got probably three neighbors for you to meet with. One in particular heard some bad stuff."

"Okay. I'm covering a meeting for Alexa Linder that morning," Alex said, putting his phone on speaker and looking at his calendar. Alexa was a fellow ADA in Raquel's unit, Special Victims, who had planned sick leave coming up. Danny, Alex knew, had worked with Alexa when he was an SVU detective before going to the Four-Four. "Should be done by eleven. Bring them in then?"

"Sure, sounds good. I'll coordinate with Sean. You headed home? It's Friday."

"Fat chance, brother. Back to the office."

At 8:00 p.m. that Friday night Alex was finally home, although referring to his little apartment as "home" was still a stretch even after two years in it. It was a small one bedroom, so the few furniture pieces he had were enough to fill it sufficiently, but there wasn't much warmth or continuity to the place. He was boiling water for ramen noodles with a beer in hand at 8:15 when his cell phone rang.

"Alex Greco."

"Mr. Greco this is Kendra Tucker, from P.S. ninety, where Hector Ruiz was enrolled. I'm an autism education specialist, returning your call from earlier today, but I just realized how late it was. I'm sorry— we can speak Monday."

"Ms. Tucker, no, this is actually fine, if it's okay for you." He turned off the stove in the little galley kitchen and went over to the couch, searching for a spot on the coffee table to set his beer among the case materials he had brought home. As it was, paper, photos and files covered every inch. "I'm just sorry you're still returning calls after eight o'clock on a Friday."

"I promise you, I return calls and take them from parents later than this," she said. "Do you have the documents the school released to your detective?"

"I do," he said, searching through an accordion file,

"just trying to pin them down. I'm afraid there's a lot of paperwork to sift through."

"I know that feeling very well," she said. "Take your time." Finally he found the school files, and invited her to start wherever she thought was most relevant. She sounded tired as she relayed information, but also sharp. She noted that Hector had been "lucky" in the sense that his neighborhood school was one of a few in the Bronx with an on-site program for ASD kids. In his case, though, it apparently wasn't making much of a difference, at least so far. He presented as almost comatose most of the time, she said, and her team had yet to establish what she called a "basal level" to even begin testing him. He was otherwise cooperative and generally quiet with school staff, her co-teachers and aides, she said. But he was mostly non-responsive.

"When you say mostly non-responsive," Alex cut in, "Were there any times he would respond?"

"I could get him to smile, sometimes," she said. "He'd react to something on television, or from another student once in a while, but we didn't see much. We did hear about some progress from a volunteer who was assigned to him in an outside program. But it was very shortly before he was killed. There should be some description of it in the records, probably brief. Are you familiar with the Haven Community Center?"

"Just meeting everyone now," he said. "But I've heard about them, yes."

"Talk to Constanza Morrell. She goes by Connie. She had power of attorney from Hector's father and attended most of the IEP meetings."

Hector, like all special needs children in the US, had an Individual Education Plan, or IEP in place. It was reviewed regularly and had to be signed off on by a parent or guardian.

"Did she sign the IEP?" he asked.

"She did. She was very involved. We've seen that before, parents signing over legal rights where education is concerned. Some parents are just overwhelmed."

"Is that how Mr. Ruiz struck you? Overwhelmed?"

"The father? No, not exactly. He seemed more unattached than anything. Definitely a cold fish. But again, not unusual."

"I see."

"Well, for one thing, Mr. Ruiz just hadn't spent much time with Hector. They only met a little over a year ago. And frankly Mr. Greco, I've worked with really conscientious parents who have been there every step of the way, and still seem emotionally unattached to their autistic kids."

Alex nodded to himself. He had heard that from therapists and other parents in a support group he and Dara once attended. Autism could be especially cruel that way. Sometimes a connection, even for the parent, was as elusive as a rainbow. Alex didn't mention it, but he knew how that felt.

He pored through the school records after hanging up with Kendra, but by 10:00 p.m. the letters on the pages were blurring. He dropped the highlighter and pulled his tie off. *Another night on the couch,* he thought, laying back and figuring vaguely he'd undress and brush his teeth later, if at all. *Thank God tomorrow is Saturday.*

Sleep took him quickly, his last conscious thought being that he might wake up chilly as the two tall windows overlooking the street were still open. A light breeze sent flat, black curtains billowing in. Then the foot and car traffic on 46th street melted into an indistinguishable buzz, punctuated by the occasional horn or siren. In his dream he was walking with Jordan beside the Potomac River in the waterfront park in Alexandria, and the river was strangely active with garishly colored boats racing noisily through the water. Jordan hooted and called after them.

CHAPTER 5

Monday, April 11

In Alex's office on Monday morning, Dr. Nicole Jaynes, Psy.D., waited patiently as Alex read through the sex-offender evaluation Jaynes had authored. The report had nothing to do with the Ruiz case. Alex was covering for his colleague Alexa Linder, who had a doctor's appointment.

Jaynes specialized in evaluating and treating sex offenders and testified regularly for both the prosecution and defense all over the city. The prosecutors who utilized her called her "Dr. Nikki."

Beside Nikki was Charlie Kolb, a perpetually bored looking but otherwise decent attorney representing the subject of her report, a soon-to-be convicted child molester named John Harney. Harney had struck up online relationships with two nine-year-old girls in a *My Little Pony* gaming chat room and had convinced them to expose themselves to him on webcams.

While Alex read, his thumb and forefinger rubbed together and created an audible hiss, a gesture Nikki noticed with a touch of amusement. Alex, she knew, was well-liked and well-respected for a prosecutor relatively new to the Bronx, particularly one who had come from such a different environment. But he was also ceaselessly intense.

"I don't want to turn this into a cross-examination," he said as he flipped over the last page of the report and looked up at her, "but if I was going to, I'd have some ammunition."

"More than you had last time, I hope," Jaynes said, the ghost of a grin appearing on her face. Nikki was not beautiful in the typically accepted sense, but she had a compelling look— pale skin, with big dark eyes, and a small cherry-colored mouth. As usual she was dressed for court in a simple but elegant black Tahari suit with a white top. She was tall and poised, with immaculate posture, something that benefited her on the witness stand.

"Touché," Alex said, looking back at her. Alex had cross-examined Nikki on one of his first cases in the Bronx, a child-predator case like many he had prosecuted in his previous life, and it had gotten borderline ugly. Testifying for the defense, Nikki recalled Alex discovering that she didn't rattle easily, and that she came prepared.

"I know this isn't your usual gig," Charlie said in a monotone voice. "Alexa asked you to cover this meeting because you handled a bunch of these when you were in Virginia. We're trying to come to an agreement on sentencing, and I know she listens to you. We're willing to plea to the top count, in exchange for your office to agree that Mr. Harney can be released to intensive probation with time served. Dr. Jaynes' report supports that."

"I've seen a lot of sex-offender evaluations, Charlie," Alex said, taking off his reading glasses. "And I've seen a lot of John Harneys."

And I'll bet you don't miss either, Nikki thought, looking discreetly at him behind his desk. His chair was slightly re-clined and he had his legs crossed tightly, the way women normally cross them, but he struck her as one of those men whose masculinity actually seemed accentuated by it.

"Look, my client is pleading guilty either way," Charlie said. "But assuming he's low risk to re-offend, why hit him with any more time? This wasn't a hands-on abuse case, Alex. He's a creeper, I get it. But he was never actually within a thousand miles of either girl. Let him get the help he needs on probation. He'll get nothing in a jail cell."

"It's a big assumption that he's a low risk to reoffend," Alex said, frowning. He turned back to Jaynes. "It sounds like the basis of your opinion is that Harney was...forth-coming with you. Or something to that effect."

"It's more than that," she said. "But Mr. Harney's truth-fulness is significant to me, yes. He appears to have no interest in lying, even to a degree that's socially awkward."

"You acknowledge that Harney was uncooperative in group sessions, correct?" Alex asked, flipping to a section of the report. "Verbally abusive, even?"

"I did. Mr. Harney can be, well, a highly unpleasant in-dividual in many respects."

"He's got anger problems?"

"Yes, mostly self-directed."

"But he's told you he has no plans to re-offend," Alex said, now aiming his gaze at her. "And you believe him." Jaynes paused before answering, forming her words as if she was on the stand.

"I'm satisfied that, among Mr. Harney's anti-social traits, prevarication isn't one of them. He strikes me as many things, but not a liar. He's developed specific strategies to keep from reoffending, we've discussed them, and I believe he'll follow them. That's what I'd be willing to testify to. And frankly, it feels like I just did." She punctuated this with another tiny grin.

"It's my job to question the report on Alexa's behalf," he said, softer, like he knew it was time to take it down a notch. "And I'll admit I didn't get very far disagreeing with you when we were in court."

"You didn't have much to work with that time," she said. Alex looked ready to acknowledge that fact when a detective Nikki recognized popped his head in. He was younger and rugged looking but had a great smile. Danny something, she remembered.

"Are they here?" Alex asked. Danny nodded, and then popped out again.

"I'm afraid I've got witnesses I need to meet with," Alex said to Nikki and Charlie. "And in any event, I don't think we're going to reach an agreement."

"It was worth a shot," Charlie said with a sigh. He gathered his files and rose to leave along with Nikki.

"Well, like you said, it's Alexa Linder's case, not mine. She'll be in touch with you, but I won't recommend she agree with time served. Anyway Charlie, it was good to see you." He shifted his eyes to Dr. Nikki, and she saw something vaguely wry in his look. "Always a pleasure, Doc."

CHAPTER 6

Elopement, Alex thought. That was the term, used in in autism circles, to describe the tendency of some kids to just up and walk away from their surroundings. Maybe they followed something that caught their attention. Maybe they were suddenly anxious and felt they had to leave. Or maybe none of the above; they just wandered. No one really knew for sure. It was a concept Alex hadn't thought about since he and Dara were preparing for Jordan's journey through life. Jordan, of course was too young to start eloping, but it was something they were aware of.

He was hearing about it again from one of the witnesses Danny and Sean had brought in, namely how Hector apparently walked out of his house on occasion. From what the witness, a dour-faced, short and stout Latina woman named Angelica Esparza said, it drove Norman to fits of anger. She was one of three neighbors Alex would hear from that day who had seen rough treatment and a lot of anger from Norman toward his son. But this account was the most disturbing.

Esparza was around 60 and lived in the row-house two down from the Ruiz's. She wore a long, black skirt and a thick sweater even though it was in the mid 70's outside and clutched a beaten black purse as she sat in Alex's office.

"Sometimes Hector would walk away from the house," she said in accented but accurate English. "A few times the police came."

"You mean he ran away?" Danny asked. She made a see-saw motion with her hand.

"Not exactly run away. Walk...like down the street. Just wander. Norman would find out he was gone, then come outside after him. He would get so mad. He would grab the boy, Hector, by the arm or...how do you say? Scruff. Of the neck."

"Did you see him hurt the boy, ma'am?" Alex asked, and then regretted the word choice. 'Ma'am' was a southern way of respectfully addressing a woman, but he was finding that a lot of women in New York, particularly female judges, with whom he would always use 'ma'am' if not 'your honor,' hated it. But it was a hard habit to break.

"Not exactly," she said. "But it was like he was dragging him, and with the boy screaming sometimes." She paused, then continued, "He wished Hector dead. I heard him say it."

"What did you hear?"

"The last time Hector walked away from home," she said, her tone going flat. "Not long ago. Middle of March, maybe. He walked out of the house. It was cold, and he had no coat. Norman came out a few minutes later, he was screaming. Hector fought with him. Finally Norman said, 'you want to walk away and get killed? I'll do it myself.'" She looked up at Alex and the two detectives, as if this last statement particularly merited eye contact.

"Are you sure those were his words, Mrs. Esparza?" Alex asked.

"I'll never forget them," she said. "Never." Alex nodded and was about to respond when his phone went off. It was Margaret from the ME's office. He excused himself and turned in his chair to take the call as Danny went over a few more details with Mrs. Esparza.

"What does your afternoon look like?" Margaret asked.

"Are you asking me out?"

"You should be so lucky. Can you come by?"

"Sounds important, whatever it is."

"It's two things, actually. I'll be here late. Text when you park, okay?"

CHAPTER 7

The photo Alex was staring at was of a white man, maybe mid-thirties, lying in a patch of dune grass either on or just off of a beach. He was dressed for colder weather, in jeans with a hooded sweatshirt and a stylish jacket over it. His eyes stared straight up toward the sky. His throat had been cut open, leaving a corona of dried blood spread across the scrub and sand beneath him.

"He was found almost two weeks ago, April second, at a park in Lido Beach," Margaret was saying as Alex absorbed the photo. It was crime-scene quality and had been taken probably at dawn. Lido Beach was a small seaside community just outside the city limits on Long Island. "It's in Nassau County, so we didn't get the case."

"Huh. Five days before the Ruiz murder. Do we know who he is?"

"No, he's unidentified. There was no wallet on him, just some cash and an MTA card in one pocket. Because of the transit card they assume he was in the city at some point, but no one knows where."

"Nothing on CODIS?" Alex asked. CODIS was the Combined DNA Index System, the massive database maintained by the FBI. It could match crime evidence to potential suspects, but it was also used for identifying human remains. It was used to identify hundreds of victims after 9/11.

"Not yet. Looks like he wasn't on anyone's radar." She drew another photo from a manila envelope on her desk and handed to him.

"Good God," he said under his breath. The dead man in this photo looked younger. He was also throat-cut, his body sprawled across a bare mattress. "Where was this?"

"Yonkers," she said. "Westchester County, just north of the Bronx. He was found first, about a week before, in a budget motel. Again, we didn't get this case because it didn't happen in the city."

"ID on this one?"

"Yes. Ryan Isoli. Twenty-three. Someone was able to ID him on the scene, and the name was traced back to a family in the Bronx. You haven't been here long enough to know, but the Isoli family has been known to NYPD going back I don't know how long."

"Hmmm. Italian last name. Mine is too, so I can say this. Are they mobbed up?"

"They might have been once, but I doubt they were ever that high in anyone's organization. Ryan's father did time in prison in the eighties and was always in trouble. There was an older brother who was shot to death in the Bronx, probably fifteen or twenty years ago. Ryan was the youngest. He worked as a barback or bartender at a few places, but also dealt drugs, stolen goods, and who knows what else. He had a rap sheet going back to when he was a teenager."

"No suspects though? For either murder?"

"Not yet. The unidentified guy, they don't seem to have a clue. He was well-groomed and well dressed. Didn't look homeless or deprived. That one is a head-scratcher. Isoli, on the other hand, was a sleazy guy and a known grifter from a family of them. Plenty of guys probably could have killed him. That's what Yonkers is sorting through with NYPD's help."

"I'll ask Sean about that one," Alex said. He sighed and set the photos down. "So, how could this become my problem?"

"We don't get many of these," she said. "The throat-cutting thing. They happen, but not as often as the crime shows might suggest, at least certainly not since the early nineties. If these two homicides had taken place in the city, I would have been aware of them before now, and I would have said something. As it was, I made inquiries to ME's outside the city, just to see if anything like this had taken place nearby."

"You've reviewed both autopsies?"

"I have."

"Are there physical similarities in terms of the cut?"

"I wouldn't call it a signature by any stretch, but yes. Look here. The cuts are clean on both. No sign of a struggle or panic on the part of either victim, much like with your case. Remember I told you we usually see a jagged pattern of some sort, when the victim is struggling? Not seeing it here."

"Suggesting what? Surprise?"

"Perhaps," she said. "Either that or they were asleep, maybe, or drugged. In Isoli's case he was on a bed. It's hard to say, but it doesn't seem like either one saw it coming."

"And given the rarity of these to begin with..."

"Exactly," she said. "Three homicides in this manner, within a few weeks and within this radius is odd. I'm not saying it suggests a pattern, or a serial situation. But it's worth noting, and I have to do so."

"I'm glad you did," he said with a shrug. "I'd rather know now than be surprised somewhere down the line. What's the second thing? I almost forgot." With that, Margaret pulled out another file, this one with X-rays attached.

"I got films back from QG," she said. "Sure enough, there was an old fracture under that abnormality I saw on Hector's left wrist. It looks to me like it was either never treated or treated poorly. That led to it healing incorrectly. Post-traumatic wrist arthritis is a probable result. I can explain it in as much detail as you want, but basically what it means is that he had cartilage damage and irregular bone development in a very delicate place. He would have been in pain quite a bit of the time, probably shooting pain up his forearm, maybe into his left hand also."

"I can't find any records from his time in the DR," Alex said, scribbling down the basics of what she was telling him. "I haven't seen anything in his US medical records, but I'll keep looking."

"Well, keep in mind, he may not have reported the fall, or whatever it was that caused the injury in the first place. After that, I think he probably just thought the pain was a part of him. Too many kids with disabilities go through that. They don't even know to complain."

CHAPTER 8

Tuesday, April 12

Alex had many acquaintances in the office after two years, but no real friends. One potential exception, though, was Alexa Linder, the ADA whose meeting with Dr. Nikki he had covered the day before. Alexa was a few years younger and had been in the Bronx DA's office her entire career.

"Lex," he called out when he saw her, approaching the courtroom where her case was to be called after the lunch break.

"Lex," she called back, smiling at him. That they had gender specific versions of the same name facilitated early on their connection in the office. Professionally, he sensed she looked up to him as he had a few more years of experience and had spent much of his time on special victims cases in Virginia. But he had come to depend on her as a source for knowledge of New York law and procedure that he was still struggling to master as a newcomer. She was a brilliant trial lawyer and smart as a whip. On a personal level, he had been reluctant to get to know her well, as he was with pretty much everybody since his life had changed. But slowly he was finding himself opening up to her anyway. She seemed both steadfast and loyal.

"Here to watch me cross examine your favorite psychologist on the Harney case?" she asked. "Thanks again for covering that meeting, by the way. We're hearing testimony on his sentence. I talked to Charlie last night. I didn't agree with time served either."

"Jaynes? I heard Charlie called her on direct before lunch. How is she?"

"Nikki? How is she always? Kind of a bitch. When she's on our side I love her. Right now, not so much." Alexa was maybe five-three but seemed taller and always wore impressive heels. She had luxurious dark-red hair and green eyes that were remarkably expressive- alluring when she wanted them to be and stonecutting when the occasion called for it. "How's your case? You saw Margaret already, right? Autopsy done?"

"Pretty much. No big mystery as to cause of death, but there were a few things she caught. What about you? Ready to take Dr. Nikki on?"

"Yeah I suppose. It won't be as entertaining as your battle with her, I can tell you that. I'll pin her down on the self-reporting thing, but I'm not going to linger. I doubt it'll take ten minutes." Alex nodded approvingly. Alexa was the kind of litigator who understood that cross-examination was a little like surgery. You didn't do it unless you had to do it, and if you did, you went in, got it done, and then got out.

True to her word, Alexa's cross of Nikki went to right about the ten-minute mark. Alex watched the brief argument that followed, and then left the courtroom. Nikki was already outside, talking with another ADA on a different case. That ADA got a call from a detective and walked off to take it, leaving Nikki and Alex alone. The two seemed to simultaneously and awkwardly take note of the moment.

"I don't see you here as much as I thought I would," she said finally.

"Could be I've been seeing you first, Doc," he said. Her dark, little mouth flattened into something of a grin.

"Clever as always, Alex Greco. So...you saw that. Alexa made her points and knew when to stop. She's wrong in asserting Harney poses a high risk to the community, same as you. But still, she's very good."

"She's not wrong to believe John Harney is sexually excited at the thought of undressed little girls."

"Of course not. No one denies that, including Harney. Frankly, I knew it before he told me. Have you ever interviewed a sex offender in depth?"

"Not that I'm aware of, no."

"There are things they can hide, or lie about. There are things they can't. When Harney described what he saw when those girls took off their clothes on camera, it was obvious to me he was excited by it."

"I'm sorry, was he standing in his underwear while talking to you?"

"Pleasant thought, but no. And that response, actually, some of them can control. It was his eyes. They dilate when a person is sexually excited. That's a tell no one can control, in my experience. But Harney didn't deny anything. He told me what he saw, and I asked him how it made him feel. What he told me is pretty much what I observed. That's not the whole puzzle, but it's an indication. He didn't try to minimize anything. We started from that place, a place where I could be confident Harney was telling me the truth. It's been that way ever since. We can't cure the man of his pathology. But we can minimize risk, and we can make a fair judgment about risk. That's what I did."

"Sorry, Doc, but even if you're right, I'm not of the opinion that an utter asshole like John Harney should be walking the same streets as me. Or people I care about."

"Then make that argument. If the state wants to punish John Harney for being something they don't like, then let them say so. Not every utter asshole is a repeat sex offender. Part of my job is not letting Harney's personality or pathology cloud my judgment. Most of us can stand to be reminded of the importance of that."

"So you do your job and I'll do mine, I guess," Alex said.

"Fair enough. Good day, counselor."

CHAPTER 9

Wednesday, April 13

"Nothing yet on Rolando Garcia," Danny said, with a shrug. "He hasn't been at work and hasn't used so much as a credit card, last five days." He and Sean were in Alex's office after lunch on a rainy and chilly afternoon. "The super at his building is watching, but hasn't seen him. He doesn't have a camera up though, so he might be missing him if he's coming or going late at night. Supposedly he keeps weird hours and he's quiet as a mouse."

"Five days," Alex said, shaking his head. "His job doesn't have any idea?"

"No, it's a little place. One old guy owns it. He says Garcia misses work sometimes. They think he's got emotional problems or something, but they don't know details. They're kind of used to him not showing up sometimes."

"Any rap sheet?"

"No criminal record, but he was picked up once as an EDP," Danny said, using NYPD-speak for an Emotionally Disturbed Person. "He was in a park off of Fordham Road, screaming at people. He was at Bronx Psych for a day or two, then released. Three years ago."

"Christ," Alex said with a sigh. "Okay. Stay on it, you'll find him." He looked over at Sean. "Any I.D. on the throat-cut guy from Lido Beach?"

"Nope. Nassau guys don't know where to start."

"We know Ryan Isoli, though, right? The body in Yonkers?"

"Oh yeah," Sean said. "Isoli was from the Four-Five, down Tremont Avenue. His family has been in the same neighborhood, going back to when it was mostly Italian. Most of that area is Hispanic now, but there are pockets left."

"Margaret said he was a bad guy. And that it runs in the family."

"It does," Sean said. "The Isoli's have always been low level, but definitely wrong. Ryan was mostly a drug dealer, but it wasn't a street thing. He dealt pharmaceuticals, club drugs, stuff like that, out of the bars he worked in. He also sold stolen goods, credit card numbers, that kind of thing. He was a ladies man, too, kind of an alley cat. Could be he was found with the wrong girl. Or he just ripped off the wrong guy. Chances are, Yonkers will solve that one with our help. Isoli was the kind of guy you expect to end up dead. Someone knows who did it. Eventually a name will bubble up. It usually does."

"What's it got to do with us?" Danny asked. "The M.E. thinks it could be a pattern? Like a serial thing?"

"She didn't go as far as that, but she thinks it's possible all three people were killed by one person. Or it could look that way."

"So, if it's Norman we stay focused on for murder- just argument's sake- we're saying it's possible he did all three? Like he's connected to these other bodies?"

"No, that's not really our theory," Alex said. "Unless

he really is ganged up, like you suspect. Then maybe he's some kind of hit man, a guy who does wet work for a crew. That way, killing his own kid wasn't too far out of the box for him, whatever his reasons. It's a stretch, I know."

"We need to look into his background anyway," Sean said. "You know there could be an opposite theory."

"Like?" Danny asked.

"Like Ruiz is a victim also. Like some other guy killed his kid and the other two."

"Exactly," Alex said, nodding in his direction. "If it's Ruiz we stay focused on, this pattern thing could constitute a defense. Crazier things have worked."

"But what's the connection?" Danny asked, crossing his arms and frowning. "A normal looking white guy, a Guido with a rap sheet and a little autistic kid? What the hell's that about? Who kills all three?"

"I'll start digging around on Norman's gang ties," Sean said. "I've a couple of guys I can ask. You two are heading over to this community center, right?" Alex nodded.

"Haven. The kid spent a lot of time there."

CHAPTER 10

The once fashionable Grand Concourse was the wide boulevard designed by Jewish immigrants in the late 19th century with the Champs Elysees in mind. It no longer held that sparkle, but around 165th street, where Haven Community Center welcomed its clients, the concourse was vibrant and well-traveled. Haven took up the first floor of a surprisingly modern looking mixed-use building, free-standing on one side. Alex was impressed from the outside. He had heard through the grape vine that HCC wasn't just some plucky storefront operation.

A minute or two after checking in at the reception desk, a woman came out to greet them with some files under her arm. She had a motherly look to her, and also seemed a little bohemian with flat, black hair, a bit long for her age and parted carelessly in the middle. Neither thin nor heavy, she was dressed typically for someone running a non-profit, with a kind of no-frills, over-worked and under-paid vibe, and looked to be a few years older than Alex. But something about her gave Alex a sense that the woman was more than she seemed.

"Mr. Greco, Detective Lopez," she said, moving her eyes from one to the other as they rose to shake her hand. Her posture and diction were immaculate; she walked into the room not with any arrogant air, but with confidence, like she'd been announced. Now Alex saw it, the thing that had looked out of place before. Despite her aging, hippy-chick appearance, she was poised and cultured. Through Dara's family, Alex had gotten to know people with money, including old money. That's how she struck him— old money.

"Ms. Morrell?" Alex asked.

"Yes, Constanza," she said. "But please, call me Connie. Everyone here does. And frankly I hate my real name. Come in." She led them through an inner door and then down a narrow hallway past various bright, natural-lit rooms where children played, some with parents and grandparents in tow. Mostly young people- case workers, presumably- walked in and out with clipboards and files. Alex noticed that almost all of the children appeared to have cognitive delays of some kind, many with intellectual disabilities, the term that had replaced mental retardation. There were some, he could tell, who were probably autistic, on various points on the spectrum. Seeing them sent memories slicing through his otherwise ordered thoughts about the case, the witnesses, the particulars.

Connie's office was at the end of the hallway, a corner space with big windows that looked out onto a small playground. She settled in behind her desk and Alex and Danny took chairs in front of it.

"Can I get you something, Mr. Greco? Detective Lopez?"

"No thank you, but please call me Alex."

"I'm good," Danny said. "And likewise, Danny is fine. We appreciate you seeing us."

"I'm happy to," she said. And then her face darkened. "I hate the circumstances, that's all."

"Yes, ma'am," Alex said, then caught himself. *Women fucking hate that up here!* But Connie seemed okay with it. "Can you tell us a little about the facility, and how you came to know Hector Ruiz?"

"Sure. Where you are now is our community and counseling center, part of which you passed through on your way in. This area contains the bulk of what we do. We focus on finding services or directly providing them, and our focus is on intellectually disabled and autistic kids, as you may have heard."

"I heard a little," Alex said. "I have some experience with autism. Has that always been your focus?"

"It has," she said. "If we continue to grow we may branch out, but I like to stick with what I know best. I'm the executive director. I run things with my partner, who you'll probably meet today. He's taken up running, and he usually goes out around this time of day."

"One thing I noticed," Alex said, "is that HCC isn't a contracting provider for OPWDD. With all of the state-approved services Hector had, he still spent more time here. That's not a bad thing. It just seemed odd to me." Connie nodded, seeming unsurprised at the observation. OPWDD was the state's Office of Persons With Developmental Disabilities.

"People are often surprised to find out we don't contract with the city or the state to provide services," she said. "The truth is, we don't have to, and we enjoy our flexibility. I'm insured of course, but I don't jump through the other hoops."

"But in terms of funding," Alex said, "you all are okay without it? Like I said, I have a little bit of experience with this, that's why I ask."

"I come from a wealthy background, Alex," Connie said plainly. "It's not a secret and our 990s reflect it. I know I don't look the part, but that was us. Mexican industrialists on my father's side if you can believe it."

"Not hard to believe," Alex said. "Did you spend time in Mexico growing up?"

"Quite a bit, yes," she said. "In Mexico City mostly, and on the coasts. You want the truth? I lived like a princess." She shifted her eyes from Alex to Danny and back, and made a face. "And I *hated* it. I left that life many years back. It's a long story but suffice to say it left me on my own, but also with some funds. I've put them to the best use I know how."

"Understood," Alex said. *So, she walked away from another life also, then.* Alex was feeling a fast connection to this frank, seemingly open-hearted woman, and he made a mental note to be aware of it. She was still a witness, and he had to remain neutral. But he liked her.

"So, what I can tell you about Hector?" she asked. "It breaks my heart just to say his name, I hope you know that."

"We can imagine," Alex said. "We're here because Hector spent so much time here, and it looks like you had some power of attorney where his education was concerned." She nodded and sighed.

"Mr. Ruiz was never very concerned, frankly, about Hector's development or condition. Not in the year or so we knew them. We handled some school decisions, yes, because he asked if we could. We coordinated with the city and state providers of course."

"Did Norman spend time here?" Danny asked, scratching on his notepad. "Any regular involvement?"

"I wouldn't say regular. He'd show more interest when he needed something, or when there was a potential service change for Hector. To be blunt, he tended to show up when it looked like there was something in it for him. He let us do most of the paperwork on the services Hector got and didn't pay much attention to the details. Most parents we deal with are less than stellar, that comes with the territory. But Norman Ruiz seemed more out of touch with his son than most. I'm sorry if this sounds harsh. I'm just being honest."

"That's what he need," Alex said. "The young woman who found him on April seventh, Joseliz. Was she paired up with Hector under your program?"

"She was," Connie said carefully. She frowned and seemed to search herself for a moment. "The thing is, our volunteer agreements don't provide for the kind of in-home assistance Joseliz was doing with Hector. So technically, she was on her own when she visited him, although we would never just leave her that way. I went over with her in the beginning, and we still look in on her from time to time. As you've seen, the home lacks a woman's touch, shall we say, but it's livable. And Mr. Ruiz, whatever other faults he has, treats her respectfully."

"We've talked to her," Danny said. "She seems like a great kid."

"She is," Connie said. "She has a heart of gold and she's very bright. She's wants to teach kids with autism also, so Hector was a good fit for her. She had a real connection to him, as I'm sure she'll share with you."

"When I spoke to his teacher," Alex said, "She told me Hector was mostly unresponsive at school, but he might have opened up a little here. Do you recall anything?"

"There were a few things we saw," Connie said, seeming wistful. "Not much. But Joseliz? I always thought she might be able to reach him."

"Reach him how?"

"Well," she said, cocking her head and appearing to think about it, "I'll give you a *for instance*. There was a picture game she would play with Hector. She'd sit him down at a school desk, and then lay out a few photos of us, staff members, one or two of his classmates. She was always taking pictures of things and people in Hector's life. She used them like study aids. Then she'd ask something like 'Hector, who did we play a game with this morning?'"

"This was in English or Spanish?" Danny asked.

"All Spanish," Connie said. "I don't think Hector had any exposure to English other than maybe what he caught on TV, or in school. Much of the time, he wouldn't answer. But sometimes, he'd very slowly point to the picture of the person they'd been with, and smile. It was a glorious thing to see." At this, Connie looked like she was going to cry, and Alex paused to give her a moment. She composed herself quickly. "I'm sorry."

"Please don't be," Alex said.

"Did anyone else from HCC visit Hector at home, or provide services?" Danny asked. "Other than you?"

"Sure, from time to time. Mostly to support Joseliz. We arranged transportation back and forth from here to the home. It's less than a mile away, so that was never a big deal. Joseliz has a key to the house, but she keeps it here. We weren't usually over there without her unless she was ill or something, or in class. But we brought him to the doctor a few times, and to a couple of IEP meetings at school."

"Did you see any signs of abuse or neglect?"

"Nothing remarkable, no. Hector would show up with the occasional Band-Aid or minor bruise, but nothing that stood out, and we're trained to watch for that kind of thing. He often seemed uncomfortable, though. He tended to grip his left arm, or forearm."

"His wrist, maybe?" Alex asked, remembering what Margaret had told him.

"Possibly, yes," she said, after a moment's thought. "You know it's tough with autistic kids sometimes, to know if they're even in pain. I've seen them fall flat on their faces and not react at all. It can be scary. Really scary if you imagine how many dolts out there don't think autistic kids feel pain at all."

There was light knock on her door.

"Connie?" It was a man's voice. He opened the door slightly, and she beckoned him in.

"There he is," she said, standing and smiling as he came over and kissed her. It was light kiss, friendly mostly, and sort of straddled between lips and cheek. Alex couldn't be certain, but he assumed they were a couple. "ADA Greco, Detective Lopez, this is my partner, Bruce Eldrich." Bruch turned to them and smiled, giving each a handshake.

"Partners in name only," he said. "She's got all the money and she does all the work. Good to meet you both." He was a friendly looking man, average in size and shape with thinning dark hair, graying around the temples. He had a high forehead, thick eyebrows and a 5:00 shadow over healthy but slightly ruddy skin. Alex judged him to be in his late forties. He was dressed in baggy running shorts and a damp sweatshirt.

"How was your run?" Connie asked.

"Painful. I'm too old to run in the rain." And then to Danny and Alex, "You're here on Hector's case, I guess?"

"We are," Danny said. "Looking to talk to anyone who worked with him and get impressions."

"That's all of us," Bruce said. "He didn't say much, but he smiled. All the time. Lit up this place like a Christmas tree."

"Can you tell me about your interaction with him?" Danny asked. "Day to day, or whatever?"

"I saw him at least weekly," Bruce said, frowning and seeming to think it over. "He was at school most days, and they had their own transportation set up for him, but he was home by two or two-thirty each day. Joseliz was with him...hell, three or four days a week I guess. She has classes in the morning, so her schedule and his fit well. Most of the time they were at the Ruiz home, but she was with him here quite a bit. If I was with him, or them, it was probably about transportation. I drive the van here most of the time. Hector felt comfortable with me also, at least I think he did."

"He definitely did," Connie cut in. "Bruce was one of the few who could assist or guide Hector physically without freaking him out. The thing we talked about before, how he'd sometimes look like he was nursing his arm? Bruce caught that early and told the father about it."

"How did he respond?" Alex asked. "Ruiz didn't say anything to us about it. I was alerted to the possibility of discomfort from the medical examiner. Apparently, he had an old injury that might not have healed correctly."

"He thanked me for pointing it out, but otherwise he didn't say much of anything. I'm sure Connie told you, he was mostly disinterested. He was polite to me. I can't say different. But he never seemed dialed in. To Hector, I mean."

"That's the impression we're getting, I'm afraid." Alex said.

"I'm not judging," Bruce said, putting a hand up. "I don't have my own kids. God only knows how I'd be if I had to raise a child alone with a disability the way Norman did." He paused then, looked down, and then back up at Alex. "But if he killed him? And that way? I don't even know how to think about that."

"Did you all see Hector the day he died?" Alex asked. At this, Connie seemed to visibly deflate.

"We were supposed to," she said. He could see tears welling up in her eyes. Bruce, his face downcast, just shook his head. Connie started to speak, but then put up a finger as if to ask for a moment.

"This month was Hector's first anniversary with us at HCC," Bruce said. "We were planning to have Hector over for a small party around five that day. He never made it."

"I see," Alex said. "Was Joseliz the person who was supposed to bring him here?"

"We hadn't even worked that all out yet," Bruce said. "Their house is just a few minutes away. On nice days, sometimes Joseliz and Hector would walk. Otherwise I'd go get them, or someone else on staff. Joseliz was going over there that Thursday anyway in the afternoon. She was going to spend some time with him, and then bring him here to see all of us." Bruce paused and blew out a breath. "I'm sorry. It's all still very raw."

"The details of that day," Danny said. "I know it's painful. Do you think we could go over them with the two of you?" His phone went off then and he apologized, excusing himself to take the call.

As Danny stepped out, Connie sat up straight, and Alex could see her force the emotion from her face. "Of course, we'll go over everything. We're grateful for your efforts. We work with a lot of kids, but we were very paternalistic with Hector. He felt like family."

"Better than most family," Bruce said with a small grin. "Mine, anyway." Much as with Connie, Alex felt a pull to like Bruce almost immediately. He seemed down-to-earth and unassuming. Alex wondered what their personal life together was like.

"Are you a New Yorker?" Alex asked him. "I'm a transplant, so I wonder about others."

"Yeah, I grew up in Throgs Neck," Bruce said, "east of here off of Tremont Avenue. My last name is Scottish or German, I don't know which. My father never knew or cared. But my mother was Polish, and there were a ton of us in Throgs, back in the day."

Danny stepped back into the room at that moment, and the expression on his face told Alex there was something new that needed dealing with.

"Everything okay?" Alex asked.

"Something's up. We should go out on it," Danny turned to Connie and Bruce. "I'm sorry, it looks like we have to respond to another issue. I'll reach out in a day or two, and we can go over stuff then."

"Certainly," Connie said. To Alex, she looked a little relieved. "We'll walk you out."

"So, what's going on?" Alex asked as they approached Danny's car. "You've got a look on your face like it's important."

"The uncle. Rolando Garcia. He was picked up."

"Whoa. Picked up? In relation to this case?"

"Not exactly," Danny said, firing up the car. "EDP again. He was on a subway platform waiving around one of those little umbrellas and screaming at people to stay away because he had a knife."

"Jesus, really? That's what I'd call emotionally disturbed, yeah. Where?"

"Woodlawn, at the four stop near the cemetery. Five-Two guys subdued him and called for a bus. They took him to Lincoln ER and then Manhattan Psych. That's where we're going." A 'bus' in cop speak was an ambulance, but usually specific to EDP situations.

"Did they find a knife?"

"No, just the umbrella. Looks like a psychotic break, or something. We can talk to him now though, they're saying he's calm. Buckle up, I'm gonna step on it."

CHAPTER 11

Nikki Jaynes did part-time contract work at the Manhattan Psychiatric Center and regularly did intakes for EDP's. It was she who caught Rolando Garcia's case earlier that afternoon. Garcia had come in on what was called a "2PC", meaning a two-physician certificate. That meant either police or EMT's had brought him to an emergency room, and that two doctors there had agreed he needed further psychological evaluation at one of the city's psych centers. Manhattan's, on the otherwise non-descript outcrop known as Wards Island in the East River, was by far the biggest. By the time Nikki saw him, sitting in one of the industrial drab interview rooms on the third floor, he looked utterly calm and collected. Also in the room was an orderly for security's sake.

"Mr. Garcia, how are you?" she asked, his file in hand.

"Better," he said. He looked up at her, a thin, graying man who looked to be around 50 but was probably younger. "I'm really very sorry about all of this. Once I was finally in custody, it's like I just snapped back into place."

"They gave you something at Lincoln," she said. "That might have helped. Do you have any better recollection of the incident?"

"A little. I know I was...terrified. Screaming. Waving something around."

"It was an umbrella," she said. "The reports say you were yelling something along the lines of 'I'm next, I'm next.' Is there anything you recall about that?"

"Not yet, no. But sometimes, after a while, things come back to me. I'd guess the paranoia stemmed from what happened to my nephew last week."

"That seems likely, yes, especially since it's been quite a while since you've had a reported breakdown like that. If I may ask, do you feel threatened? I mean, is there any actual reason you know of to fear for your safety?"

"No, nothing like that. I think I just...broke down."

"I understand you requested an appointment to have your meds checked, a couple of weeks ago. So maybe it just didn't happen in time."

"I guess not," he said, shaking his head. "But with my nephew's murder..." he trailed off and stared straight ahead. "I don't know if it would have made a difference."

"It's okay, Mr. Garcia. It sounds like you've had a series of bad breaks. You're not in any legal trouble. We just need you to meet with a psychiatrist and have your medications reviewed. You'll be released soon."

"I understand from the orderly there are police here who want to talk to me about my nephew's case. Can I speak with them?" He seemed eager, which struck her as odd.

"There's an assistant district attorney and a detective here, yes," Nikki said, slowing her speech. She hoped he understood what those men were likely there for. "Whether you want to speak to them is entirely up to you." She didn't mention what seemed obvious, that Garcia was probably a suspect. It wasn't really her place. Still, he was in her care.

"As long as you know you can wait to speak to anyone until you feel completely well again. They're investigating a murder. I assume it's the one you've mentioned."

"I'll speak with them," he said. "Please. Wherever it's convenient."

"We meet again, Doc," Alex said to Nikki when he and Danny encountered her in the hallway. She was in slacks and a sweater. Nikki didn't go for lab coats, most of the time. "How is he?"

"He seems stable. He's willing to talk to you both also. I don't know that I would do that in his situation. But I'm not his lawyer."

"Right now, he doesn't need one," Alex said with a shrug.

"Maybe, maybe not, but we know how quickly that can change, Mr. Greco."

"How long until he's released?" Danny asked. He looked like he sensed tension between Alex and Nikki, his eyes going back and forth between them.

"He has to meet with a psychiatrist about his medication. That's all I can really tell you, but Mr. Ruiz may fill in the rest. He should be out of here tonight. Go ahead to room three-eleven, down the hall. He's in there." With that, she turned away and walked down the hall.

CHAPTER 12

Gray was the first thought Alex had as Rolando Garcia rose to shake hands with him. The man looked almost entirely gray, from his head to his feet. His hair was darker than that, but very thin and strung across his forehead. He had a drawn, long face devoid of much color, and wore a simple work shirt and pants that blended in with his general gray look.

Alex expected a similar kind of "gray" look in his eyes, either something exhausted, confused, bereft, or the like. He had seen eyes like his entire career. But when their eyes met, Garcia smiled and Alex saw something like a twinkle.

"Mr. Garcia, thank you for speaking with me," he said. "First things first, please accept my deepest condolences regarding your nephew's death."

"Thank you," he said, his voice smooth, and just above a whisper. "I'm just sorry for the trouble I caused today. I still don't have much of a memory about it."

"Yes, sir. And clearly, these are odd circumstances. Do you feel okay talking to myself and Detective Lopez? We're investigating your nephew's murder. I'm sure it's affected you deeply aside from what you've been through today."

"More deeply, I'm afraid, than I thought," he said. "I think what happened today was the culmination of several days of near-psychosis. I heard about Hector late on Thursday afternoon. I honestly don't have many memories since then. I have a condition, as I guess you know."

"We understand that," Danny said. "And given that you might be a witness in a case at some point, do you think we could get your consent to see your medical records? Mostly just on the basics of your condition."

"Yes, that would be fine," Rolando said, and, again oddly to Alex, he seemed almost cheerfully agreeable. "What I suffer from is classified as a generalized anxiety disorder, but on the severe side. Sometimes with hallucinations."

"That must be difficult," Alex said. "I'm sorry to hear it."

"It has been, yes. Mostly my condition is stable, but I've had bad periods, most recently, of course, in the wake of last week's events."

"Can you account for your time at all over the last few days?" Danny asked. "Or do you know anyone who could? I asked at your job if they had seen you, and at your building, but no one at either place seemed to know where you were."

"I'll think back," he said. "With time, I can usually reconstruct where I've been. Other times I've had a break like this, I've mostly just wandered around. I don't eat much. I think I tend to sleep a lot. I'm sorry I can't be more helpful right now."

"The day in question," Danny said. "It's obviously pretty important to know where you were then, too."

"Of course," he said. He sighed then, but the corners of his mouth turned up into the slightest grin when he said, "I know how this might look. Truthfully, I think the crisis I went through was starting before I found out about Hector. I know I didn't report to work that day. I think I felt it coming on. I went walking. Just walking. Some of that I remember."

"Do you remember who informed you of Hector's death?"

"His name is Oscar," Rolando said, his face reflecting a strange and sudden brightness. "He's related to Norman, Hector's father. He called me that afternoon to tell me. I'm not sure how he found out."

"Do you know how I could reach him?" Danny asked.

"Oscar? I'm afraid not. He's a gang leader of some kind. He uses different phones and I never know where he's calling me from, not that he calls often. I only know he's in the Bronx someplace. His last name is Carrera." Danny nodded and scribbled the name down. He didn't seem to be picking up on it, but Alex was all but certain: There was some part of this, however unconscious, that Garcia seemed to be enjoying.

Alex wasn't entirely surprised by it. He had encountered people like that over his years as a prosecutor, people who seemed lonely, ignored, or left-out, and thus enjoyed—on a level however buried or unconscious- the idea being interviewed as a potential witness. Even in Garcia's case, where he was also a possible suspect, there was something brighter in it than the usual dull palette that life probably offered him. For a moment at least, maybe he felt like someone important.

"Well for now, we'd appreciate any insight you have on Hector or his father," Alex said. "But beyond that, I'd be grateful if you could tell me about Hector's mother, and maybe give me some background as to the family before she passed away."

"Of course," he said, nodding, that maddening shadow-grin still there. Alex also noticed that Garcia almost never moved. He sat perfectly still, like a talking mannequin.

He spoke for a few minutes about some of the things he had seen. Most were similar to what Alex had heard from others. Norman as bitter and uninterested. Norman blowing up at Hector and whoever else was nearby for things as inconsequential as a spilled glass of apple juice. There was no 'smoking gun' in his accounts, but they were sobering. Then the conversation turned to Bianca, Hector's mother.

"My sister never saw the United States. You know that, right?"

"I do."

"I got lucky, I suppose. I was able to come to the US when I was still in school. I wanted Bianca to come, but she wasn't very ambitious. Santo Domingo was all she knew, and she was content. Not everyone imagines another life." He looked at Alex for understanding, but like most Americans he lacked it and didn't try to pretend otherwise. "Norman, as you probably know, came to New York when he was a teenager. He was naturalized, as I was. But he went back regularly. My family and his are from the same town, just outside of Santo Domingo."

"We've heard," Alex said. "Apparently he connected with Bianca over there?"

"He did," Rolando said, the disgusted edge back, and the odd grin finally fading. "He went after her. He charmed her. Norman could do that, once. Bianca was very traditional. I was surprised when I found out she was pregnant. But Norman had a way with her. He has a way with many people. You'll discover that about him, I'm sure." The grin was back. Just barely there.

"A way, meaning…"

"He fools people, Mr. Greco. He draws them into his schemes. He's taken money from family members here and in the Dominican Republic. Friends also, I'm sure, although I don't know that he has many left. Did he tell you he sent money back to Bianca?"

"Actually, yes."

"He might have, as a token. But he's taken far more from our family than he ever contributed. He never acknowledged Hector as his child. Not until Bianca got sick. Then, finally, he agreed to go back, marry her, and bring her to the US with Hector. This was the only place my sister had a chance. For Hector, it was probably already too late for his development. But for Bianca, maybe something could have been done. Anyway, she didn't make it. She died working at a T-shirt factory with my nephew languishing in daycare."

Alex nodded in sympathy, wondering if he should look around for a box of tissues, but Garcia was utterly dry-eyed. His eyes were almost bright, if anything.

"Bianca was what she was," he continued. "Like I said, not very ambitious. Not terribly smart. She loved Hector, though, and wanted something better for him. She wanted to come here and form a family with Hector and Norman. Norman would never do that. He probably wouldn't have done it if the boy was healthy, let alone with the autism."

"When I talked to Norman, I got the impression there was pressure put on him to go back," Danny said. "I mean to retrieve Bianca and Hector." At this, Rolando almost smirked.

"You could say that, yes. Pressure was put on him, from people in both his family and mine. He owed money to some, favors to others. There were a few people even Norman couldn't shrug off or make excuses to. So yes, he went over, married Bianca, and made arrangements to bring them both back. She deteriorated quickly, though, while he was there. She died within a couple of weeks, and then he came back with Hector." He paused for a moment and seemed hesitant to say the next thing. "I thought about seeking custody of him, when they arrived. But it wasn't possible. Clearly, I'm not well. I can care for myself, usually, but no one else. For that reason, I was grateful when HCC found Norman. They were at least able to provide some meaningful care."

"Did you interact with Connie Morrell or Bruce Eldrich? We've spoken to both of them. They seem sincere."

"I believe they are," he said. "Connie and Bruce and their staff proved a great asset to Hector. I know there was a young woman very close to him also. She was there when I visited a few times."

"Joseliz Perez."

"Yes, thank you. I know she meant much to Hector. And of course, all of these efforts gave Norman a free ride. That's what he looks for. All the time." The grin was back. A little more apparent than before. Now, Alex could, see, Danny was noticing it.

Dr. Jaynes poked her head in then. A psychiatrist was waiting to see Mr. Garcia. Danny confirmed Garcia had no plans to travel, and that he had a way to get home from the psych center. He and Alex left a little before 8:00 p.m.

CHAPTER 13

"So, where the hell are we now?" Alex asked Danny as the two waited for a late dinner at the bar of a reliable cop hangout called "Coogan's" in the Washington Heights section of Manhattan. "Is this guy a suspect or a distraction?" Danny shrugged and waved at the bartender for another beer.

"Garcia? I don't get a guilty vibe from him. He's a little creepy, though."

"Yeah, I noticed that. And he has a psych history, and right now, no alibi. So, he's the perfect guy for a defense attorney to suggest might have done it, if Norman's charged."

"I'll try to fill in the alibi with him," Danny said. "If he remembers more, I might be able to corroborate it and we can keep him out of the spotlight. Our focus should probably stay on Norman. It's still the thing that makes the most sense."

"Yeah but there's something about it you don't like," Alex said. "I can tell." Alex had been sensing this from the first interview actually and had been waiting for the right time to bring it up. It was funny, the dynamic between a DA and the lead detective. Sometimes it seemed like a marriage.

"What, about Norman? Who says I don't like him for murder?" He gave Alex a sideways grin. Alex didn't return it. Overhead, Billy Joel's "No Man's Land" beat broodily. Nearby a group of cops and firemen were fixated on a hockey playoff game.

"There's something that doesn't seem right to you. Tell me, please, because I need to know."

"Who the hell am I? I just gather stuff, bro. You're the one who puts it together in front of a jury. What do you think?"

"I'm a trial lawyer. It's a different skill set. My brain doesn't work the way yours does. So tell me."

"I wish I *could* tell you," Danny said, light frustration in his voice. "The guy seems like an asshole, but...I don't see him yet as the killer. He had the motive and the opportunity, I know. It looks like he did it, I know. But..."

"But what?"

Danny sighed. "Fuck, man, it's like...like he he'd rather have the kid around almost, just to feel sorry for himself. He's the type who'd rather have something to bitch about. You know?"

"Not exactly, but I think you know."

"I don't know anything for sure," Danny said. "Anyway, you've got to do what you've got to do. It probably is him. He's probably ganged up. And now this guy Rolando mentioned? Oscar something? Ganged up also, and related to Norman, right? I'll run that, down, too."

"I appreciate the work. Just keep me posted on what you're feeling. It's easy to get myopic in situations like this."

"Myopic?"

"Overly focused. Too narrow. And to be honest, I kind

of want to hate the sonofabitch." Alex paused and looked through his glass. "What that kid was going through already was bad enough."

"If he killed his own son, especially as helpless as he was, he deserves to be hated." At this, a pang of something, guilt, regret or just sadness, cut through Alex and sank into his gut.

"Yeah, but that's not the job. The job is bringing charges, if I believe it and we can prove it. Right now, that's the case. But if you start to feel differently, speak up, okay?"

"Don't I always?" he said, flashing a smile. "Come on, let's do a shot. You'll sleep better." After a few hand motions, two whiskeys arrived. They tossed them back and the glasses clanked down hard on the bar.

CHAPTER 14

Woken from what was probably a heroin-induced doze by Sean Regan's nudging shoe, Edgar Pedilla sat up in a fright, the plastic tarp below him crinkling as he blinked up into sundown's fading light.

"Relax, Edgar. It's Sean."

It was a little before 8:00 p.m., an evening that was capping an absolutely beautiful weekend in the city, weather-wise. The two were under the Deegan Expressway just west of Undercliff Avenue, not far from the massive interchange where George Washington Bridge traffic on I-95 filtered through the entrance to the Bronx. Sean knew why Edgar liked that spot, same as a lot of guys like him. It was an easy walk to a few points on the twisting, concrete ramps where they could panhandle in traffic.

"Jesus, Sean, don't do that," he said, rubbing his face and sniffing loudly. Edgar was bone thin, probably around 35 but looked much older, and wore loose-fitting work pants and a dirty Yankees T-shirt. "Anyone see you?"

"I've been doing this a long time," Sean said tiredly. "No."

"Whatchu want?"

Sean sat down on his haunches next to Edgar. In twenty-three years of policing, he had developed a remarkable network of underground intelligence throughout the Bronx and beyond. His principal CIs–confidential informants–were guys he had busted over the years for various things, some of whom were still attempting to "work off" charges by providing information, and some of whom were just vagrants, addicts or both, looking for a few bucks, which Sean could procure through the use of confidential funds provided by the department.

"Norman Ruiz," Sean said, taking out a photo. He passed it toward Edgar, let him get a good look, and then pulled it back. "Heard of him?" Edgar frowned, and rubbed his face again. Sean knew it might take a few minutes for Edgar to come out of his drug haze, although as a long-time heroin user a guy like Edgar barely felt the high anymore and kept using just to prevent withdrawal effects. Sean produced a cigarette and Edgar took it.

"Shit, man," he said, shaking his head. "That dude's being investigated for cutting up his kid, right? Little retarded kid."

"Autistic," Sean said. "Seen him around?" Edgar seemed to think for a long moment, staring straight ahead at the concrete pillars of the overpass in front of him. Over top, a steady stream of tire and engine noise melted into a constant, low rumble.

"I never saw him with the kid," he said. "I saw that shit in the paper."

"I'm not talking about the kid. I'm asking if you've seen him with any crews."

"In the Four-Four?" Guys like Edgar, having regular interaction with the police, picked up on their jargon as well.

"Anywhere," Sean said, and then passed him a folded twenty dollar bill. Edgar took it without looking at it and slipped it into his pants pocket.

"He's got a boat," Edgar said, drawing heavily on the cigarette. "Decent sized fishing boat, right?"

"Correct. You've seen it?"

"No, I don't go out there. But people know about it."

"Who knows about it?"

"There's a crew that hangs out around an old tire shop. It's near the Mt. Eden stop. There are two brothers. They run the crew, probably out of the shop. Juan and someone. I only met the one guy, Juan. Your man hangs around with them. I've seen him down there."

"What does this crew do?" Sean asked. Edgar looked down and to his right, toward Sean, but not at him. Silently, Sean fished out another perfectly folded twenty and passed it over between two fingers. Like the first, it disappeared into Edgar's pocket.

"One of the brothers has a van with North Carolina plates. They bring cigarettes up." Edgar paused for a moment. "Probably guns, too." Sean nodded at this. Edgar didn't even have to say the "guns" part. In Sean's experience, guys who ran cigarettes from the southeastern US often ran firearms as well. Like the cigarettes, they were cheap and plentiful below the Maryland line. "Lately, though, they bring girls in. Turn 'em out."

"Girls? From where?"

"Shit, I don't know. Anywhere, I guess. Jersey, Pennsylvania, Central America, I don't know. But your man, there. He runs them back and forth to parties, and bars and shit. And there's that boat he's got. They go out there, too. Guys talk about it."

Sean nodded and stood up. His hamstrings ached. The gang unit and Bronx Anti-Crime, he knew, might be able fill in many of the blanks from here. There might be surveillance footage also. But this created a good starting point, and probably confirmed the suspicion that Norman Ruiz was, in fact, 'in the life.'

"What do I always tell you?" Sean asked, looking down at Edgar and passing him one more cigarette. Edgar swiped it away and shook his head.

"Yeah, yeah. Detox. One of these days."

"Forget detox, Edgar, just get your ass to a take-out. Get some food in you, you look emaciated."

"Been busy," Edgar said, staring blank-faced in front of him into the gathering dark. "Watch yourself walkin' out of here, okay? I don't need a trail comin' back to me."

CHAPTER 15

8:25 p.m.

In the quickly fading evening light, the last few scraps of yellow and black police tape, wrapped around wooden stakes, whipped in a stiff, offshore breeze on Lido Beach. The four year-old, Liam, had been warned away from the taped-off area by his parents, one of whom, his father Jeff, followed thirty or so paces behind him on the beach scratching out a message on his cell phone. The crime scene, just in front of the dunes, was no longer cordoned off. But most of the local residents avoided it anyway and felt spooked by it. Lido Beach wasn't crime-free, but it also wasn't the place throat-cut bodies appeared bled-out in the sand, either.

Liam wandered between the two remaining stakes, through the area where the unidentified male had been found, and then to the edge of the dune grass itself. There in the grass, something had caught his eye. It was a baggie, like the kind of sandwich bags his mother used. But this baggie didn't have a sandwich in it. It had something far more interesting.

"Liam!" the man called out, looking up from his phone and realizing his son had wandered all the way up to the edge of the dunes. Were his ex-wife here to see this, he knew, she'd probably deny him weekend visitation absent a court order. "Liam, get out of there!"

"Daddy, look!" he announced, holding up the baggie. He tried to free the contents, pulling at the plastic.

"Liam, drop that!" his father yelled, cursing to himself and breaking into a jog. He reached his son and swiped the baggie out of his hand.

"Don't pick up stuff on the ground," he said, wagging a finger. He glanced around and fought off a shudder. It had been a gorgeous April day, but it was almost full dark. And it was like they were standing in a graveyard. But worse.

"Lollipops!" Liam said. "Daddy, can I have one?" Jeff inspected the bag. Sure enough, that's all it was. Three ordinary looking lollipops, all yellow.

"I'll buy you a lollipop," his father said. "I don't know where these came from." With that, he took his son's hand and walked quickly through the area and over the dunes, depositing the baggie and its contents into a trash barrel.

CHAPTER 16

Tuesday, April 19

Alex knew as soon as he set eyes on Danny and Sean. They were waiting in his office when he returned from an afternoon meeting with that healthy, self-satisfied look detectives wore when they had discovered something big on a case. Still, they weren't smiling.

"I think we've got it put together," Danny said. "I went back over everything with Connie and Bruce. Sean talked to Joseliz. There's a timeline."

"Hang on," Alex said. He left and came back wheeling in a portable white board. Picking up a marker, he looked at Danny. "Okay, shoot."

"Norman told us he left the house a little after three, expecting to be back in a half-hour, forty-five minutes. There was the money pick-up, and then the hardware store on one seventy-fifth. That's where Sean found him at three-forty. We confirmed that with security video."

"So, he expected to be home sometime between three-forty-five and four o'clock?" Alex asked, writing the times down.

"Right," Sean said. "He probably wouldn't have been in the hardware store more than another four or five minutes, and it was a two-minute drive back to the house from there. But Joseliz got there first and let herself in right around three twenty-five. That corresponds with the responding officer- Murphy- who called in the body at three twenty-seven." Alex nodded and recorded the times on the white board.

"The thing is," Danny said, "she was early.

Turns out she was supposed to get to the house around four o'clock."

"Oh, damn," Alex said, recording the time and standing back from the board. "So maybe he was surprised by her. Figured he'd have time to get back from wherever he was before she showed up."

"Exactly," Danny said. "She had been at HCC. She got there after her classes let out, maybe two-thirty. She was supposed to go see Hector around four. But Connie asked her to go over earlier, around three-fifteen."

"What was that about?"

"I interviewed Connie and Bruce again yesterday," Danny said, thumbing through his notes. "They filled in some of the blanks. Bruce says he saw Norman twice that day. Once, when he was picking up Hector from school. That was around one forty-five. He says he reminded Norman about the party they were having for Hector, and said Joseliz would be over around four o'clock to pick Hector up. Norman said he wasn't sure if he'd make the party, but that he'd be there when Joseliz got there."

"Okay," Alex said, noting all of this in different columns on the white board. "Then he saw Norman again?"

"Yeah, he saw him in his car on Walton Avenue, near

the cross-Bronx. That's a five or six minute drive from the house. That was at three eleven. And Norman was alone."

"Ah. So he figured the kid was left alone? How do we know the exact time?"

"Bruce snapped a picture, through the windshield, at Norman's car at a stoplight. He sent that as a text to Connie, and then another one behind it that said, 'guess who?.' I have a printout of texts and the photo. You can't see Norman very well, but the car looks like his.

"Anyway, Connie texted back "uh-oh." That was at three-twelve. At three-thirteen, Bruce was driving again, so he called Connie instead of texting. He says he asked her if Joseliz was at Hector's or if Hector was at HCC. Connie said Joseliz was at the center and hadn't seen Hector. Brice told me it wasn't that big of a deal, that Norman was known for going out when he wasn't supposed to. But they both figured they should send Joseliz over early if she didn't mind going. Of course, she didn't. So, she walked from HCC over to the house. Took her maybe eight or nine minutes. She found him when she walked in."

"Do we know what he was looking for, once he got to the hardware store?" Alex asked, looking over at Sean.

"Trash bags and cleaning stuff. The counter guy remembered. He was looking for bags in one of the aisles when I came in with patrol."

"Jesus," Alex whispered, putting it together in his own head. "So, he kills the kid, then runs out for stuff to clean up with." He looked from the white board over to them. "But why the first stop? I mean, if you just killed a child, and you need to start covering your tracks, why run some extra errand? I know he thought he had time, but still."

"You're right, it's weird," Danny said, switching back

into the present tense as speculated about Norman. "But yeah, he figures he has the time. Joseliz isn't supposed to be there until four o'clock. So as long as he's home when she gets there, he tells her the kid is asleep, or tired, or not feeling well. They can reschedule the party, it certainly wasn't a big deal to him. He didn't even mention it to me when I interviewed him the day of. So, then she leaves. Norman finishes up, waits till dark, and gets the body out the side door and into his trunk. Then he goes over to the boat, takes it out, and dumps him."

"And to explain the disappearance," Alex said, staring blankly in front of him. "Elopement."

"You got it," Danny said, nodding. "He can say the kid just walked out once he woke up or felt better. Went...who knows? Drowned in the river. Got picked up by some as-shole, whatever. Never seen again. Eventually it just becomes a missing persons thing. Stays open, but..."

"Seems risky," Alex said. "There'd be a full search of the house, all that stuff."

"If he cleaned up well enough?" Sean asked, shrugging. "Who knows? People have gotten away with sloppier jobs. The tub was a convenient place. Caught almost everything." Alex pondered it all for a minute or two, staring at the board.

"Motive?" he asked finally. "Anything concrete?"

"We can only speculate right now," Sean said. "If Danny can break him down, get him to talk, maybe we get some idea of what was in his head. But as it is, we've got people who heard Norman saying some awful things to him."

"It could be he snapped and just killed the kid," Danny said. "Maybe got pissed because he wouldn't get out of the tub. Or, maybe he'd been thinking about it for a while, and he figured now was the time, with the kid sleeping in a place that would catch the blood."

"Okay," Alex said. "Yeah, this is probably it. I'm meeting with Raquel before the end of the day. I'll update her. Any sense of how easy it'll be to pick him up if I authorize an arrest?"

"Shouldn't be a problem," Danny said. "We know where he is and patrol goes by every now and then. We'll coordinate with you, whatever you need."

CHAPTER 17

7:15 p.m.

Alex never saw the three men watching him, following him with their eyes in sync as he walked down 161st street toward the Yankee Stadium subway station. It was a couple of hours after he had authorized an arrest for Norman Ruiz, and he was on his way home, his phone to his ear, listening to a voice mail message from a lawyer on another case. It was still light out and the air was breezy, dry and cool.

He had just walked past a small bodega when two of the watchers walked out behind him, following him at a few yard's distance. Now thumbing through emails and texts, he almost bumped into the third man, this one facing him and standing in his path. The man was of average build in baggy jeans and a hooded sweatshirt. His hands were in his pockets, but he looked poised, utterly calm and clearly ready for anything, including a confrontation. He was dark-skinned, Latino, Alex figured, and had a handsome, but tired, prematurely lined face and a tattoo Alex couldn't see that sprouted from his shirt up onto his neck. There were no two ways about it, he looked like a gang-banger. Now Alex looked behind him and saw the two men who had followed him from out of the bodega. They were younger and looked a good deal rougher than the one he was talking to.

"Alex Greco?" the man asked, in a polite tone. His voice was higher than Alex would have assumed, and almost raspy. Alex looked back at him. In over fifteen years of prosecution, he had never been seriously pursued or bothered by anyone he prosecuted. Most defendants either didn't notice the DA at all or accepted that they were just doing a job like anyone else in the system. It was defense attorneys, because of the more personal nature of their representation, who had more trouble with angry defendants.

"I am," Alex said. He looked briefly around him. The street was still busy with school kids, old people, delivery drivers and others walking back and forth. A Yankee game was underway at the stadium up the block and the cheers were audible. For the moment, anyway, he didn't feel threatened although the hair on his arms was standing up a little. "Can I help you?"

"I need to speak with you," the man said. "Just for a minute. Do you mind?" He gestured into the open door of a pizza and gyro place, one Alex had been in from time to time. It was empty except for two small children and an old woman way in the back. One guy was behind the counter and watching the man who was talking to Alex with an air of familiarity.

"Are they coming too?" Alex asked, gesturing slightly with his head toward the younger guys behind him.

"No," he said, again politely. "They'll wait outside. *Neno! Espera aca. Ahorita vuelvo.*" Then, to Alex, "Come on in. It'll just take a minute."

Once inside, the man asked Alex if he wanted anything. Alex politely declined and the two sat at a table by the window. Outside, the two guys on the street talked and watched passersby.

"Do you know me from the DA's office?" Alex asked, once they had settled in. The man nodded.

"Of course. And I know this is unusual for you. But I mean no harm. No disrespect, either."

"Likewise," Alex said. "But whatever this is, my office wouldn't approve of it." The man nodded, as if this made sense to him.

"Hector Ruiz," he said. "The boy. With the condition, who was murdered. You caught that case." It wasn't a question. Alex thought for a moment about declining to answer, but then just nodded. The man nodded back. "His father. Norman. He's the one who did it."

"Well, that's a possibility we're looking at," Alex said with a shrug. "If you've got information on it, I'd be a lot more comfortable if I could put you in touch with a detective…"

"No," the man said, still calm. "Just you. I don't talk to cops."

"Okay."

"Look at this." With that, he pulled out a smartphone and thumbed over it until he found a video. He handed it over as it began playing. In it, a man who looked a lot like Norman Ruiz stood with a knife in his right hand, in a field someplace with lush, green mountains in the background. The recording was shaky, but clear enough. The man eventually came upon an animal- a goat or a lamb, Alex figured, although he wasn't quite sure of the difference- and then straddled it. He looked at the camera and smiled. Then he lifted the goat's head back and slashed its neck open. Blood sprayed from the wound and the goat wobbled around for a second or two and then collapsed. Cheers were heard from the crowd. He climbed off and wiped the knife off with a rag from his pocket.

"That's Norman Ruiz?" Alex asked as the video ended with the killer's hand freezing on the bloody rag, a ragged grin on his face. The man took the phone back and stuffed it into a pocket.

"Yeah. He's a cousin of mine, on my father's side. That was in the Dominican Republic, where we're originally from. Norman's good with a knife. A few of us in the family have videos like that one."

"Okay."

"He *enjoys* it, mister. I've seen him cut lots of animals. It's what he does. It's the only time he smiles."

"That's a lot different from cutting a child, though..."

"It was him," he said plainly. With that he reached into his pocket and handed Alex a battered, black flash drive. "That same video is on this memory stick. There are others also. Can you use them?"

"It's possible, but only under certain circumstances, like maybe if he were to testify at a trial or something. I can't use it right now." The young man's face didn't wrinkle with disbelief or frustration. It was like he figured that was the answer. "But it's good for you to know," he said. "You get the point."

"I do. I'm just not sure what I can do with it. Any idea where that knife is?"

"I thought about that," he said. "But no, I don't think so. This was over there, and it was probably someone else's he used. From the size of it I doubt he'd travel with it. But he's got other ones. Believe me."

"We're looking into that," Alex said. "For now, all I can tell you is I'll keep it in mind. Do you want me to take contact information for you? Do you want mine?"

"I know how to find you," he said. "And I know how to call your office. I just see you on this block, so…"

"I should probably shake up my routine," Alex said, mostly to himself. The man almost smiled, but not quite.

"You need to make this right," he said, letting his eyes rest in Alex's. They were bright and intense. He was smart, whoever he was.

"If he's charged, I'll do my best," Alex said. "That's all I can tell you."

"You make it right," he said. "He's family, or I would have made it right by now. But I'll leave it to you, and the law, this time. If it's not right, someone will make it right."

"You know I can't be a part of anything like that," Alex said. The man nodded.

"Of course not. I'm just telling you how it is. You can go now. Thank you for speaking with me."

"Yeah, sure," Alex said. "Thank you, Mr…"

"You can call me Oscar," he said. "You ask anyone in this place if you need me. They can reach me, and I'll find you."

"The detectives I work with," Alex said. "I have to ask. Do they know you also?" At this Oscar smiled thinly.

"Some do, some don't. It's all good, Alex. I just don't talk to them. But I'll talk to you. Have a good night." With that, Oscar stood up and left without another word.

CHAPTER 18

9:45 p.m.

Norman rubbed his wrists and glanced momentarily around him in the Four-Four interview room as Danny took off the handcuffs. He had been arrested without incident about thirty minutes before, and now Alex sat across from him with a clipboard that contained the script ADA's used when interviewing suspects. Since Danny was present and witnessing the interview, Alex was cleared to take his statement. The only other person in the room was a camera technician from the office named Vince Boyer, a whippet thin, hipster looking guy with a beard and mustache. Vince had his small video camera mounted on a tripod, along with a light that illuminated the table where the interviewee sat.

"Is the light okay?" Vince asked from behind the tripod, either to Alex or Norman, Alex was unsure which. "It can be a little bright, but the overhead lights produce heavy shadows."

"It's fine," Norman said. "I'll answer whatever you ask. I told you I didn't do this thing."

Alex went down the same path of questioning Danny had at the first interview, basically covering the day Hector had died, where Norman had been when the police found him, and what he'd been looking for at the hardware store. Norman acknowledged he had been buying cleaning products and trash bags, but insisted it was for his boat, which was rigged for fishing and still hadn't been fully cleaned since going into the water around mid-March. Then Alex turned to the issue of Hector "eloping" from the house.

"The street is dangerous," Norman said, "and Jerome Avenue is right at the end. There's a lot of traffic there. So sure. When he just walked out like that? I got scared. Sometimes, I got mad. But I never hurt him. Not on purpose."

"Did you ever drag him, though?" Alex asked. "Maybe drag him back inside, by his arm?" At this Norman looked up, and into Alex's eyes. Alex felt a chill; the guy's eyes were a cold, kind of dark gray color, just short of blue. But instantly they flicked away.

"Sir, have you ever had to deal with a child like my son?" he asked, his chin rising slightly, again in that proud, almost but not quite defiant way.

"No, sir," Alex said. It wasn't a completely true statement of course. Jordan had died much younger, but Alex had dealt with the meltdowns and tantrums and a dozen other things. But this wasn't the time or place to elaborate, as much as a part of him wanted to. *Yes, you son of a bitch. I have. And I didn't murder him.*

"Then you don't know. Grab him by the arm? To get him off of the street? Sure. I did that.

I did what I had to do to keep him safe. He would go out the front door, sometimes. I could never tell when. It didn't happen so much that I was ready for it. But it happened enough so it could take up my whole day. From work. From providing for him. So yeah, I would follow him.

114

And yes, usually I had to grab him. I don't know how many times. You want to know if I cursed at him? Or if I said bad things that maybe some neighbor heard? Sure, probably I did. But it was just talk."

"The knives we found in your home," Alex asked, switching gears. "Can you tell me about them?"

"I use them for fishing, mostly. We clean the fish ourselves. You need knives for that."

"Have you killed other animals as well with knives, Mr. Ruiz?" Alex glanced over at Danny, who nodded minutely. He had given Danny just a few details about the run-in with Oscar and what he had been shown.

"Yes," Norman said, as if he, like Danny, also expected the question. "You ask because I've slaughtered lambs and goats for family events. In my father's country."

"Do you mean you've cut their throats with knives, Mr. Ruiz?"

"Yes," he said, and for a split second his nostrils flared and the dark storm in his eyes was back. But then it smoothed. "We do things the old way there. We have no choice, to feed our families or to celebrate important things. There's no money to buy meat that's wrapped so pretty, like in the store."

Alex glanced over at Danny, who gave a barely perceptible shrug. There wasn't much more they were likely to get from him. The camera was shut off and Norman rose, putting out his hands to be cuffed. He eyed Alex as he did so.

"You ask me questions about how I kill animals to eat," he said as Danny clicked the cuffs on. "What is that for, except to make me look like a monster?"

"The interview is over, Mr. Ruiz," Alex said. "Please don't speak to me."

"I do what I have to do to feed my family. Don't you?" Alex looked over at him to remind him again that they couldn't converse, and saw that Norman's eyes had narrowed on him, almost squinting. "Or do you even have a family?" Alex opened his mouth to speak, not sure for a terrifying split second what might come out.

"Move it," Danny said then, and there was unfamiliar steel in his voice. He nudged Norman forward toward the door. "And fuckin' keep quiet."

CHAPTER 19

"Oscar Carrera," Danny said, dropping a couple of black and white photos on Alex's desk. It was a little before 9:00 a.m., and the case against Norman was about to be presented to the grand jury. "The one Rolando Garcia mentioned. Is he the guy who approached you, the night we picked up Norman?"

"Yeah, that's him," Alex said. The photos were dark and had been taken from some height, like from a wall or a light post. "What do we know about him?"

"He's a known quantity in the precincts south of the cross-Bronx," Sean said. "He's ganged up, for sure. He's upper level, though, and very quiet."

"What's his business?"

"Drugs, mostly. There are smaller, street-level crews who kick up to him through other people. He did time on a distribution charge a few years ago, but he keeps a low profile now. No history of violence, but at his level you don't have to do it yourself."

"He's no joke," Danny said. "The guy is a boss."

"I already told him," Sean said, nodding toward Alex,

"he's nuts for not calling one of us when it happened."

"The guy was a perfect gentleman. I don't know what to tell you. And he didn't do anything remotely illegal."

"He threatened it, though," Sean said. "'Making it right.' So he'll smoke Ruiz if you can't get him convicted. Fine. But you're sure it wasn't you he was talking about?"

"I didn't get that vibe from him," Alex said. "He wanted to give me the video more than anything." With that, Alex plugged into his laptop the flash drive Oscar had handed to him. The video was the only file on it.

"We can't use this thing, right?" Danny asked when they had seen it. Alex shook his head.

"Not at this stage, no. And probably not ever, unless he testifies, either at Grand Jury or at trial, that he's never used a knife that way, or something like that. I won't hold my breath for that to happen."

"And Carrera doesn't think the knife is one Ruiz uses now?"

"No, the video was shot in the DR. You can barely see the knife in it anyway."

"It's interesting, though," Sean said. "I agree there's a big difference between using a knife on a goat for a barbecue and on your own kid. But it's interesting."

"I've seen my people do some fucked up things to animals," Danny said, shaking his head. "But there's a different mindset over there. You kill things. You eat them. I'm with Sean, though. It's something else for us to consider."

"It all goes into the mix," Alex said. "I'll make a note to the file. Let's go put this thing on."

CHAPTER 20

Bronx Grand Jury panels met for five days a week in roughly month-long shifts, twenty to twenty-five borough residents of every imaginable description and circumstance. They sat for roughly eight hours a day in a dingy, theater-style classroom setting, as if meeting at some college on the verge of bankruptcy. Their job was to listen to the presentation of felony cases, usually dozens over the course of a typical month, brought by Alex's office.

Because they usually met for four weeks, grand jurors got to know each other. They gossiped, argued, shared food, and so on. The group dynamics created a distinct personality for each panel. Many ADAs dismissed grand jurors as busybodies, morons and assorted others not ambitious or connected enough to avoid month-long service, but the better ADAs knew them to be valuable. For better or worse they represented the community, and their impression of a case was a decent reflection of how strong it was, and how the community was likely to value it.

Alex called Rolando, Joseliz, the neighbor Mrs. Esparza, Sean, and Danny in quick succession, and things went swimmingly. At times ripples of disbelief and head-shaking anger went through the room. When Danny testified, wearing a French-blue dress shirt with a stylishly loosened tie, most of the female grand jurors perked up. After Danny, the Medical Examiner, Margaret Hettinger, testified confidently and quickly. The case had taken about three hours to present, and it was almost time for the 1:00 lunch hour. Alex was almost whistling as he left the grand jury room. Then his phone vibrated.

"Alex, it's Rick Melendez." Rick was a well-respected attorney with an office in Manhattan as well as the Bronx and had been an ADA in the Bronx before Alex's time. Alex had not tried a case against him yet and got along with him. "I've got the Ruiz case."

"You know it's in grand jury, right?"

"Yeah, and I'm calling to tell you he wants to testify." There was a pause as Alex absorbed this. It was highly unusual for defendants to testify at the Grand Jury. Rarely was it in their best interests, as whatever they said was recorded and could be used against them at trial. Plus, they could be cross examined. If a defendant was interested in testifying, it was usually because he thought there was a possibility of it getting 'kicked' at Grand Jury. That meant betting on the Grand Jury to vote not to send the case on for trial, denying what was called a "true bill." That that was rare, though, even in the Bronx. The legal standard of proof for a true bill was very low.

"He wants to what?"

"He wants to waive and testify. I can be there with him tomorrow morning, when the panel starts if that works for you. Can you have him brought over?"

"I'll draw up a transport order," Alex said, masking a sigh. His mind was spinning with the information.

"Great, thanks. I'll talk to him tonight at Rikers. He'll be ready." Nothing in Rick's tone seemed to indicate whether he thought Ruiz testifying was a good or bad idea, and in any case it wasn't Alex's place to ask him. Instead he thanked him for the heads up, then headed back to the office to get the paperwork going.

"What the fuck?" Alexa asked rhetorically as Alex showed her the transport order, about an hour later in his office. He shrugged as he took it back from her. She shook her head. "No way Rick will let this happen."

"It's not his choice."

"I know that. But Rick is good with client control. He'll probably talk him out of it. If not, whatever. Let him come in and hang himself. Rick gets paid either way."

"Maybe. In any event I've got an all-nighter ahead planning a cross exam. Any thoughts?"

"He thinks he can get it kicked," she said, staring straight ahead as she thought it through. "Thinks he can charm them, maybe. I've seen it with pimps. It's a psychopathic move, but sometimes it works." She looked up at him. "But I thought this guy came off like an unlikable asshole."

"He does. He generally acts like the whole thing is a big nuisance, like having a car towed. But I think he can clean up and present well for a grand jury. He might come off like a victim. We were on him, fast, in terms of the investigation. He could say he was ganged up on, I don't know."

"It shouldn't matter," she said, "but this *is* the Bronx. If he does manage to sound decent? Be careful how you challenge him. Don't take this the wrong way but remember what you represent to most of those people."

"The big white guy," he said with a sigh.

"Yes. The Man, as it were. I'm sure they like you. Most

people do. But if he comes off as sympathetic for whatever reason and you go after him, there could be a backlash. I'd keep the cross very technical. And short. Just get some concessions that coincide with your theory, and let it rest. Don't worry, hon. They'll indict."

CHAPTER 21

Friday, April 22

Norman seemed taller as he entered the Grand Jury room, his posture no longer slouching and his chin high. Coming in after him was Rick Melendez. Rick was an imposing figure, tall and heavy set with a smiling, round face, olive skin, and sleek but thick eyeglasses. Above the glasses a wide forehead swept back to a lick of black hair. As Norman's attorney, Rick was allowed in the room and would listen to his client's testimony, but he was not allowed to ask questions. He could, however, object to them, either ones that Alex asked or that the grand jurors themselves asked.

As was his right, Norman wore civilian clothes so the jail jumpsuit he was otherwise living in wouldn't prejudice him before the panel. He wore dark slacks, a short-sleeved white shirt and a thin black tie, like a 60's engineer. He looked respectable and non-threatening. His eyes swept across the rows of jurors who stared back at him intently. *They probably haven't seen a defendant testify,* Alex thought. Then he went through the waiver and swearing in with the court reporter. "You've indicated you wish to make a statement to the Grand Jury, Mr. Ruiz," Alex said.

"You may do so at this time." Norman nodded to him, cleared his throat, and turned to the jurors.

"My father brought us to this country," he began, slowly and sonorously. "My mother, my brothers and me. I was a boy, no more than six. The first winter, I thought I would die from the cold. I cried all the time. I'm not ashamed to say it." Alex looked over at the panel and saw an older Hispanic woman, whose face had been a mask of anger when Norman walked in, soften and crack a small smile. "But my father told me. He told me that feeling- the cold- was how life was supposed to feel. It was, he said, how you felt when you woke up. That's how it was for us, when we came here. We woke up. We saw what life could be, if we worked hard and were lucky enough to be in America. I've worked my entire life to be the person my father wanted me to be."

"Mr. Ruiz," Alex said, stepping in as Norman drew a breath to continue. "I have to ask you to confine your statement to matter at hand. You can explain the circumstances of Hector's birth and how he came to the US to live with you, but how your family came to the US isn't relevant to how he died."

"This is who I am," he said, almost apologetically. "I don't know what else to say."

"Well, sir, you have to confine your statement to the facts around your son's death. You can provide some background, but it has to be relevant to Hector only."

"I think it's all relevant," the woman in the back said, the older one who had smiled before. "He's here to tell us his side, right?"

"Yes," Alex said carefully, "but the rules of evidence dictate that what he tells you has to be directly relevant to the case."

"I think it's relevant," a young white woman in the front row said, turning around to see if others agreed with her. A few nodded, and a murmur went through the crowd. Alex was about to say that it was his job to make that determination, but then thought better of it.

"Mr. Ruiz," he said, "go ahead. Just please, tell them about Hector if you'd like, but then the details you want them to know about the day in question. That's what we need to hear about."

"I'm very sorry," Norman said, giving Alex a direct but respectful look. "I won't waste their time. Or yours." He turned back to the room. "I can't say I'm proud of how I treated my son or his mother- my late wife- until I came to my senses a couple of years ago. I sent money while Hector was growing up, back to the Dominican Republic where they were. But I didn't acknowledge them as my family. That was wrong, and I have to live with it. It took my wife's illness to finally make me see what my duty was to her, and to Hector. You may have heard that my wife- we were married shortly before she died- did everything she could for Hector when I wasn't there. She got cancer, and that's when I went to get them both. She died and I brought Hector back with me. I've been on my own with him ever since." He stopped and glanced at Alex sheepishly. "Can I say more?" Alex wanted to throw something at him. This was not the person he had encountered before today. Not by a long shot. Now the grand jurors were glaring less at Ruiz and more at Alex.

"It's your statement," Alex said. "But we do need to hear about the day in question."

"I understand," he said, and then turned back conversationally to the room. "I worked that day, picked Hector up from school, and was home with him about two o'clock that afternoon." With that, he told them basically what he had said on camera, and then described being found at the hardware store, something he described as an arrest. "The next thing I knew, there were police all around me. A detective was in my face, telling me my son was dead. And in the most...horrible way." He paused for a second as if to collect himself. On a clipboard, Alex was making notes of the things he would cross Ruiz on, but he kept second guessing himself and crossing them out. He was sorely tempted to be aggressive on cross and attack the guy for various inconsistencies, but he had to remember Alexa's advice. Ruiz was sounding like a grieving father. Going after him with an aggressive cross could play right into his hands.

"The police took me to the precinct," he went on. "I had no time. No time to think. No time to mourn. I've had no time since, really. The police believed immediately that it was me who did this to my son. They never asked about anything else. They never asked anyone else about me, except to ask if they had seen me hurt Hector. They asked for dirt." He paused and looked over at Alex, who stared back impassively and felt the eyes of the grand jurors on him with increasing judgment. "I'm sorry, but that's what they did. They asked people who don't like me, and who didn't like Hector. He was an embarrassment, I guess, to the neighborhood. He got out sometimes, and I had to bring him back so he wouldn't hurt himself. He made noise. He couldn't help it. I know there were people who didn't like us. The police found people who would say bad things about me, but I didn't do this thing." Norman finished the last sentence and his head drooped forward. A few of the women in the room were tearing up. Some of the men shook their heads. The rest just stared straight ahead, seemingly perplexed. Inwardly, Alex wanted to scream.

"Mr. Ruiz, is that all you'd like to say?" Norman didn't answer for a few seconds.

"I lost Hector's mother," he said finally. "Now I've lost Hector. To some...monster. Some monster who is still out there." He pointed toward the windows at the back of the room, and a couple of the jurors turned their heads in knee-jerk fashion. Then he turned back to Alex. "But the police decided that day what happened. Now I guess your office has decided also. I have nothing else to say."

"You understand I have to ask you some questions now, sir?"

"Yes, of course."

In a short and methodical cross examination, Alex clarified that Ruiz was never "under arrest" at the hardware store, and that he was told that fact. He clarified the timeline, and Ruiz's belief that Joseliz wouldn't be at the house until 4:00.

"But you were surprised to find out she arrived early, correct?"

"Sure," Norman said. "But that would have been okay. Hector loved her, like I said."

"You didn't expect Joseliz to be there by three twenty-five, Mr. Ruiz," Alex asked carefully, "did you?" Now, in an almost imperceptible flash, Alex saw in Norman's eyes the same bright anger he had seen previously. Then it was gone.

"No. But she had a key. It would have been fine if she came early. I just thank God she wasn't hurt by whoever did this." At this, another murmur went through the crowd. Alex could feel the muscles in his neck starting to ache. He was sweating, and thankful he had a jacket on.

He turned back to the jurors, ready for the part he was seriously dreading.

"Are there any questions for the witness?" he asked. Too many hands went up to count at first. Alex clamped down on a sigh and took note of them, then beckoned for Rick to come over to where he was. The way it worked was that Alex went from person to person, knelt beside them, and had them whisper the question to him. If it was legally appropriate, and if Rick didn't object, he would ask it, on the record, to Ruiz. Most of the questions weren't too thorny and had to do with the usual childcare arrangements, when Ruiz worked, and things of that nature. Rick had no objections, and Ruiz answered each without trying to add commentary. It seemed to be winding down; some of the jurors with hands up lowered them, their questions apparently asked by someone else. Then Alex came to an African-American man in his 70's or early 80's in the back row. The man had a great white beard and thick glasses, and stared at Alex intently as he whispered the question.

"Who does he think did this to his son?"

"Well...sir, I'm not sure if that's relevant," Alex said. "I mean, his speculation about..."

"There was a small window of time," the man said, eyeing Alex carefully and drawing out the word 'time.' His voice was clear and deep, and he spoke with confidence. "If it wasn't him, it was someone who knew he was leaving the child alone. Maybe someone who was watching. Don't you agree?" Alex took a deep breath and looked over at Rick. Rick just shrugged.

"You wouldn't object?" Alex asked. Rick shook his head.

"No objection" Rick said. "I'd prefer it be asked, actually. If you don't agree, we'll have to see the panel judge."

Alex frowned. Rick favored the question. Alex could provide a legal excuse for not asking it, and perhaps he and Rick could bring it to the presiding panel judge for a final ruling and move on. But then Alex's reluctance might alienate a grand juror, particularly one with a possible theory, and not to mention one with the gravitas of age and presence.

"Okay sir," Alex said to the old man. "Mr. Melendez and I agree it's appropriate. I'll ask it." He stood and took a deep breath. "Mr. Ruiz, the question is…who else do you think could have done this, given that there was a small window of opportunity while you were gone?" Every juror in the room perked up. Norman absorbed the question and his face darkened. He shook his head.

"I'm afraid there are many people, actually," he said. He gave a tired, almost defeated shrug. "I've had a difficult life. Some of it my fault. Some not. My wife's family—they all hate me." Alex tensed up at this. Rolando Garcia, his brother-in-law, had testified the day before without much reaction or any questions. But now the grand jurors had a face to put with a family member who supposedly hated him. And Rolando's face was not a very sympathetic one.

"There are the gangs also," he continued, his voice a little lower. A few grand jurors leaned forward to hear him. "And I know they watch me. I don't like to say what I'm about to say, but for my only son it needs to be said. I have made enemies over the years, both here and back home in the Dominican Republic. I know things. Things about gangs, and drugs. Dangerous things. I have made mistakes in my life. I will not deny that. I have been desperate for money at times, with no idea how I would support my family. I have tried to stay away, now, from that life. But I know people in that life and some of them hate me. They also know very, very bad people. They know people who will kill anything. Anyone. They don't always come for you. Sometimes they come for the people you love." Another murmur. Jurors were now taking notes and whispering to each other.

"Is there anything else?" Alex asked, looking around. Silently he thanked God as no other hands went up.

"Thank you, Mr. Ruiz. I'll now ask that you and your attorney please step outside." They left the room, and Alex turned back to the jurors. Before he could say anything, a woman in the second row with a Jets jersey on spoke up.

"Is that it?"

"I'm sorry. Is that what?"

"Are there any other witnesses?"

"No, there aren't," Alex said. "In a few minutes I'll come back and read the charges, but you all are up for a break first."

"So that might be all you have on this man?" she asked, giving him a quizzical look.

"Oh, give me a break," a Hispanic man about Alex's age called from the back of the room. "You believe this guy?"

"What did that man say that sounded like a lie to you?" she said. "And what about that creeper of an uncle?" The other man started to reply but Alex interrupted as gently as he could. "Folks, please. I'm not allowed to listen to you deliberate. Take a break, and I'll be back in a few minutes."

Thirty minutes later, he was pacing in front of the Grand Jury room as deliberations went on. And on. When it came to deliberations and a vote, no one other than the court reporter was in the room, and she was sworn to secrecy. Alex could hear muffled arguing.

Finally, the battered wooden door opened. The court reporter, a tiny cocoa-colored young woman named Ceci, scurried out without giving Alex a glance. Behind her, the grand jury foreman, a middle-aged Hispanic woman in jeans and a flowered blouse, walked over to the door with her arms crossed.

"True bill," she said, matter-of-factly. After a week or two in Grand Jury, the jurors picked up the lingo. Alex let out a sigh of relief he could not contain.

"Okay. Thank you for your time."

"Good luck with this one, counselor," she said, the last 'r' dropping so it came out 'counsella.' "You're gonna need it."

CHAPTER 22

The door to his apartment was unlocked when Alex finally got home around 7:00 p.m. That was why, despite fumbling with his key in the ancient lock and cursing up a storm, he hadn't been able to turn it. He pushed the door open slowly and peeked inside. His front door opened into the living room, facing the street. The bedroom and bathroom were just past the galley kitchen to the right. He leaned in a little more, suspicious and cautious, and then smiled. From the kitchen, the smell of tomato sauce, savory and rich, reached his nose. There was music also, from the living room speakers. It was Frank Sinatra's "Summer Wind." He smiled and loosened his tie.

"I guess you knew I wasn't bringing anyone home," he said.

"I made enough for her if you did," Nikki Jaynes said. She smiled at him, a glass of wine in hand. He took the glass, drank, and then kissed her.

"I'm glad you're here," he said. "It was a long day."

"I suspect that's an understatement," she said, her eyes searching his. She ran a soothing finger down the side of his face, then nodded toward the stove. "That's simmering. We've got about twenty minutes. Get me out of this skirt."

CHAPTER 23

Thursday, May 12

"So, what do you think?" Alexa asked, sitting cross-legged on a chair across from Alex's desk and digging into a carton of Chinese food. It was a stormy Thursday night, two weeks after Ruiz's first court appearance before a calendar judge. Interestingly, the case had been marked for the "rocket docket," a relatively new experimental program designed to minimize delay in getting cases to trial. The judge, Alphonse Messaria, had set a motions schedule and was overseeing the discovery process whereby Alex would share information with Ruiz's attorney. Trial was targeted to start before the end of the year. Now it was time to create a war room and plot out initial trial strategy, the details of which would set the tone for the next several months.

"You know what I think," Alex said. It's all circumstantial." He gazed at his office wall, one he had stripped and covered with poster-sized pieces of paper with various case details and timelines on it.

"True," she said, "but it's fairly tight. You have that really nice timeline. He was obviously surprised by Joseliz. He was buying cleaning products and plastic bags on his way home. And he made threats." She watched as Alex walked over to the window and peered out at the shopping center next to the DA's office. It had been nicknamed "Perp Plaza" for longer than even Tony Washington, the current, almost 30-year D.A., had been around. Outside it was storming, bringing the kind of lashing wind and lightning that usually bore down after a humid, summer day. Raindrops streamed down the window.

"A murder weapon would be nice," he said.

"So would a signed confession, hon."

"You gonna break my balls all night?" He turned and smirked at her.

"Oooh, check out who's learning the local lingo," she said, smiling. "Think of it this way: You don't have an identified murder weapon, no. But you have a guy with several knives that could have done it, and he's someone who knows his way around them."

"And if I'm really lucky he somehow testifies and claims he never hurt anything with a knife, and I get to cross him on the thing with the goat or whatever."

"Doubtful, but sure. In the meantime, let's focus on something you have that's not on your little war room charts yet."

"Which is?"

"Motive. You've got it for miles with this guy. And by the way, you need to frame it in your opening."

"Mmmm." Alex scrubbed at the stubble on his jaw and seemed to search the paths of evidence and information plastered to the wall. "Yeah I get that. But in an opening statement, you're making promises. You don't deliver, and the other side eats your lunch. As to motive I'll be guessing, no matter what I come up with. The kid embarrassed him? I don't think that's enough. Expenses? He could meet them. And he had plenty of help. So...what? He snapped after a year and a half of having to put up with it all? Maybe, but why then? There's no trigger we're aware of."

"Either pick one and go with it, or find a way to express all of those," she said. "It's got to be put in their heads early."

"Motive isn't an element, darling."

"It might as well be. You need to be able to explain why he did it. Juries have a hard time with the reality of what parents can do to their own flesh and blood. You know that." Alexa saw Alex tense up then, as if he'd been momentarily shocked. Whatever it was, was gone in a second, but it struck her as odd.

"You're right," he said, seeming to smooth over again. "I have to be able to answer that question- why he did it- even before they start asking it."

CHAPTER 24

10:30 p.m.

A couple of miles from Alex's office, Joseliz Perez woke to the velvety, rumbling sound of thunder. The sky through her bedroom window was still stormy, the latest band of showers and lightning sweeping east. She was grateful it hadn't been a nightmare that had woken her, although that wouldn't have been the least bit unusual. What little sleep she'd been getting as the spring slipped by in a numb haze was ruptured by tortuous dreams where Hector was reaching for her from the tub, blood dripping in sheets from his arms. There were ones where he was screaming even though his throat was cut clean through, his eyes wide with terror. She'd been seeing a really nice therapist— Jill— since finding Hector dead. Jill had told her the dreams were trauma being processed, and that with time and therapy, they would fade.

Joseliz knew that was probably true. Already, after about a month, she could feel the worst of the horror loosening its grip on her, both in sleep and wakefulness. But there was something else, two things actually, below both the shock and the terrible emptiness of Hector being gone, that either kept sleep at bay or, like tonight, set in on her the moment she woke up. One was an almost maddening question she could not answer. The other, plain and simple, was guilt.

The nagging question was *why*, in the last weeks of his life, Hector would make his way to the bathtub in the hallway bathroom, on his own.

She had seen him a few times, lying there in the middle of the afternoon with no water in the tub and his clothes on. He would smile, like it was some sort of happy place.

She could usually cajole him out, but why was he going there to begin with? She could get him to bathe, the same way she could get him through other tasks. But the bath was never a thing he looked forward to. It wasn't— in her experience anyway— some sort of place he would escape to for security or pleasure. She had checked more than once. There were no bath toys he was interested in. No stash of candy or snacks she didn't know about. This pull to the bathtub was the one thing in his behavior–which she had learned so much about over the year she had spent with him–that she couldn't mostly predict or understand.

Oh, for God's sake, what do you know anyway? You were making it up as you went along!

Well, not exactly. But she *was* being guided by books and YouTube rather than credentials or professional experience, which she didn't yet have. She wasn't even in a "Sped" program yet, meaning a Special Education teaching program. She was just a general ed student at a community college. In the meantime, she had been working with Hector on her own and had told almost no one about how far she had gotten in terms of getting him to communicate. She really didn't know what to make of it herself. In most other volunteer programs, she would have been significantly more monitored, but HCC wasn't like that. They just didn't ask a lot of questions. And Hector's father Norman was all but invisible. If he was there, he was civil to her but not much else. Sometimes he wasn't home at all, even though he was supposed to be unless someone else was there to watch Hector. That someone was supposed to be "qualified," but outside of the school providers it was usually her, or someone else from HCC.

As it was, Joseliz was the closest person to Hector, and certainly the person who knew him best. For that reason, and because of her successes with him, she had developed a breezy confidence about his care and development. She'd felt an almost proprietary sense about him. A motherly sense. But that was reckless. And in the end, it made no difference. Norman had still butchered him. The last thought made her blood run cold.

She turned back to her thoughts— it was better than picturing him again in the tub. Had she seen anything at all that made his attraction to the bathtub make sense? Down the hallway, she heard her little brother cough. She could hear her grandmother snoring lightly in the next room. She searched her memory but nothing came forward. She curled up, giving in and hoping for sleep to find her.

The pictures?

She sat up again and looked to her right, to her desk and the big binder where she kept the pictures and photographs she used in her "first, then" exercises with Hector. She had kept a log of sorts with how Hector was using them. Soon, maybe, she would look them over. She couldn't bear to do it now. And anyway, who knew what they meant? And who could she tell? *Hey, I was kind of experimenting on the boy who died. What do you think this means?*

She sighed and clutched a pillow, employing a breathing exercise Jill had taught her and letting herself cry softly as a now numbed but still terrible sadness moved though her. *Soon*, she thought. *Soon I'll face this. And then I'll tell what I know.* Sleep found her again a few minutes later, her face still tear-streaked as she sank into slumber.

CHAPTER 25

Friday, May 27

"No I.D. yet on the body found at Lido Beach?" Alex asked, loosening his tie. "Still?" Danny and Sean had joined him, in his office as usual, at the end of the day. Sean shook his head.

"Not yet, no. It's like that guy fell from the sky. What's up?"

"I had a discovery conference with Ruiz's attorney today. He's definitely focusing on the other two bodies, I can tell. I have to assume he'll bring out the issue of the possible pattern through the M.E. I think he's going in the direction you suggested, Sean."

"This thing where Ruiz is the victim of some kind of a serial killer?" Danny asked. "Even in the Bronx, that's crazy."

"Rick won't suggest a Ted Bundy type," Alex said. "It'll be more like an assassin, for a crew. He can take it from the story Ruiz told in Grand Jury, about how he was in the life and there were people out to get him. If Rick is creative and careful about it, he might be able to concoct a boogey-man, some nameless guy out there who killed three people pretty much the same way and around the same time. The last one was a kid. Norman's kid. Remember, they don't have to identify anyone. They just need to plant reasonable doubt, suggest some other monster. If Ruiz comes off as well at trial as he did in Grand Jury, it could work."

"But why is the kid killed if this is gang stuff?" Danny asked.

"A warning, or punishment, maybe," Alex said with a shrug. "Norman said something like that. 'They come for the ones you love,' or something. It doesn't much matter if they can suggest another killer, or even the possibility of one. Norman has proven he can act more likable when he wants to. You get a jury of people that don't want to believe he could do it, and with a circumstantial case and some other bad guy to imagine? That equals reasonable doubt."

"It's a risk, though," Sean said. "We've talked about that, too. Who says Norman didn't do all three? He doesn't have an alibi for either of these other cases. We know Ruiz is involved with some pimps, running girls around the place. Isoli could have been a part of that, somehow. Could be Isoli pissed someone off in Norman's crew. So, they bring in Norman, with his penchant for cutting things, and Norman gets rid of him."

"Okay," Danny said. "But this other guy at Lido? He's a normal looking white guy who wore Tommy Bahama. How is he mixed up with Ruiz?"

"No idea, admittedly," Sean said. "But we get guys like that, living two lives and coming down here from the suburbs for all sorts of bad behavior. I'll keep digging."

"We'll have to see how it plays out," Alex said. "If Rick tries to make Norman look like a victim and gets into his past, I might be able to claim he opened a door to some questions on cross, maybe about how he uses knives, or something like that. It'll be tough, though. And even if I can show he's really the one who's a natural at butchering things, will a jury believe he'd do that to his own kid?" Sean shrugged at this.

"That could've been just Norman being Norman. Maybe something pisses him off- in this case his kid- so maybe he gets rid of the kid, same as he's paid to do with other people. Most of us are guilty of letting what we do at work spill over into our other life."

"Yeah ain't that the truth," Alex said, as much to himself as anyone. When he had a life, his work did spill over into it. It was impossible for him to argue, especially with Dara, without her accusing him of 'acting like a lawyer.' For a moment he relived one of those exchanges. They were bad, sometimes, but they were sweet and funny others.

"Let us know what else we can do," Danny said, shaking Alex back to the present. "Whatever you need."

"Thanks. I'm close to ready for trial at this point. Rick will file some motions over the summer and push things out a few more months. I'll be assigned to other cases in the meantime. I know you guys are catching again also. But let's use the time we have. Keep digging on Ruiz and his gang ties. The more information we have, the better. If he does try to duck this thing by playing the victim on the stand, I want to be able hit him between the fucking eyes on cross."

PART II: SUMMER

CHAPTER 26

In the end, it was Detective Regan's number Joseliz decided to call with the information she had about Hector. It wasn't that she didn't like the other one— Detective Lopez. *Danny,* as her friend Elena had dreamily referred to him after meeting him once at school when he had come to speak to Joseliz.

He *was* hot, but whatever, that didn't phase her. There was something about Detective Regan she sensed was really warm, like a dad, kind of. He seemed gruff, but she could tell, he was a nice man. Her own father had died when she was young, Joseliz barely knew him. So maybe it was that. She had taken several psych classes and was extremely sharp to begin with. It wasn't hard to discern what she was looking for and to be honest with herself about it: *He feels like a dad, and right now I could use a dad.*

There was a part of her that wanted to tell Connie first, meaning tell her everything including these new things troubling her. It wasn't like Connie and Bruce didn't know she was working with Hector and using the pictures. They also knew it was more than just a picture game, although perhaps not to the full extent of what she was attempting.

But Joseliz felt a distance now from Connie. She wasn't sure if she'd even remain at HCC when fall classes started. Since Hector's death, their relationship had changed. Connie seemed tense around her, almost like Joseliz reminded her of some terrible mistake she had made. It wasn't that she sensed Connie blamed her for anything. It was more subtle than that. Or maybe it was just sadness, a chasm of loss compounded when they were faced with each other.

In any event, she had to tell someone, and for the time being, Connie didn't feel right and Detective Regan did. She felt miserable for hiding it for so long. But Regan would get it, right? She held her breath as she dialed his number. He barked his name.

"Regan."

"Detective Regan, hi. It's Joseliz Perez. I'm sorry to be bothering you."

"Oh...yeah. Hey, Joseliz. What's shakin'?" She smiled inside. It was going to be okay.

"Can you meet me today? I need to talk."

CHAPTER 27

Sean took in Joseliz's family's neat, little living room as she sat down in front of him with three items: A simple three-ring binder, an old notebook cover cut to create a makeshift tablet, and a stack of laminated photographs with Velcro squares on the back. They were in the apartment she shared, she had told Sean, with her mother, little brother and grandmother. Her mother was working. Her grandmother had headed to the kitchen when Sean arrived.

"I feel pretty awful about this," Joseliz said. "I hope I'm not in trouble. But I don't care anymore. I have to tell someone."

"I doubt it," Sean said, putting reading glasses on. "I'm glad you called. Tell me what all this is." Sean looked up when he heard Joseliz sigh, watched her bite her lower lip in deliberation.

"You know autistic kids don't process stimuli the way non-autistic kids do, right?" she asked. "At least that's part of it."

"Yeah, I guess. There's perception problems, or something? Communication doesn't get through?"

"Yeah, among other things. I'm not an expert. That's

why I feel so bad about...trying this stuff with him. But it was *working.*"

"Joseliz, relax. It's just us. Tell me what you know." Her grandmother came in with a mug of coffee for Sean. He smiled and thanked her, and also noticed the look the older woman gave to Joseliz with raised eyebrows. It seemed very clearly to say *be honest and do what he tells you, young woman.*

"Okay," she said, seeming to organize her thoughts. "I think, with autistic kids, it seems like the world is coming at them really fast. They get anxious and they freeze. They can't listen to commands, or at least they can't process them. But sometimes you can sort of slow things down, and get them through simple tasks by breaking the tasks down and showing them what's coming next." She handed him the old notebook cover, and Sean noticed there were Velcro squares attached to it as well, in two columns of three each. "See how I made this into like a tablet? With the Velcro, I can attach these pictures to it in whatever order I want." She spread out the photos on the coffee table. Sean noticed they all appeared to be of things in Hector's house. There was a photo of his dresser, and one of a pair of pants, underwear and a shirt neatly laid out. There was one of a toothbrush and toothpaste. There was one of the sink and bathtub. There were also ones of toys, and food. All of them had Velcro squares glued to the back. Sean could see it now, how they could be stuck and then un-stuck to the surface of the notebook cover. "I had these all laminated at a copy place. That way he could handle them without them getting smudged. He really liked them, actually."

"So...you put these pictures up. In some order, depending on what you're trying to get him to do?"

"Yes," she said, a look of sadness darkening her face. He would bet she hadn't handled the pictures at all since the day she'd found Hector, and the memories were flooding back now. Sean felt for her. He thought about suggesting she take a break, but then she was clearing her throat and directing his attention to the photos again. "Let's say I want Hector to brush his teeth. If he does this for me, I want him to know he'll be able to play with something he likes after. He had some toy cars and trucks he loved. This is a photo of them. What I'd do, then, is put the photo of the toothbrush and toothpaste up first. That's the 'first' picture. Then, I put up the toy picture. That's the 'then' picture. That way, Hector knows that, first he brushes his teeth, and then he'll get to play with his cars."

"Ah," Sean said. "So, you can do that with just about anything."

"Yeah, pretty much," she said. "I started with just the two pictures. 'First,' and 'then.' That's a common tool. After a while, I could put more than two pictures up, though, so we could almost plan out a day. Like this— I could put up a picture of him getting dressed. Then a snack. Then some TV. It didn't always work. He'd forget, sometimes. But usually I could bring him back to the pictures, and then he'd go and do the task I asked him to do."

"The school," Sean said, thinking out loud. He looked up at her. "They never got this far."

"They didn't," she said softly. "At least I don't think so. From what I know, he was mostly unresponsive there."

"But he opened up to you."

"Yeah. I guess so."

"Do you know why? Why only you?"

"Not for sure," she said. "I tried to find out. I read once

about a thing called 'selective mutism,' where some kids like Hector just open up to one person, or only in a certain environment. That might have been it. He felt safe with me. And at home."

"Gotcha. Listen, do you mind if I pass this on to the DA, Mr. Greco?" he asked. "He might need to know."

"Yeah, of course," she said. Sean knew he didn't need to ask her permission, and he figured Joseliz sensed that. Anyway, asking was the right thing to do.

"Let me ask you this: Did Hector ever use the pictures, or just you?"

"No, he did," she said, brightening. "Really, that's why I called you. I've been thinking about this for a while." She paused, her brow knitted. "Sometimes, Hector would switch out the pictures, or try to. So, if I put up a picture of his toys all neat in the box, he knew that meant I wanted him to pick up his toys. Then I'd put up a picture of a snack, or some candy. He loved lollipops, especially toward the end. I actually created a picture just of a lollipop. It was his favorite treat after a while."

"You had a lollipop for him," Sean said, carefully as he knew this was a painful memory, "the day you found him, right?"

"Yeah." She stopped for a moment, tearing up. Sean waited and after a short time she seemed collected again. She was, he could tell, a tough kid. "Anyway, sometimes he'd switch out the snack or the lollipop picture for something else, like TV. That meant he wanted to watch TV instead of eating something. Maybe he wasn't hungry, or who knows? But it meant he could make choices, you know?"

"I think so," Sean said. "It sounds like the really important thing was that he understood the consequences of them."

"Exactly," she said, pointing in his direction as if he'd articulated something she had been struggling to express. "Like at first, there were a few times I put up the picture of the toothbrush, and then one of his toys. But he'd switch out the toy and pick up the picture that had a lollipop or a cookie on it. But he couldn't have those things after he brushed, so I'd have to try to explain that. It was all in Spanish. It didn't always work, but he really got, well, better. His choices started to be more rational."

"Okay," Sean said. He was following her. He was also deeply impressed. "So, what about this started to concern you? You said his using the pictures was why you called me." She paused and frowned, as if she was considering how to lay it out clearly.

"Here's the best example I can think of," she said, handing him a picture. It was of the bathtub. "Hector would take a bath, but he didn't look forward to it, at least not that I saw. This wasn't, at first anyway, a picture he would hand me or paste on the tablet to show he expected it as a reward."

"So, it wasn't like a picture of a snack, or TV. The things you'd expect he'd look forward to."

"Yes. But toward the end, sometimes, it seemed like he *was* using it that way. He would switch out a "then" picture of the TV, or even his toys, for a picture of the bathtub."

"Like...he wanted to be in the tub?" Sean asked. "Like that was the reward he expected?"

"Yes. Like he wanted to be in the tub. Sometimes he'd stick a picture of a lollipop or some candy up there with it. But the tub seemed like his focus to me."

"When we interviewed his father," Sean said, looking at the bathtub picture, "he told us Hector was going there on his own, toward the end. Like it was a place he just wanted to be. Felt safe or something."

"We all saw it," she said, shaking her head. "I've been racking my brain over this, trying to figure out what about the bathtub was pleasurable for him."

"Well, Norman didn't know either. But I guess that's not surprising."

"Norman didn't care," she said quietly, and sighed. "Anyway, I don't know if this has anything to do with it. But I had to tell someone."

"I'm glad you did," he said, arching his back a little and wincing. He had been fascinated by what she had told him and was now sore from being in one position for so long. "What's in the binder, anyway?"

"Oh that," she said. "That's a log of how he used the pictures. Every time we sat down with the pictures and the tablet, I recorded what I was putting up, and then how the exercise went, meaning if he followed the task or had trouble. It got more complicated after he started using the pictures also, but I tried to keep up. Basically, I drew a simple chart like this-" she pointed to one of the pages- "and made a bunch of copies of it. I loaded them into the binder after each time we worked together. It shows how he was developing, or at least it's supposed to. The pages are dated."

"Really? You did this every time?"

"Everything I saw on this exercise, or read about, said you have to keep a log to see exactly how the child is pro-gressing. I figured one day, maybe, I'd show it to someone. I should have. I never got the chance."

"It's okay," Sean said, sensing her close to tears again. "I'll write this all up, everything we talked about, and give a report to Mr. Greco. That's my job. He might follow up with you, but I don't know. If he does, I'll be there."

"Okay," she said. "Again, I'm sorry I didn't say something before."

"I don't think you have anything to be sorry about it, Joseliz. Tell me this, though. This isn't what you study in school, right? Not yet, anyway."

"No, not yet. My classes are basic. I'm applying to get into a special ed program. But now...with this? I don't know if anyone would take me."

"I think you'll be alright," he said, winking at her. "Don't sweat it, okay? Day by day, for right now."

"Okay. Thank you for being kind. Do you need to take any of this with you? It has sentimental value to me, but it's also painful to even touch it."

"Not right now," he said, standing to leave. "But keep it in a safe place, just in case." He looked at her closely for a moment. "Where did you learn all of this stuff anyway?"

"Books," she said, with a little shrug. "And online. You can kind of find anything."

"That you can," he said. "That you can."

CHAPTER 28

Sunday, June 13

The first place Alex went with Sean's information from Joseliz was Nikki. He showed her the DD-5, or detective's report, Sean had written up over the weekend on his meeting with Joseliz. The two were seated on her balcony which looked out over Columbus Avenue, on Manhattan's Upper West Side. Nikki's apartment was also small, but warmly decorated and homey, a welcome contrast to Alex's place.

The night was warm and still. Street traffic in front of Nikki's building was a lot heavier than on Alex's block, and even twelve stories up he could hear the bustle from the street, people of every description walking to and from bars, restaurants, and shops. Alex had a beer and an ashtray beside him. He was smoking more these days, something Nikki didn't like, but understood. She was happiest that he seemed to be, in little but important ways, opening up to her more and more as the months went on. The very fact he was spending more time at her apartment and away from the more sterile confines of his own was heartening.

"I'm not an autism specialist," she said. "But this girl sounds like a natural, at least. A genius at most." She took her reading glasses off and looked over at him. "She has no background in this stuff?"

"No formal background. Looks like it was books. And YouTube."

"Not even a sibling with ASD?"

"Not that I know of. She's a bright kid, what I can tell you?"

"She didn't tell anyone at HCC about this?"

"Not fully, until this week, after she spoke with Sean. I talked to Connie today."

"Was she freaked out?"

"Nah, I think she knew Joseliz was up to something. There was a game she played with him at HCC, where she'd get him to match pictures with people they'd seen that day. Connie knew about that. They knew she worked with him on this stuff. I don't think it mattered as long as Connie figured no one was getting hurt."

"Maybe," Nikki said. "But this isn't just a game Joseliz was playing. It's an established therapeutic method. She was teaching him about choices. But not just making them. It was about *communicating* them, and how he felt about them."

"Pretty much."

"So, this was really about expressing himself," she said, stealing a sip of his beer. "That's what she was teaching him to do. She was unlocking him."

"Yeah, I guess she was," he said. "Like an Annie Sullivan, Hellen Keller type of thing." He paused and looked out over the skyline. "This kid had nothing. But then he had her. And it was almost enough, you know?" There was a flash of anger in Alex's eyes. It was almost scary. And, if she was going to be honest, a little hot also. He shook his head. "Almost. But he had Norman, too. The poor, goddam kid had Norman."

CHAPTER 29

The face staring at him, when he emerged from the court-room, was familiar. *Gray*, he thought. *Oh yeah.* It was Rolando Garcia, Hector's uncle. He was wearing pretty much the same outfit as when they'd first met. His face was void of expression, but his eyes seemed to fix on Alex. He looked a little thinner than Alex remembered, and ghost-like as ever. Marcie Bauer, a rookie assistant who had been covering the calendar docket with Alex, looked at him and frowned.

"Do you know him?" she asked, talking out of the side of her mouth.

"Yeah, it's okay," he said. "I asked him to call me. I guess he decided to visit instead."

"I'll take the folders back," she said. "Be careful. He looks like the Grim Reaper."

"I decided to come by instead of calling," Rolando said as he and Alex walked down the stairs of the courthouse. "I hope that's okay. I needed the walk. Your office said you would be here."

"Oh yeah, it's fine," Alex said. "There's a place outside we can talk." He led Rolando to a courtyard behind the

Bronx Hall of Justice along 162nd street, and they took seats on concrete benches under a tree. The humidity was blessedly low, and in the shade the afternoon was a pleasant one. "How much time have you got?" Alex asked as they settled in.

"I'm afraid I've got all day. I've had a bad couple of weeks. I'm not working at the moment."

"Oh. Related to your condition, or..."

"Yes, it is. I feel a little better today. Often, walking helps. It can be tough, though, being around people. I hope I didn't frighten your assistant. I tend to fixate when I'm not doing something with my hands. I work on cell phones, and computers. I'm not so good with social situations."

"Oh, Marcie? No, she's fine."

"I know the effect I have," he said. "It can be unsettling."

"I'm pretty familiar with mental health issues, Mr. Garcia. Please, don't feel self-conscious. You've been nothing but polite and responsive to me."

"Thank you. So, what can I do for you?"

"I'm just following up on a few things. One thing I never asked you was when you last saw Hector, or talked to Norman. Do you remember?"

"Maybe a week before Hector died, I was over there. I talked to Norman, but rarely. All he ever wanted from me was money, and I don't have any, so I wasn't worth much to him. But I came by from time to time. I'd bring little things for him. Simple toys. Or *chupetes*. That means..."

"Lollipops," Alex said, nodding. "I lived in Mexico for a while."

"Exactly, lollipops. He really loved those, especially the last few months. And red licorice. Sometimes he would try to tie knots with the licorice. He was very tactile, Hector.

He liked to hold things in his hands. I think, if he had been given the chance, he might have been a little like me. Someone who could work with his hands, even if he wasn't so good with people."

"Thanks for the detail" Alex said. "You never know what's valuable. Also, was there anything else you remembered about where you were on the day Hector died? I'm sorry if that seems intrusive. We have to ask."

"Of course, it's fine. As I said before, I think I felt a breakdown coming even before the news. I wasn't at work in the morning. In the afternoon I was doing what I'm doing now. Walking. I'm afraid that's not very helpful."

"Do you remember where? Or do you have a usual route? If we can confirm anything, it might help us keep diversionary tactics at bay."

"Ah, like Norman trying to suggest it was the crazy uncle who slaughtered Hector," he said, bitterness clear in his voice. A little bit of the creepiness resurfaced also, as if the thought was somehow amusing. "He would do that. Sure."

"Usually it's just a few questions the attorney tries to plant strategically," Alex said. "Maybe it generates some reasonable doubt. Hangs a jury. We just want to be prepared for anything. I don't think you're in any legal danger."

"There's a cemetery, in Woodlawn," he said, looking away. "It's very peaceful. I go there frequently. It's a couple of miles from my shop."

"Is someone buried there you know?"

"Oh, I wish I could say there was," he said. "I know how it sounds, but no. I just like the stillness."

"It sounds normal to me," Alex said. "We all need quiet time, I think. God knows I do."

"May I ask how the case is going? Other than this possible issue with my whereabouts?"

"We're gearing up," Alex said. "It's a circumstantial case, which can be difficult to prove. I'll do the best I can."

"I appreciate your efforts," Rolando said. "I can only hope justice is done. Frankly I think Norman has been evading justice for a long time."

Alex nodded at this, unsure of how else to respond. "We've uncovered a few things about Norman that are somewhat disturbing. He doesn't seem like a particularly good guy."

"It's more complicated than that, Mr. Greco," Rolando said, and fixed him with his eyes, now twinkling for sure. "If I may ask, are you a religious man?"

"I'm not, no."

"I'm not either. But Bianca was. She was very spiritual. She was also somewhat old-world in her views on religion. She had a saying about Norman. She liked to say he lived among the dead."

"I'm not sure I understand."

"She meant the way he interacted with people, including her, at least after he had charmed her into bed. She told me, shortly before she died, that Norman moved through life like a dead person breathing. Like no one mattered to him. Like there was no joy in it for him. He only smiled when he beat someone at something or took something from them. To Bianca, that wasn't really living."

"What you're describing sounds like psychopathy, or something approaching it," Alex said. "I'm not a psychologist but I have some background in it. The condition is marked by a lack of empathy, an inability to connect with others. For some, the only pleasure they feel is when they're getting over on someone."

"It's quite possible that's Norman's problem, or a part of it. My sister described it her way because it was all she knew to compare it to. In the third world there's a different relationship with death. A more intimate one. Animals die, often at our own hands." Alex pictured Norman cutting the goat's throat on video. "When relatives die, they're usually not embalmed. The family buries them. My point is that Bianca knew death, particularly when it came for her and she had to face it at a young age. She saw something death-like in Norman, some way in which he seemed to invite it."

"And you see it also?"

"For years, I've seen glimpses of it. There was a time he could appear charming, or sympathetic, especially to get something he wanted. Now I think anger and bitterness have finally exhausted him. So mostly he's dismissive, barely there. But there are times you can still see the thing in him. The thing that was once smiling and now just...stares out from him. Like it's forgotten how to mask itself. I'm probably not describing it well. But the idea of something overwhelming Norman and causing him to kill his son is not something I find impossible to imagine."

"Actually, you're describing it very well," Alex said. For a moment he saw again the ugly flash in Ruiz's eyes at his post-arrest interview.

"It's not something you could use in a court of law, though is it?" he asked. "This characterization of him."

"You mean these impressions of him? No, I'm afraid not. But this is valuable insight. Thank you."

"You said you had experience with mental illness," Rolando said, appearing to change the subject. The grin was gone again, like a moment had been broken. "Was it personal, if you don't mind me asking?"

"It was my ex-wife." Alex wasn't sure why he was comfortable letting that out, but out it came. "She struggles with depression. And mood disorders. It's tough."

"Not dissimilar to what I have," he said. "I appreciate you sharing that with me." He paused. "You know I had a feeling," he continued, and a ghost of a smile was back. His manner now seemed less off-putting and more sincere, at least to Alex. But Alex also suspected it was because he was getting to know the man. Objectively, pretty much everything Rolando did made him appear a little sinister. "I had a feeling you understood my condition. A little, I mean. Most people don't. Or maybe you're just an empathic person, Mr. Greco."

"Call me Alex," he said. "I try to be."

"It's just that I sense a loss about you," Rolando said, his voice low and his eyes moving over Alex's face. "Like a sadness, maybe. But I guess we all have something tugging at us." Alex felt a coldness slide through him. Nothing like that had been intimated about him for a long time. Certainly not from a stranger. Rolando seemed to sense his reaction and snapped back to a detached and now apologetic tone. "I'm very sorry. I do this sometimes."

"Don't be," Alex said, smiling. "Thanks for making the time to come by." With that, he walked Rolando to the gate, and watched as the man, bent and sad looking, padded off into the neighborhood.

CHAPTER 30

He nearly has a grip on Jordan's right hand as his feet lift off, as if he's about to float away, from the top step of the basement stairs. Alex grabs for his son, everything happening in maddening slow motion.

Then there's the feel of his skin— Jordan's— as his fingers connect with Alex's. But the little fingers slip from him and Jordan begins to fall backward, staring back at Alex with eyes wide open. He is silent as he falls backward into some impenetrable blackness. There is no sound— no tumbling or bumping. Only the darkness swallowing his child. Until a scream from Dara erupts behind him.

His heart pounding, Alex sat up in bed and held his head in his hands until the worst of the last image left him. The alarm clock on the nightstand read 3:04; he had been asleep for maybe two hours. No more sleep tonight.

He hadn't seen Jordan fall. He wasn't even aware Dara was having such a bad morning with him until he heard the scream— the one from her, unbridled, coming from the basement itself. He was upstairs shaving and the razor in his hand slipped and cut a groove across his chin. Bright-red blood sprang from it, mixing pink with the shave cream.

He'd grabbed a towel then bolted down the stairs. Lately, Jordan was sometimes a holy terror. A month from his fourth birthday, he was responding a little bit to the intense intervention therapy they had arranged for him, but meltdowns were still common when Dara or Alex tried to get him to do anything, especially eat or bathe.

And Dara was on the edge. He was perilously close to a breakdown of some sort also, but he had always been able to manage stress better than Dara, who just wasn't built for the situation they were in. There was something deeper going on also, something in her that had reared its head from time to time since childhood. Jonah hated psychiatrists and hated the idea of Dara being diagnosed as some sort of mental patient. But the fact was, Dara had issues. She was making it worse lately by drinking too much and sleeping almost never. In recent weeks she seemed as prone to meltdowns almost as much as Jordan was, often meeting his screaming fits with her own. At first, it had seemed that's what this was too: Jordan losing it and Dara giving up and screaming at the ceiling.

But this scream was different.

He had taken the stairs two at a time in his underwear, his heart beginning to pound. In the kitchen on the table was a smudged glass and over-turned bowl of cereal, dripping milk over the side. No Dara, no Jordan. His eyes shifted to the basement door, flung wide open. None of the light that usually emitted from down there. Just darkness. And then another scream.

Oh God, no.

He was scarcely aware of getting to the bottom of the stairs as Jordan's figure became visible in the gloom, lit by watery, gray light from a high basement window. His son was hideously positioned, lying on his side with his right arm wedged behind his back. His face was staring straight up, right angled from his body. His eyes were blank. Dara kneeled beside him, moving her hands around his body but terrified to touch him. He looked like a broken doll. Alex crumbled to his knees beside her and she screamed again, high and hopeless.

He barely remembered calling 911 but had a recollection of wondering if his brother, an EMT for the city, was working that morning. It was a little after 7:00 a.m. And then, he had called Jonah, Dara's father. To the last day of his life he would be unsure why. It wasn't anything Dara had asked for. She had been incapable of asking anything at that moment, sobbing uncontrollably and wanting to cradle her child, the one she had just pushed down the stairs. Dara, she would whisper to Alex later, snapped after Jordan flipped his bowl, jumped from his chair, and ran at her, pounding his fists in a rage. At first she was just scooping him up. She would swear to any god who would eventually sit in judgment of her, that's what she thought she was doing. She was going to scoop him up, like always, brace herself for the thrashing, like always, until he calmed or she could get him to a safer place.

But then he spit something at her and bellowed in anger. She had felt herself rejecting him, thrusting him away from her, her arms locking with the effort. And then he was flying backward, his little face still contorted and red with rage. But it wasn't a wall he hit, or a stretch of tiled floor. It was the wall under the banister, the one that led down fifteen wooden stairs to the concrete surface of the basement. The door to the basement stairs was open— she had left it that way when she'd come up with a light bulb for the hall bathroom.

Then, like a vision of hell, Jordan was plummeting into that dark space, hitting the wall, then turning and falling, his limbs going limp. The terrible sound of him tumbling and eventually hitting the concrete was something Alex had been spared. There was only the scream, Dara's scream, wretched and curdling.

Jonah was there within minutes, slipping in just after the first ambulance. The EMS team was already downstairs, down to where his wife was, wailing, beside the boy. It all seemed surreal, like a milky dream. But then Jonah was there, gripping Alex by the shoulders, looking into his eyes. The two were alone in the front hallway, the sound of radios and calls between the responders echoing from the basement. Distant sirens were droning from outside, a second wave and advanced life support.

"What happened?" he whispered. Alex opened his mouth to speak but nothing came out.

"Wait," Jonah said, "Just wait. Go upstairs and put some clothes on. I'll be there in a second."

In the end, Alex didn't know what exactly Jonah had said to the EMS supervisor. Alex only knew that he, the supervisor, was asking Alex if he had seen Jordan scrambling after the toy and falling down the stairs, and Alex was numbly answering in the affirmative. Yes, they had all been in the kitchen. Jonah had been also, because he'd come over early to see his grandson and daughter before a trip to New York later that day. They all saw the same thing: Jordan flipped his milk bowl and jumped out of his chair, seeing something on the ground that attracted his attention. Dara had sprung for him, yelling that he had to stay put. Jordan had paid her no mind, and went after the toy, accidentally kicking it down the stairs. And then he had broken for it, chasing after it not sensing there were stairs in front of him.

Jonah was the most collected, and the supervisor had responded to him, his presence, his certainty. The only thing Alex was aware of other than dawning horror and the beginnings of grief was how confident Jonah seemed to be in lying. It was almost like he expected a moment like this was inevitable and he had steeled himself to be ready for it.

Rolando, Alex thought as he drew on a cigarette in the living room, perched in the dark on the sill of one of his big front windows. The window was open, but the smoke drifted back in. *Whatever he...noticed about me today. That's what triggered this. Must be.*

It was a hopeful thought. Jordan had been born in April and died in early March. Nightmares— particularly that one— were becoming mercifully less frequent, but he was prepared for them around those two anniversaries. But now it was high summer and he was engrossed in trial prep, poised to be ready by November. He thought of little else, and everything in his life otherwise was stable. So why this? Why now?

CHAPTER 31

Friday, July 1

In Alex's office the next day, Sean was sweating through his dress shirt with his tie loosened, exposing a yellow ring behind his collar. He had been working almost non-stop for the last forty-eight hours. His original purpose had been piecing together information on Norman Ruiz's gang activity and contacts, but that had led inadvertently to a fairly large sting involving a local smuggling ring that included human-trafficking. Edgar's suspicions had been on the money. The men Norman Ruiz was making deliveries for moved cigarettes and some guns, but mostly they worked in prostitution, enlisting women and girls both online and in person. From what Sean could gather from a couple of lower level guys who had been arrested, Norman mostly moved prostituted women between locations in the Bronx and a few other places and collected money from them as well.

"The gang guys upstairs are talking about this bust," Alex said, an admiring tone in his voice. "Nice work, considering it wasn't what you were assigned to go after."

"Yeah, Sean's gonna get promoted away from this case,"

Danny said, texting something on his phone. "At this rate he'll be a three-star chief by October."

"I doubt that," Sean said. "But if nothing else it was overtime. Thanks. But I didn't find anything Ruiz could really be charged with."

"I'm not concerned with new charges," Alex said. "This intel is more valuable. With this out there, he may still testify, but if he does, this stuff limits him. He can open a door pretty easily to questions about this activity if Rick isn't careful."

"Unless that's his plan," Danny said, looking up from his phone. "If he still wants to play the bad guy who got in with worse guys and got burned."

"True," Alex said, acknowledging his point.

"I think he looks like shit, even if he does admit this stuff and claim it got his kid killed," Sean said. "He logged a lot of hours with some bad people. The crew he was associated with have a pipeline all the way back to Central America. Some of these girls they call for down there. Some they just pick off when they're making their way up. It's ugly. They're pretty sophisticated, too. We seized a few laptops, some other electronics. They put pictures of some of them online once they get here. The johns come in from everywhere."

"Any victims underage?"

"No one we've found yet, but I wouldn't be surprised. Some of the kids from El Salvador or Honduras? They don't even know exactly how old they are. There're no birth certificates, nothing."

"Okay," Alex said. "When you come back next week, Sean, write this stuff up. There's no rush."

He turned to Danny. "Anything on an alibi for Rolando Garcia?"

"No," Danny said, shaking his head. "The guy tries, but he just doesn't remember. Or says he doesn't."

"That's the sense I got," Alex said. "If I have him testify, even just to ID the kid, Rick can ask a few subtle things on cross examination and then boom- get the jury thinking it was the crazy uncle."

"Does he have to testify?" Sean asked.

"Probably not. I can get what I need on Hector from Connie. But Rolando is the only family member I've got. It's always better to have someone related on the stand. Someone who cared, so maybe the jury should, too."

"This isn't a gang banger who got killed, though," Sean said. "It was a kid." Alex thought about it. Sean was probably right. Best to avoid putting Rolando in front of a jury without an alibi.

"When is this thing in court next?" Danny asked. Alex blew out a breath.

"July sixth for a status hearing. Depending on what Rick wants, they should send us out on time, sometime in November. I've got other cases, but just supporting ADA's. It's mostly busy work."

"You should take a break, then," Danny said. "At least for the weekend. No offense, but you look run hard, boss." He punctuated this with his usual beguiling smile. Alex figured he looked rough after a mostly sleepless night, but he felt he had been hiding fatigue fairly well. That guise was apparently wearing thin.

"Actually, I am," he said. "I'm going to the Hamptons for the holiday weekend. But I'll have my cell."

"Famous last words," Sean said shaking his head. "'I'll have my cell.' He's right, grab some R and R. We're gonna need you rested."

CHAPTER 32

At 9:45 p.m. the last of the light was sinking behind the dunes, swallowed into the throat of a thunderstorm set to roll over the beach where they sat. Alex and Nikki were reclined in perfectly tilted Adirondack chairs, watching a previous storm disappear into the Atlantic, emitting the last gentle white flashes against the horizon. They were in a town called Amagansett, on the south shore of Long Island, at the summer cottage of a childhood friend of Nikki's who had lent it to her for the weekend. Between them was an open bottle of wine.

"We may be soaked in about five minutes," she said, craning her neck around. The rich sound of thunder rolled in from behind them, and ozone hung in the still air. Before them, a couple of kids were collecting shells in the surf. They turned to the sound of their mother, calling from the porch next door, and reluctantly walked away toward the light.

"Thanks for doing this," he said, taking her hand. She squeezed it back and smiled.

"What? Getting you out of town? Believe me, I needed it, too."

"I had no idea how much I needed this. But I did."

"Do you want to tell me what woke you up last night?" she asked then, taking a swig from the bottle. "A dream, I'd guess. Bad one?" When he turned to her, she saw he was both perplexed and impressed at the same time. She hadn't been with him.

"How the hell did you know I had a nightmare?"

"There was the smell of smoke in your apartment today. You don't usually smoke indoors. So, I figured something woke you up and had you smoking a cigarette by the window. From the looks of you today, you were up all night afterward."

"You should have been a detective," he said. A tendril of wind slipped between them and lifted her hair.

"I'm not the only detective in your life. From what you've told me, Danny knew you needed this also. Do you feel like talking about it? The dream I mean. We don't have to." Nikki was relaxed, and a little drunk. So far, their time together in this idyllic place had been perfect and she didn't want to shake things up, but with lowered inhibitions she felt herself pushing forward anyway.

"No, it's okay. It was about my son. It's a dream I've had before. I've told you."

"Oh. Yeah, you have. I'm sorry."

"It happens, but usually, it's around two big dates. Not sure why I had it now."

"Well, I'd say it's because you're immersed in a child homicide trial," she said, "but..."

"But what?" he asked after she trailed off. She sighed. Now, she felt like she was pushing it.

"Ugh, forget it, I'm sorry. I'm your lover, Alex. I can't be your shrink. And I don't mean to suggest you need one."

"Disclaimer accepted," he said. "What were you going

to say? That I'm having dreams about my kid because I'm in the middle of a child death case? That's sounds reasonable."

"Yes, but I think it goes beyond that." She paused and searched for the right words. "You live in a world framed by death, all of it violent. You put yourself there. It's a noble job and you're great at it, but I'm not sure you can step out of it. I think when you do, you tend to go backward, toward your own pain. It just sounds like a tough place to live in, that's all." Alex was quiet for a long moment. Thunder cracked behind them and the wind picked up. A drop of rain hit Nikki's neck. Then another.

"I guess it's all I know," he said at last. "I thought I was pretty comfortable there."

"You probably are. And that's okay, for now. Look, this is just food for thought. I think when we're in touch with ourselves, our subconscious is more likely to leave us alone at night."

"And if it doesn't?" he asked, standing and putting a towel around her as the rain thickened and lightning lit the clouds in momentary garish relief. She chuckled and took his hand.

"Then it's trying to tell you something."

CHAPTER 33

Thursday, July 14

"Are you sure you're going to be okay here, without me?" Connie asked Joseliz. It was 9:00 p.m. and sky was finally darkening after a long and hot day. Joseliz was in a conference room at HCC where she was set to meet Detective Regan for a second time.

"I'm fine, Connie," she said. "Security is still here, and Bruce is around somewhere. And I'm meeting with a police officer. With all that in my corner, I'm pretty sure I'll survive."

"Don't sass me, woman," Connie said, and flashed a tired smile.

"No sassing. *Lo prometo.* Get home safe."

It was a nice change, hearing Connie crack wise. Joseliz, like most people at HCC, knew Connie just wasn't in a good place. She often appeared harried and stretched thin, but lately it just seemed worse. She looked like she was awaiting disaster around every corner. It was exhausting just to see her that way.

Fifteen minutes later, Sean was across from Joseliz, apologizing for having to meet so late. His day had been a series of headaches, he explained, and he'd been on duty since that morning.

"It's fine," she said. "I got some things done, and Connie was happy you could come here. They want me to help."

"Good," Sean said. "I told you, right? No one's angry." He opened his notepad and clicked his pen. "So, what's new?"

"Well, I went back over the log I kept with how Hector and I were using the pictures in the exercises. The pages in the binder. I went over each one where Hector was using the picture of the bathtub as a reward picture, like something he was looking forward to."

"I remember," Sean said. "Hang on." He thumbed back through his previous notes. "You said there were times he'd put up a picture of candy, lollipops or something, along with it."

"Lollipops, yes. But the thing is, he didn't put the lollipop picture up with the picture of the tub. It was actually after it," she said. "I just noticed that today."

"Not sure I understand."

"Look," she said, pointing at one of the pages of the log. It was dated March 3rd, about a month before Hector was killed. "It's a little hard to decipher if you don't know what you're looking at. This list down here is what I recorded Hector doing with the pictures during this exercise. I put up a task picture, see? That day, it was putting some toys away. Then, after me, he put up a picture of the bathtub, and a lollipop. He probably grabbed them at the same time, and his coordination sticking them on the tablet wasn't always great. He usually used just one hand also, his right hand. His left arm seemed uncomfortable for him, he used to hold it a lot. I can see it now, though, how he was placing the pictures on a few of these days, especially in the last couple of months. The bathtub wasn't really the final thing Hector expected or wanted if he did his task. The lollipop was."

"But the tub came first," Sean said, piecing it together. "Like. . .I don't know. He thought he'd get a lollipop if he got into the tub?"

"Exactly," she said. "I think I get it now. The tub wasn't something Hector thought of as a reward, Detective. It was a task, like I would have thought. The lollipop was the reward that was tied to it."

"Ah," Sean said. "So, someone, maybe, was giving him lollipops specifically for getting in the tub?"

"It's all I can think of," she said. "But I don't know where he would have learned that. I usually put up a different reward for bathing, because he usually brushed his teeth around the same time, near bedtime. It was more likely to be TV time or a game he liked, not candy."

"Listen," Sean said, taking off his reading glasses, "did Norman ever seem to notice any of this stuff? The work you were doing with Hector? The progress. Anything?"

"He never seemed to notice much. He came and went. There were a few times maybe he saw us working together at the kitchen table. That's where we almost always worked. But he never seemed to pay attention."

"Was there anyone else who saw how this worked? Other people here at the center?"

"Not really," she said. "Staff people would come by. Connie and Bruce were there sometimes, to check on me or to bring things. But then we were talking about other things, or I was cleaning or something around the house. Hector and I usually did these exercises when were by ourselves. I didn't try to hide it, but that's really the only time he'd open up and respond. It kind of needed to be one on one."

"What about his uncle. Rolando Garcia?"

"He came by sometimes, usually with little things for Hector. I don't know if he saw us working, though. He was nice enough, but a little. . ."

"Weird, yeah I get it. Okay. Let's pack up, and I'll give you a ride home. I don't know what all this means, but probably Mr. Greco will want that logbook. Do you mind if I take it? Someone over there can make copies and I can get it back to you."

"Of course," she said. "Please let him know, I can answer any questions he has, at least on what I did and how Hector responded." Sean took a few more notes, and then they were ready to go. The two left the center for the Grand Concourse at 9:47.

CHAPTER 34

Sean had parked down a lamp-lit but still dark street off of the concourse, the kind he wouldn't want her traversing on her own. He assumed she felt safe with him and she seemed to, although Sean knew enough to know safety was usually a cruel illusion. He listened and engaged in light conversation as they walked, but he always had his senses tuned to the environment. After almost twenty-four years on the job, he knew no other way.

His car came into sight, technically in a no-parking zone in front of a rarely used gate, but as it was an unmarked police vehicle it had been left alone. Joseliz was, by his design, on the inside of the sidewalk. She was hugging her schoolbooks and the logbook she would eventually hand over. Their shadows grew long and short again under the streetlights. The night air was heavy from the humidity of the day, and a little rank from baking trash and the general grittiness of the city in high summer.

Across the street, between two apartment buildings, was a narrow alley. A streetlight illuminated the passage about five or six feet inward, the rest swallowed in darkness. Sean eyed it as they passed by, and then put his left arm out in front of Joseliz. She stopped and glanced over at him.

"Everything okay?"

"Yeah, I think. But wait." Something, he could have sworn, had ducked back into the shadows from the lit area at the mouth of the alley. Of course, that something could have been a cat. Or a rat. But he didn't think so. He peered down the alley but saw nothing other than the dim form of a trash bin on the right side against the wall. There was nothing but blackness the rest of the way down. "Okay," he said after a few seconds. They walked on. The car was less than fifty feet away.

About a second later he felt it. Or saw it, sensed it? He didn't know. But he knew that something— and not an animal— had stepped out of the darkness of the alley toward them. A slice of a shadow, maybe, had fallen just inside his peripheral vision. He didn't say anything to Joseliz. There was no time for that. Instead he spun around, reaching for his weapon, strapped to his right hip. There was a man standing, backlit by the light in the alley, his feet spread shoulder length apart. He had a baseball cap pulled low over his face and a dark bandana over his nose and mouth. He was holding a pistol in both hands. It was a black, square-shaped weapon like a 9mm or a .45, Sean registered in a fraction of a second. In that same fleeting moment he saw that the gun was not aimed at him, but to his right. That was where Joseliz stood, having paused and now turning around toward the direction of the alley.

There was no time to yell. No time to scream "duck" or "run" or anything else. Conscious thought left him and he reacted with a protective instinct that was a product of his training, and ultimately raw character. His arms shot out and he stepped in front of Joseliz, who was still turning toward him.

Joseliz barely registered that Sean was gripping her shoulders and pushing her forward. On a reflex she took a step back to keep from falling. Her only thought as his form eclipsed her was that he had somehow tripped on the sidewalk. She could see his face, looming over her. On it was something that to her looked like grim determination. Then his mouth opened wide and he emitted a deep, bellowing gasp, like a man clawing for breath after nearly drowning. His eyes popped wide and then froze as he began to collapse. It was at that moment that Joseliz registered the sound from the gunshot, a hollow crack that filled the hot air.

She staggered back from Sean's body, now lying facedown on the sidewalk, still too shocked to scream. The ringing in her ears continued. She opened her mouth to scream but nothing came out. The world seemed to be spinning, everything moving around her slowly, drunkenly, like she was on a carousel.

Then a light went on, an outside light attached to the building just beyond the old gate Sean had parked in front of. A door flew open and she heard steps behind her. Staggering backward, she tried to make a turn and almost fell. But she was caught by a man who then put both arms under her armpits and dragged her behind a cargo van a few feet away. As her back hit the rear doors of the vehicle, she opened her mouth again to scream. But the man was crowding her against the doors, pleading for silence with an intense stare and a finger to his lips.

"Shhh. Please." She stared at him silently, her eyes like saucers. Her breathing was rapid and shallow. "We need to get inside, but right now just be still. I don't know where he is." With that, he peaked around the side of the van, then leaned against the doors next to her and took out a cellphone.

"P-please," she whispered. "Please. What's happening?"

"I don't know," he whispered back. "I live in that building. I heard the sound and I just reacted. We need to get inside but it might not be safe. Right now, just be still. Okay? Don't move." She nodded.

"Do you know that man?" he asked. "The one who was shot?"

"Yes."

"Who is he?"

"D-d-detective," she said. "Sean." It was all she could manage. She had somehow forgotten his last name.

"He's a cop?" the man asked as the phone began to ring.

"Yes. Please help him."

"Nine-one-one," a female operator spoke, "what's your emergency?"

"I'm on McClellan Street. Between Sherman and Sheridan," the man said. He spoke calmly and barely above a whisper. "A police officer has been shot." There was a brief pause on the other end.

"Do you know the condition of the officer?"

"No. But he's not moving."

"Do you know his identity?"

"His first name is Sean. That's all I know."

"State your location again, please?"

"McClellan, in the Bronx. Near the intersection of Sheridan."

"Is anyone else hurt?"

"Not that I know of, but we're not sure where the shooter is."

"Are you in a safe place, sir?"

"I really don't know."

"Okay. Police are on the way, sir," the woman said. "Can you stay with me on the line until they arrive?"

"I can." Then he turned to Joseliz. "Are you hurt?"

"Huh?"

"Are you hurt? Young lady? Look at me." She did so, taking in his face for the first time. He was older, maybe 55 or 60, completely bald, with a high forehead, and thin, graying eyebrows. His dark skin shone in the moonlight, and she could make out little laugh lines around his eyes, a detail she would marvel at later for noticing. The eyes were deep set and stern, but they softened as she shook her head.

"No. I don't think so."

"Good. There will be police here. A lot of them, and very soon. When you hear sirens, do what I do? Okay? Do exactly what I do." She nodded, and he went back to his phone, answering another question of the dispatcher. Seconds seemed to pass with aching slowness. Then she heard them. One, then two. Then more than that. Blue lights began to flash, strafing the tops of the buildings. There was a screech of tires. The first car was approaching them, rounding the block.

"Put your hands up," he said. "Now."

CHAPTER 35

Danny received Joseliz's logbook—the one she had used to track her progress with Hector- from her a couple of hours later in the Four-Four detective squad room. Later he would also get Sean's notebook. He wouldn't be assigned to Sean's homicide, but he stayed with Joseliz through the night and the various initial interviews. The precinct itself was mobbed. High level brass and investigators converged on the building as the night wore on.

Alex joined Danny after he got his call and sat with Joseliz's mother and grandmother in a waiting area downstairs as she was debriefed. He also talked briefly with a man named Asa Green, the neighbor who ran out at the sound of the gunshot to find Joseliz on the street. Joseliz was finally able to leave around five the next morning, out of the precinct and into the hazy, first gray light of dawn.

By late afternoon, Alex and Danny, both sleepless for almost thirty-six hours, would know exactly how Sean Regan died. The bullet that struck him, burrowing between two ribs to the right of his spinal column, was a .45 caliber ACP hollow-point. It passed easily through the ribcage, deflecting only slightly, then mushroomed, per its design, and shredded the right atrium of his heart before lodging in the breast plate in front of it. He was dead before he hit the ground.

CHAPTER 36

Tuesday, July 19

Alex had been to one funeral for a police officer in Northern Virginia who died in the line of duty, a patrol officer who was killed when a suspect clipped him with a vehicle going over a bridge across an interstate. It had been an impressive thing to watch, but it didn't come close to the ceremony for Sean William Regan, who was laid to rest on the Tuesday after he was murdered. Regan was the fourth NYPD officer to die in the line of duty that year. He was the second who was shot.

Like many in the NYPD, Sean and his family lived in Rockland County, northwest of the city. But he had grown up, as had his father and his before him, in the Inwood section of Manhattan, at very northern tip of the island, a thin slice of land pushing up past the Bronx to the west, across the Harlem River. Inwood, while now largely Hispanic, was a predominantly Irish community through most of the 20th century when the immigrant population slowly and then rapidly began to escape the downtown slums. Sean's church growing up had been Good Shepherd on Broadway and Isham Street, and that's where his funeral took place. The church was an imposing stone structure, formed with granite mined from nearby quarries and topped with a Celtic cross.

The mayor spoke. The police commissioner promoted him posthumously to the rank of first grade detective, the highest possible. Sean's widow, Sally, and their four sons, ranging in age from 11 to 18, sat silently in the front row of the packed church as two priests completed the funeral rites. Alex had been invited to sit with a few other ADA's who had known Sean, but he stood at the back of the church instead. Other than his mother's funeral the year before, where he'd been obligated to sit up front, he much preferred to have an easy escape route from such events if he felt he needed it. Sure enough, as the procession for Holy Communion began, Alex felt sweat forming on his upper lip. There was a nudge of uneasiness, but he could sense it blooming toward something more like panic. If Nikki was with him he might have been able to get through it, but she had a case to testify for and couldn't get out of it.

He ducked out of the church and down the steps, then turned the corner onto the quieter Isham Street. In the courtyard to the side of the church was a 9/11 memorial sculpture garden, anchored by a large steel cross made from ruins of the twin towers themselves. Around the cross were monuments to a few of the parishioners who had died on September 11th, 2001. He paused in front of it and lit a cigarette. He was shaking a little bit, but it was manageable. Now he drew deeply on the cigarette and, within a minute or so, felt calm once again settle through him like a balm. He regarded the butt suspiciously in his hand. It was foolish, he knew, to depend on tobacco like that. Certainly unhealthy. But fuck all, it worked. Then a young woman in a simple black dress, walking in quick step down Isham Street, almost bumped into him. She was clutching a handkerchief and crying.

"Joseliz," he said quietly. She stopped, recognizing him, and wiped her eyes. He had never noticed before, but she was actually very attractive, with long, dark hair and a slim figure. He was sorry they were meeting this way not because he didn't want to talk to her but because he assumed, correctly, she had spent the last few harrowing days with far too many people like him already— prosecutors and investigators with endless questions and the sad duty of making her relive the unimaginable moments again and again. She was, he knew well, traumatized and dealing with more pain and shock than most people dealt with in lives far longer.

"Hello, Mr. Greco," she said. She wiped her eyes with a handkerchief. "I couldn't take it anymore. I wanted to stay and receive communion. But I just. . ."

"Joseliz, it's fine. Obviously, I didn't make it through the whole thing either." He paused. "And I can't imagine how much worse this is for you."

"It's okay," she said. She lifted her chin, a reflex Alex guessed was something she wasn't aware of. Maybe it was cultural. Maybe it was just her.

"None of this is okay. What is okay is feeling helpless about it. And angry. What's okay is leaving when you can't take it anymore."

"The police say it might have been a gang thing," she said. "They said he had just made a big case and that there were a lot of arrests made."

"There were. Quite a few. So, it's a possibility he was targeted because of that. It doesn't happen often. But it happens."

"It doesn't feel like that to me," she said, barely a whisper. "I told them."

"What doesn't?"

"I feel like it was something I told him. About the exercises I was doing with Hector. I feel like it got him killed." Alex was afraid she might feel that way. He had reviewed both her logbook and Sean's notes on it after they had been released to Danny. He hadn't yet interviewed her again about that last conversation with Sean, but that could wait.

"Joseliz, that's not what happened. The man who killed Hector has been in jail for months now, and he doesn't have connections that could have gotten to Sean that way. Someone else was after him. He, or they, just knew where he was, that's all."

"But it doesn't feel like Sean was the target," she said, and fresh tears filled her eyes. "It felt like it was me. Like in the last seconds he threw himself in front of me, like he twisted me around, or pushed me out of the way. It just happened so fast."

"He would have done that anyway, regardless of who he thought the target was. The moment he sensed danger he would have had an instinct to protect you. That's who he was. It sounds like that's what he did." He waited as sobs moved through her.

"Maybe," she said. "I guess. I just wish I could remember more. I wish I had seen more."

"You can't ask yourself to solve this. All you can do is step away from it and tell the investigators what you remember. First you have to take care of yourself."

"I feel like poison," she said, her tone almost bewildered. She looked up at him. "I feel like everything near me will die. And it's because of me." She wasn't crying now but breathing in shallow bursts. There was a bench a few feet down from where they were. He motioned her over to it and they sat down.

"Try to slow your breathing if you can," he said. "Try it with me. Breath deep. Then breathe out. Okay?" They did that a few times, in unison. "That better?"

"A little. Thanks."

"I've had those feelings, too," he said. She looked over at him.

"You have?"

"I've been through some of what you're going through, believe it or not. Losing people in my life. And not just that but seeing them...hurt. Even dead. When something like that happens, especially more than once, it's easy to believe you're attracting bad things to people around you. Like you're making them happen, even, just by being there. But it's not true."

"Does it go away, then?" she asked. "The feeling?"

"I think it does," he said carefully. "To be honest, I haven't fully kicked it yet. But I know the things I'm afraid of aren't true. That's the first step. You'll have to get back to me on what happens next. It does get better, though."

"I've had a pretty good therapist for a while now," she said. "There are just some things. Some things I can't even say to her. I can't come close."

"It'll be that way, for a while," he said. "That's okay, too. My guess is she'll wait for you." They were quiet for a few seconds, and then the sound of bagpipes, sad and glorious on the hot, humid air, reached them.

"I'll be ready to testify for you when you need me," she said, her voice suddenly calm. "Don't think I won't be."

"Of course, you will," he said. "That's a long way off.

Don't worry about it right now. Just take care of yourself. Try to have a good summer, if you can."

"Come with me," she said, standing up. She breathed deep and dabbed at her eyes one more time. "Please. I want to see them carry him out." He stared back at her for a few seconds.

"You're one tough woman," he said. "You know that, right? Sean knew it also."

"Then I owe him this," she said.

They walked back to the corner and then stared in silence as Sean's casket, draped with the green, blue and white NYPD flag, proceeded through the overflow crowd to a waiting hearse. Above the church, police helicopters hovered in formation. On Broadway, as far as anyone could see in both directions, was a sea of blue. There were literally thousands of officers from numerous jurisdictions. For the most part, the northern end of Manhattan island was impassible today. It belonged to Sean.

CHAPTER 37

Thursday, July 28

A string of awful, humid days finally broke with a crashing series of thunderstorms on the last Thursday of the month. Alex was on 161st gripping a much-needed cup of iced coffee when an afternoon downpour trapped him under a storefront awning. He was annoyed with the delay, but the storm itself was almost comforting. Summer's sweaty grip, as always by the end of July, was getting old. Then he heard a car horn and turned toward the sound. There was an enormous, black SUV at the curb. The passenger side window lowered, and Alex saw Bruce.

"Hop in, counselor, I'll run you back to the office."

Alex sprinted to the car and climbed in. And one hell of a car it was. To Alex it seemed more like a spaceship, with lush gray interior and sleek controls.

"Thanks," he said. "Damn, this is a nice ride. I don't want to touch anything."

"Please," Bruce said, "I love the kids we work with, but they're usually a lot messier than you are, and we haul them around in this thing all the time. No worries, shake your hair out." Alex smiled and did so. It felt better.

"What is it, anyway? The car?"

"It's a Land Rover. It's Connie's, but I end up driving it more than she does. As you can see, I'm more or less a kept man." Alex smiled at this. A lot of men wouldn't be comfortable saying such a thing, especially to another man they didn't know. But Bruce, a little like Connie as far as he could tell, seemed entirely comfortable in his own skin. It was endearing.

"I was married to a very wealthy woman," Alex said, a little surprised at his own candor. "If it means anything, I kind of know that feeling."

"No shit? Was it her money?"

"Nah, it was her father's. It was new money, though. Sounds like Connie's was old."

"Yeah, very. She hated it."

"She told me," Alex said. "How did you two meet?"

"We met when she had just gotten to the Bronx. She was looking to put together something, although it's kind of funny- she really didn't know what."

"Really?"

"Swear to God," he said, putting a hand up. "She was just this dynamo, with a bunch of money and an itch to do something decent with it. There was a babysitting service she heard about, not far from here. Well, it wasn't a "service," really. More like a lifeline for poor families. It was a group of older women, all Spanish speaking. They lived in the same apartment complex and cared for kids during the day with cognitive disabilities, mostly. Autism, mental retardation- I know we don't call it that now, but you know what I mean- Down's Syndrome, that kind of thing. They charged almost nothing and helped out families from all over the place. Some couldn't get services because they were here illegally. Some just didn't know how, or what they got just wasn't enough. Connie took one look and knew that's what she was going to do. Create a center in the community and serve that population."

"Were you in the human services field, then?" Alex asked.

"I had a kid brother," Bruce said. A shadow seemed to fall across his face. "David. We called him Davey. He suffered hypoxia at birth, a lack of oxygen. He was never right. My parents were already older, and my mother was sick. I took care of him, mostly. He died when he was seven. I was thirteen."

"Oh damn," Alex said. "I'm sorry to hear it."

"Thanks. He drowned, at a beach outing with some kids like him. Long story, they weren't well supervised. Anyway, ever since then, I was looking for something good to do, with kids like that. Before Connie, though, I was just kind of aimless. I got an associates in bookkeeping, but I didn't really use the degree. I was a handyman. A cab driver for a while. And then there was Connie. We met at a meeting I found out about, talking about her dream. That was it. We fell for each other."

"Nice story," Alex said.

"I got lucky," he said, smiling. "Professionally, HCC was perfect for me. I'm a jack of all trades, master of none, but that's what Connie really needed. Personally, I guess it just clicked between us. You know I had no idea she had any money until we moved in together? And I'm glad I didn't. That's probably how I won her over."

"Have you been married long?"

"We're not married, actually. Neither of us believe in it. Just partners. It works, I guess, because we've always wanted the same things. She wanted to build something here that would make a difference, and she had the means.

I was looking for purpose. I never really had it before her. And, I was the guy who could do most of the little things. I also know the terrain. I had a reputation."

"A reputation?" Alex asked. They had come to a stoplight, and Bruce looked over and grinned. Outside, the rain was coming down in sheets.

"Best way I can put it is, I'm the guy everyone talks to. It's been that way since I was a kid."

"Sounds like a burden."

"In a way, yeah. But it connects me to a lot of what's going on around here. I guess 'networking' is what you'd call it now. Anyway, that's what I do. I know the Bronx, and I mean the good and bad. Sometimes you have to make allegiances with rough people to get things done."

"I've seen how that works here," Alex said.

"I'm not a tough guy," he said, winking at Alex. "I just know a few of them. In the old days it was about knowing the connected guys, in my neighborhood. That's what we called them. 'Connected.' Nowadays, it's more the gangs. I don't know as many of them, but I do keep some contacts. What Connie and I do isn't controversial. Everyone's on our side. Sometimes, though, to get things done or keep something from happening, it helps to have a guy you can go to. Even if he's on the wrong side of the law. Hey, if this is too much information, I'll shut up. I respect what you do. And God knows I can ramble."

"It's fine," Alex said. "I like it here, contradictions, compromises and all. How is Connie, anyway?"

"Eh, she's a little under the weather. Truth is, she has been on and off since we lost Hector. Sorry to be so blunt. It's kind of my way." They made another turn from the Grand Concourse onto 161st.

"It's okay," Alex said. "It's been a tough few months all around."

"Sean Regan," Bruce said, and shook his head. "I was really sorry to hear that. He showed up at Hector's funeral, you know."

"Actually, I didn't." Sean hadn't mentioned it. But then again, Sean wasn't the type who would. A minute or two later they reached "Perp Plaza" and Bruce pulled in, coming to a stop facing the side of the DA's office. He put the vehicle in park. The rain was still coming down hard but starting to slow. "Give it another minute, unless you're in a hurry. Still pouring."

"I can wait," Alex said. "I appreciate the candor, by the way. About you, Connie, everything. It's not often I get to know people on my cases. It helps. And it's a nice thing."

"Connie likes you. I wish you could know her without this cloud over her head is all.

That's why I hope you get that son-of-a-bitch. He deserves it."

"He does, I agree. But I can tell you after a lot of years of doing this, criminal litigation doesn't put things back together."

"It's a start, though. Balances the books. That much I know. Looks like it's stopping, the rain. Hey, thanks for talking, like for real. When this is over, I'll buy you a beer, at least. I don't go out as much as I used to, but there isn't a bartender on Tremont Avenue who doesn't know me. Connie will tell you that, too."

"Sounds good," Alex said. "Thanks for the ride. Please give her my best. I'll be in touch." Alex gently closed the door, still treating the car like it was special.

PART III: FALL

CHAPTER 38

Monday, October 10

Alex was at his desk when a pleasant looking, plump-faced African-American man in his mid-thirties poked his head in the door. He wore slacks and a tie with his badge and weapon on his belt.

"ADA Greco?"

"I am. How can I help?"

"John Bell," he said. NYC ICAC. Can I come in?"

"Please," Alex said. From the acronym he assumed that Bell was from the city's Internet Crimes Against Children, or ICAC unit, but had to repeat to himself to make sure he got it right. There were so many acronyms to remember. "I've never met anyone from ICAC up here. Where are you all based anyway?"

"With Intel at Chelsea Market," Bell said, shaking his hand as Alex stood to greet him. Chelsea Market was in Manhattan, down on 10th Avenue. "I was in Federal Court in White Plains this morning, and figured I'd try to catch you at your desk."

"Sit down, please. Is this about a child porn case? I dealt with a few several years ago, but it's not what I handle anymore."

"This was an ongoing exchange," Bell said, settling into the chair and pulling a file from a binder he carried, "It was ratcheting up, but it got interrupted."

"Okay."

"This child," Bell said, pulling out an enlarged 8X10 and sliding it over to Alex's side of the desk. The photo was a close-up of the face of a boy, eyes closed and apparently unconscious. "Do you recognize him?"

"Oh, dear God," Alex whispered. He looked up at Bell. "This is Hector Ruiz."

"Yes. We found twenty-seven photographs of him and two short videos, all in the same room, and all in a bathtub except for one where he's bent over a toilet. He's not being penetrated in any of them, but his genitals are exposed in some, fondled in others. He looks unconscious in most of the photos, but there are a few where his eyes are open, and glassy. Probably drugged."

"Jesus. Where did these come from?"

"These images were found on a seized computer, along with about nine-hundred other CP images and videos," Bell said, using the usual "CP" in place of child pornography. "Among the images were chat conversations." Bell took out another photo and set it before Alex. It was the booking photo of a stone-faced, somewhat startled looking white man who looked to be about Alex's age. He had a buzz-cut, tight against his scalp, a pale complexion, brown eyes and thin lips. He looked neither evil nor angelic, just utterly mundane. "This is a guy named Corey Timmons. He lives south of Killington, Vermont. There's no reason you'd know him, but he was in communication with someone who had access to a child in the New York City area. Timmons was willing to pay for video of that child being sexually molested."

"And we don't know who was providing access," Alex said, mostly to himself. Of course, if they had, he would know.

"No, not yet. The IT address of the New York party is encrypted by TOR. Darknet. You know about it?"

"Very little. TOR is the network that encrypts web traffic, right?"

"Correct. It bounces from IT address to IT address all over the world. There have been some breaks, but it's mostly impenetrable. We have the username for the party in New York, but that's it. It's not one we've seen before, at least not that I've discovered yet."

"How do you know the party was in New York?"

"It was discussed, the general area of where the kid was. Maybe at some point, the child would have been offered to Timmons for in-person contact. But it never got that far."

"What's the username?" Alex asked. "The one from the New York party?"

"Angel2221. Does it mean anything to you?"

"Not a thing. How was this guy busted? Timmons?"

"He was picked up at his job after CP was found on a work computer. The ICAC team in Vermont got a warrant for his home equipment. They scrubbed it and this came up. In chat conversations with the other party, Timmons asked for and received the pictures. He said he was interested in watching sex acts being done to the child. The other party described the kid as mostly out of it. That was okay with Timmons, as long as he got to see what he wanted to see. One troubling thing was that he wanted the kid recorded in the bathtub. Could be that's just a fetish, but it might be worse, in a practical way. Some of these guys, they want to see kids on camera get cut up, or even killed. A bathtub is a good place to do that. It catches blood."

"Was the child identified by name in the chats? Any name?" Alex asked, looking over the other photos. In one, there was a finger inserted into Hector's mouth, the finger covered by a blue latex glove. Hector's eyes looked glassy and blank, lolling upward. He was lying face-up in the tub, as he was in most of the photos, except for one where it looked like he had been turned over, exposing his behind.

"No. Just the pictures, and a rough description of his height, weight, and condition."

"So how was he identified?" Alex asked. At this Bell smiled, grimly.

"This is what we do," he said, the pride unmistakable in his voice. "Although here the credit goes to the Vermont team. They analyzed every pixel of these photos." With that, he tapped on one of them that showed a part of the bottom of the claw foot tub, where it met the floor. "See this? Magnify it and enhance it, and you'll see the markings the manufacturer used in the design. Now here, they got a little lucky. Claw-foot tubs aren't super common, but they are out there. You can order one through a Lowes or a Home Depot. Most are made overseas, and they're pretty similar. But this one wasn't. It's not custom, but it was made by a much smaller manufacturer out of Easton, Pennsylvania. Kind of boutique, almost."

"Okay. So, they ID'd the manufacturer, but then what?"

"Then they traced the distribution pattern. This model went almost exclusively to the northeast. Most went through independent orders. But a few went to a smaller plumbing supply store in the Bronx, middle of last year."

"I'll be damned," Alex said, suitably impressed. "They traced the sale?"

"They traced a few, but yeah. One was sold about seventeen months ago to a Norman Alberto Ruiz, of 178th Street in the Bronx. Once Vermont had that, they reached out to us. I tracked down Norman and then found out he's at Rikers awaiting trial for murder. Sean Regan was on your case, I saw. Did you know him well?"

"I did," Alex said. "Did you?"

"No. I was at his funeral, though. Sounds like a good man."

"He was."

"When is your trial scheduled for?"

"It should start sometime next month. Although this could throw a wrench in it. Any idea of when these were taken?"

"Assuming they were concomitant with the chats, it would have been early this year. Timmons confessed to the chats, but he swears the conversation just ran cold right around the end of March. He says he only received the two videos we found."

"And he has no idea who he was talking to on this end?"

"Apparently not. The last communication they had was March twenty-eighth. In that chat, they started talking about price and payment for more graphic videos. Timmons wrote again a day later, wanted to know about cost and how to make payment. That was it. No further replies."

"Can you run me a transcript of their communication?" Alex asked. Bell pulled his lips taut and handed him a large envelope.

"This has everything on the case. They're your copies, including the photographs. You just have to sign for them."

"Thank you," Alex said. "That's one less thing I have to do. Let me ask you this. The party on this end, is there any analysis of the syntax, words used, spelling, anything?"

"Not really. There was the usual internet shorthand. A lot of these guys use acronyms or abbreviations for sex acts or physical type, but this was straightforward. Timmons is well educated, like a lot of these guys. His English was clear and direct. The guy on the New York end wrote in simple phrases, but they were largely accurate."

"I'm asking because Ruiz isn't a native English speaker. He's a US citizen and his language skills seem okay, but he's a blue-collar guy. Not sure how he writes. We didn't find a computer in his possession either. Still, he was associated with a trafficking ring in the Bronx that got busted over the summer. They were tech savvy, apparently."

"We know about them," Bell said. "Ruiz doesn't own a computer and has no online trail himself, but sometimes the parents aren't actually brokering the deal. Instead they're providing access to their child for money, to someone who knows how to use the system. That someone also needs to know where the markets are for this kind of thing. How to access them. That's where TOR and Darknet come in, if you know what you're doing. Someone here did."

"Got it. So, it could be Ruiz was approached by someone and propositioned, or he knew who to ask. This is all assuming it was Ruiz, of course. At this point I have no idea."

"This child was extremely disabled, right? Did he have other regular caretakers?"

"Yes," Alex said, leaning back and trying to keep his head clear. This news was hitting him like a hammer. "He was mostly un-responsive. Didn't communicate." He paused for a moment as Joseliz popped into his head. "Except with one person."

"Who is he?"

"She, actually. She was a volunteer. Caregiver. She was the first person who found him dead, also."

"Any reason to suspect she'd deal him out to someone?"

"Joseliz?" Alex said, as if Bell would recognize the name. "Christ, I don't think so. She's a college student."

"Oh, wait a minute," Bell said as the thought dawned on him, "she's a witness in Regan's murder, right?"

"Yes. She was there, right beside him."

"Wow. She's got to be in bad shape."

"She is. She's pretty tough, though."

"Will she testify in your case?"

"Yeah, she will. I guess you'll want to interview her on this stuff?"

"I don't have to reveal a lot of details," Bell said. "No pictures, nothing like that. But yeah, I will. Is she comfortable with you? If so, I can arrange to speak to her here."

"She is, yeah. The lead on the case has gotten to know her also. Danny Lopez, from the Four-Four."

"Lopez? I don't know him, but it's a big department. I'll reach out to him also."

"So, you'll be the primary person working this?" Alex asked.

"Yes, but we may not be able to do much. The subject child is dead and Timmons is in custody on a bunch of other stuff. He'll likely plead in federal court and I've got a ton of other things going on. Still, we'd love to know who the seller was- the person on this end. You and Lopez are closer to this situation than anyone now. If you come up with any theories or make any new determinations on who had access, motive, etcetera? Let me know. I'll follow up with you personally. In the meantime, his photo is in a secure data base monitored by us nationwide. If he pops up again, we may get something additional."

"Thanks for coming by," Alex said, walking him out a few minutes later.

"I'm sorry to throw this wrench into things," Bell said. "I tend to leave a lot of bad news in my wake."

"This wrench is just another in a series," Alex said. "No worries."

CHAPTER 39

Tuesday, October 11

Alex's grandmother was fond of saying nothing good was on the other end of a phone line that rang after 10:00 p.m. It was an antiquated sentiment, but not an entirely unreasonable one. On this Tuesday night, while Alex and Nikki tried to relax with a binge-watching session of *Breaking Bad*, the call was from his brother Peter.

"Everything okay?" she asked when Alex returned from his bedroom. She was curled up under an old but incredibly cozy throw blanket, one of the only possessions he still had from his old life.

"Richard, my father's law partner died," he said with a sigh. "That brings their official run to a close, I guess."

"I'm sorry," she said. "I didn't know they were still working."

"They weren't full time anymore," he said, settling back in next to her. "My father hasn't done much in a few years, but Richard still had a trust and estates practice. He's been sick for a while, it wasn't a surprise."

"Will you go down?"

"I really don't want to."

"You kind of have an excuse," she said with a shrug. "You're approaching trial."

"Yeah, but we're kind of at the 'hurry up and wait' stage. For the most part I'm ready to go. Richard was good to us, Pete and me. We grew up around him, at the law office in Old Town. He was more patient with us than my father was, most of the time."

"That's nice," she said. "Then yes, you should go. Take the train, you can work at least. When is the service?"

"Thursday. I can leave that morning. It'll give me a chance to see Pete and Sam and the kids also. It's my father I don't want to deal with. Or Dara."

"Dara wouldn't be at the service, would she?" Nikki asked. Alex had told the broad strokes of the ugly history, the lawsuit involving his father and Richard, and Jonah Schwartz. It was over a development deal near an old train tracks, and apparently, where Alex's father was concerned anyway, it had bankrupted the firm. Greco and Tramlin were never the same, and his father believed the suit mostly derailed his career. Alex had also told her that it all took place about a year or two before he and Dara eloped.

"Not the service," he said. "She'll know I'm in town, though. She just will."

"Are you okay with seeing her?"

"I'm really never okay with seeing her."

"I can only imagine," she said softly.

"It's not because of her, Nik. I loved her once. I don't now."

"I understand that," she said, giving him a look which seemed to say that was obvious to her. "But that's only one part of it. You lost a child together."

"It's not that either," he said with a sigh. He opened his

mouth to say more, to begin the torturous and, as he saw it, necessary process of really inviting Nikki into his life with the divulgence of an awful truth she'd only seen the edges of. "It's just..." he trailed off, fighting back emotion and utterly at a loss for words, which was unusual for him.

"Alex, it's okay," she said, and he felt a cool wash of relief cover him as she simply let him off the hook. She leaned in and kissed him lightly. "Go, be safe, and come back to me. We'll talk then."

CHAPTER 40

Thursday, October 13

The reception Alex got from his former colleagues and friends at Richard Tamlin's funeral was overwhelming in its graciousness, and also closely observed by one person in particular. That person, Alex eventually sensed, was Kevin Crane, a rival and former colleague in his old office who was now beginning to organize the campaign of another former colleague, Steve Paulson. Alex, Kevin and Steve had all started around the same time in the Alexandria Commonwealth's Attorney's Office, fresh out of law school. After almost fifteen years, Steve was now angling hard for Commonwealth's Attorney, the job everyone, including Alex, in another life, believed he would eventually hold.

As usual, he was grateful but conflicted as he walked from his rental car to St. Mary's, the beautiful old stone church in the heart of Old Town where Tramlin's funeral was. He was greeted warmly by every familiar person he met, mostly attorneys but also cops, judges and others. He shouldn't have been surprised and in a way, he wasn't. Alexandria was home, and he had left there on good, if tragic terms. But there was a dark part of him tempted to wince at the smiles and handshakes. That part was guilt-ridden.

Inside the church, he noticed his brother Pete, his sister-in-law Samantha, and his niece and nephew up front with his father. His father was alone as Alex's mother Martina had died almost a year to the day after Jordan. He would have liked to have greeted the kids, but that meant dealing with his father, and there would be time enough for that later. The plan was for Alex to be at Pete and Sam's for dinner that evening.

It was at the graveside that the former colleague, Kevin Crane, finally sidled up to him as the crowd began to disperse.

"Alex, you got a minute?" he asked as they both emerged into the bright sunlight outside the burial canopy. It was a brisk, clear day but windless. Puffy clouds bunched in sharp relief against a crisp, blue sky. Alex turned to the sound of his voice, unsurprised. He had noticed Kevin studying him more than once during the mass and the burial.

"Sure Kevin." Alex had mixed feelings about Kevin Crane. He was an adequate attorney and had been a good guy to work with in the early years. But as time went on, Kevin seemed less intent on developing trial skills and more on developing another skill—toadying—which he eventually came to do with shameless precision, first to Craig Clemmons, the current Commonwealth's Attorney and Alex's former boss, and now to Steve Paulson, who looked to be next in line. Kevin never seemed to turn on Alex, even when things had gotten terribly dark just before he left. But there was also something in him Alex couldn't bring himself to trust. Kevin wasn't a bad guy, but he was weak and he could be bought. Or threatened.

"Listen, walk with me a second, okay?"

"Any way but that way," Alex said, nodding to his left. 'That way' meant the location of Jordan's little grave, which was in the same cemetery.

"Jeez, of course," Kevin said, hunching his shoulders and pulling his overcoat around him. He was of average build and height, graying at the temples with a soft, roundish face that was often flushed and pink. He seemed nervous, the pink face a darker shade, and Alex took note of it. "Listen, Alex. First things first, welcome back. Everyone's glad to see you."

"Thanks. And?"

"Well, the thing is, there are some rumors floating around. Stupid shit, mostly. But it's stuff I'd want to know about, if I were you."

"What does it matter? I'm leaving here tomorrow morning."

"Are you?" Kevin asked, stopping and turning to him. They were in front of an old, small crypt with a stone angel standing guard. "If so, for how long?"

"What? Why?"

"You did a lot of palm pressing today. I noticed it. And I'm not the only one."

"So that's what this is," Alex said, his eyes narrowing. "Jesus. You're carrying water for Steve Paulson now?"

"Insult me if you want to," Kevin said with a shrug. "I was never the stalwart guy you are, and I know you look down on me for it. Believe it or not, though, I'm looking out for you." Part of Alex thought that might be possible. But he also knew there was something else at work.

"Okay, so what's the issue? Steve thinks I might move back here next year and challenge him in a primary?"

"It's not a ridiculous scenario," Kevin said. "You went away because of grief, and you dealt with it. You kicked ass in the big city. We've all heard about your victories up there. So now maybe you want to come back, fresh and ready to take the reins where you came from. It's been done before. People would like it."

"Jesus, I can't believe this."

"You're still well-liked," Kevin said. "You'd also be well heeled, if you ran and Jonah backed you. And I think he would, wouldn't he? You two are still friendly, right? Despite splitting up with Dara."

"What are you getting at?"

"Look," Kevin said with a little bit of gruffness, as if it was a sad duty he was executing. "I'm not trying to hurt you. I'm clueing you in okay?"

"About what?"

"Things have changed since you left. There's a progression happening, I know you've heard. Steve Paulson is the man for the job, and he'll probably run unopposed. If you came back and wanted it, though, it would be a race. That's made some people uncomfortable. With you, I mean. I think if you tried to run, they'd try to make things difficult for you. That's what I'm trying to say."

"It's what you've been told to say," Alex said. He was flashing back to that now long-ago conversation with Jonah at Yankee Stadium. As usual, Jonah had been right. The man knew the playing field, really any playing field, like no one else. "So just say it."

"Fine," Kevin said, clearing his throat. "I'm not the enemy. And by the way Steve has nothing to do with any of this."

"Sure. Go on."

"It's true. This goes beyond the CA's office. It affects the political landscape all over town. There might be a judgeship in play. The police department expects certain things. If you were to come back and shake things up, some people would be angry about it. And they might start digging."

"Just tell me," Alex said, feeling suddenly drained. "What the hell is it they think they have, whoever 'they' are?"

"Jordan's death," Kevin said at lower volume. "I was on the death investigation team. You know that."

"Of course."

"There was pressure on us— I never knew from whom or what— to close it pretty quickly. And we did. But there's a file, still. It could be re-opened."

"And what would be in there, Kevin?"

He sighed heavily, and then said, "Dara's story was that Jordan fell down the stairs chasing a toy."

"He did."

"Right. And supposedly he never hit anything on the way down. He just tumbled down the stairs. God, I'm sorry to bring this up but..."

"Just tell me."

"There is a series of photos, of an area of the wall, just below the banister. I'm not sure if you saw them or not. The drywall there was indented, Alex. Not much, but enough to see. A roundish patch, maybe a few inches in diameter. Not very deep. But there was no stud behind it. You could put your fist right through it, or your elbow. It's also the kind of indentation a kid's shoulder could have made."

"You mean if he was thrown down the stairs and hit a wall first."

"Yes. I'm sorry, but yes. That's a possibility. There was a bruise on the shoulder. Sure, the fall could have caused it. But not necessarily. There were finger marks on one of Jordan's arms, also. You know that."

"She gripped him to wake him up," Alex said, feeling his heart start to pound. He concentrated on controlling his breathing and keeping his voice from rising. "He was unresponsive. That's where the damn finger marks came from. This is covered territory."

"Okay," Kevin said. "I get it. All I'm saying is, there could be questions. New questions. No one— I mean no one— wants to go there. But if you did decide to return and run? I don't know what would happen. Please don't kill the messenger. I don't want this either. I'm simply telling you how it is. In confidence."

"I know what you're doing," Alex said, pausing and lighting a cigarette. He inhaled and gazed past Kevin to the tree line where the sun was preparing to set, slowly burning from pale yellow to orange. Alex paused as the smoke moved through him. The smartest thing that could come out of his mouth next was the truth that he had no intention of returning to Alexandria and challenging fucking Steve Paulson. But Paulson was a smug prick and Alex just wasn't in the mood to be mollifying.

"Tell Paulson to go fuck himself," he said. "I don't know what I'm doing next year. Right now, I have a murder trial to win. But I'll tell you this: If he, you or anyone else thinks I'll be bullied into crawling away, you're wrong. I've got nothing to hide." With that, he turned and walked off between the rows. After a moment, Kevin called after him.

"What?"

"There was never a toy found either," Kevin said, looking at him quizzically, almost sympathetically. "At the bottom of the stairs. Maybe it was moved, I don't know. Maybe it rolled under the water heater. But it was never found." Alex opened his mouth to answer, then thought better of it and left Kevin alone in the darkening graveyard.

CHAPTER 41

There was a running joke between Alex and his older brother Pete that the scowl etched on their father's face would become surgically irremovable in time. That night, as dinner wound down and Samantha collected the dessert plates, it seemed less a joke and more hard reality. His father had been drinking, a lot, since before dinner, first wine and then bourbon after the meal. He had been silent through most of it, cheerful enough with the children, but otherwise somber and withdrawn. Now he stabbed at the last of his apple pie with his fork, and the scowl deepened. Alex glanced at his watch. He had probably stayed long enough. If things could just remain quiet for a few more minutes, he'd be able to make a polite exit.

"So...how's the Bronx?" his father asked without looking up. He pushed some pie around and then stabbed at it. Dominick Greco was a little shorter than his sons, gray and mostly bald, with a prominent, brooding forehead and eyes that seemed to peek from under it. He still had gravitas as a well-known and older attorney in the lawyer's town that was Alexandria, but bitterness and resentment had long ago stained it. It wasn't all because of the fallout after the legal battle against Jonah.

There were a few other bad turns. But that had sealed it.

"It's fine, Pop," Alex said.

"Just fine? Come on, it's the front lines of prosecution. The big city."

"Dad, do you want a cup of coffee?" Samantha called out. Curbing his drinking would be a good thing, she knew, and he usually loved her coffee.

"No. Actually, I'd like to hear how Alex is doing. But he's been suspiciously quiet. Like he had a rough day or something." Alex sighed. He could tell by their faces that Pete and Sam hoped Dom would avoid picking a fight with his younger son this night, for the sake of the kids if nothing else. But Devyn and Hunter had been excused a while ago and were downstairs watching a Disney movie. Samantha was busying herself in the kitchen, leaving the three Greco men to themselves for the moment.

"Everything is good," Alex said. "I'm very busy. I'm glad I could be here for Richard's family."

"Oh, you were a hit," his father said, fixing him with sleepy, almost predatory eyes. "Everybody was so happy to see you. Almost like you were coming back for good."

"Well, I'm not," Alex said, taking a sip of beer and setting down the glass carefully. It was as if the less noise was made from any source, the better. Dinner time tension was something both Alex and Pete had known all their lives, and the strategies to ameliorate it were all but second nature to both of them. "I'll be on a train tomorrow morning. Trial starts in a few weeks."

"Everyone except for Paulson's lapdog, I should say," his father went on, as if he hasn't heard a reply. "What did Kevin tell you, anyway? I saw you two at the cemetery. Huddling up."

"Nothing, really. We just talked."

"About what? Your big upcoming trial? That animal who slashed his kid's neck open? Kevin wouldn't know about that. It doesn't happen here."

"It was really nothing," Alex said. "Please, just drop it."

"Can you tell us anything about that trial?" Pete asked, busying himself rearranging silverware in front of him. "You got great press on that case from last year. What was the name, Prince?"

"Yeah, Shawn Prince," Alex said. "Drug dealer from South Carolina. That was a great outcome, thanks."

"Samantha saved a couple of the clippings. She's gotta be the last person on earth still saving newspaper clip..."

"He threatened you, didn't he?" Dom broke in. Pete went silent and minutely shook his head.

"No, Pop," Alex said slowly. "He didn't. And I'm not sure where this is going, but..."

"The word's out, they're onto you. Locking you out. And you won't challenge them, will you?"

"There's nothing here I want."

"No, of course not. You'll serve in that zoo up there instead." He picked up his bourbon glass and took a drink, then shook the ice. "Anywhere but here, I guess. And Steve Paulson will just waltz right in."

"Please don't start, Pop," Alex said, meeting his father's carnivorous gaze with a cold one of his own, but measuring his tone. Nikki's voice was strong in his head, and while he wished she was with him, he wouldn't wish this experience on her for all the whisky in Ireland. In his mind, she was telling him to *Consider the Source*. She was also telling him to use every word he spoke with the undivided goal of ending the conversation and getting the hell out of there.

"They've got you neutered," Dom said. "You could come back. You could make something of yourself. Here. Even now. But you won't. You'll run. Just like last time."

"Pop, stop this," Pete said, speaking through gritted teeth.

"You gave up," his father said, almost spit really. "You gave in. And you're doing it again."

"Dad, stop!" Samantha called from the kitchen, her voice high with anxiety.

"Who told you this?" Alex asked, his voice purposely low as it was barely controlled. "Who told you Kevin or Steve or anyone else was looking at me?"

"It's a small bar," his father said. "Word gets out. What are you, dense? That's what was supposed to happen. Kevin was just batting clean-up today, making sure you heard it. Loud and clear."

"I've got nothing to hide."

"Are you sure about that?" Dom asked, his voice rising. "What about my grandson?! What the hell happened to him? What do you know about that?" Alex opened his mouth to answer but found he couldn't form words. His father continued. "It breaks my heart every day. But I warned you, didn't I? That spoiled, rich, nutcase of a girl. You married her anyway, and now look at you! Look at all of us!"

"Jesus stop it!" Alex said, his teeth clenched.

"What she did killed your mother also!"

"Enough!" Pete called out finally. He slammed his beer on the table and foam poured out of the bottle mouth. An EMT in the Alexandria Fire Department, Pete had a beard and mustache, a barrel chest and generous beer gut, and the same bellowing voice Alex and his father employed regularly in courtrooms. For a few seconds everything went quiet. "This is my house," he said at lower volume. "I won't have this." Samantha came into the dining room and stood beside him, folding a hand towel and then crossing her arms in solidarity with him.

"I'll go," Alex said, and stood to gather his coat and keys. "Sam, please give the kids my best. I'll see them around the holidays." He hugged his brother and sister-in-law, and then glanced back at his father, who stared straight ahead, stone-faced. Since Pete's outburst he hadn't said a word.

Then he paused and looked at the old man more close-ly. His father had almost always made him and Pete feel like sources of disappointment, but now, for the first time in his nearly 40 years, Alex had a sense of what that re-ally meant. It wasn't just that his father expected-— hell, *courted*-- disappointment. It was as if he craved it. He was difficult and hostile when dealing with the disappoint-ment he seemed to divine in everyone around him, but he was actually worse when the source of it was taken away.

Now Danny's words about Norman Ruiz floated up again, from the conversation at Coogan's over beers back in April. *He's the type who'd rather have something to bitch about.* That was his father, when it came to pretty much everyone in his life. Whatever the struggles or circum-stances of the people around him, whatever their limita-tions or triumphs, they were, in the twisted, sad world of Dominick Greco, disappointments. He treated them all as such, like perpetually unsatisfying burdens. It was wrong, though, to believe he wanted rid of them, or even to change them. Alex wasn't sure if Pete, the more dutiful son and the one now absorbing most of his father's dis-dain, even saw the pattern although Alex was pretty sure Samantha did. Dara and Jordan were gone. His mother, obsequious for years in the face of her husband's derision, was gone. Now Alex was gone. Dom was faced with nothing to lament.

"You know, you've given me a lot to think about," Alex said to him. "Thanks for that, if not for much else. Take care, Pop."

Alex could feel his anxiety begin to wane as he shut the door behind him, and almost instantly his thoughts started to churn back toward the case, the usual cacophony of figuring, second guessing, and planning. He needed a decent night's sleep and then a fast getaway in the morning, back to the reality of his life and the task at hand. He was about to stuff his phone into his coat pocket when, on his brother's front walk in the chilly air, he heard a text chime. It was a distinct but familiar one he almost never heard anymore. The alert sound was called "popcorn." She had programmed it into his phone a few years ago, and he had never bothered to change it.

Dara.

CHAPTER 42

Dara Schwartz was simply pretty, and in the most subtle and un-coaxed way Alex had ever known. There was nothing vampish or striking about her; she didn't have Alexa's electrifying eyes or even Nikki's understated but provocative mouth. She was of average height and build, a little pear shaped, with generous lips, dark, heavy eyebrows, and a cute, pug-like nose with a sprinkling of faded freckles around it. Her hair was perhaps the most alluring thing about her; it formed a corona of rich, brown, naturally curly lushness that went past her shoulders. On top of it tonight she had on a small red beret, and over her body was a black, stylish overcoat that went about midway to her knees. She stood in front of Jordan's gravestone with a little bundle of flowers, her lower lip curled slightly downward in a gentle pout. The cemetery around them was well-lit, but still shadowy and shrouded by trees at almost 10:00 p.m. Dara hated anything "creepy," but she seemed always to want to meet Alex at this place, day or night.

"Can't we just meet in a goddam bar one of these days, Dara?" He asked as he approached from the narrow, cemetery side road. His gaze shifted downward to Jordan's still-gleaming little monument which contained his name, the dates that encapsulated his life, the words "Beloved Son," and the carving of a reposed lamb over the letters. The color Dara's mother chose for the granite was called Autumn Rose; it was one of those details Alex would recall often and usually for no reason.

"I can't drink with this medication," she said. "Anyway, I wanted to visit him. I'm sorry."

"Don't be sorry." He could tell she was "visiting" quite a bit lately. There were flowers and toys and cards that were all distinctly in Dara's taste, gathered around the stone. "And please, while we talk, don't say you're sorry every five seconds, okay?"

"Okay, I won't, I'm s…" She stopped herself and smiled at him. That smile, impossibly honest, sweet and un-staged, sunk into Alex as it had since he'd been in sixth grade. He felt helpless before it momentarily, and then regained his composure. The lurking knowledge that he usually had to play the adult when the two of them were discussing something serious brought him back to level.

"How are you, Dara?"

"I'm okay," she said, looking at the stone, then up at him. "How's your family?"

"Eh. Pete and Sam and the kids are fine. My father…not so much."

"Is he sick?"

"Not really. I just…can't talk to him. It's okay."

"He hates me," she said plainly. "More than he hates my father even."

"He hates himself."

"I don't blame him one bit," she said. Then her gaze fell to the stone, and her face fell with it. "I'm so sorry, sweet baby," she breathed.

"Dara, you have to let this go."

"It should be me down there," she said with dead evenness, her eyes fixed on the grave.

"No. It shouldn't be either of you."

"But I pushed him," she said, almost quizzically, as if it was just occurring to her for the first time. She looked at Alex and blinked, and suddenly a look of horror spread across her face that sent a shockwave through him. Before he knew it, he was grabbing for her and embracing her, attempting to support her as she collapsed to her knees in the cold grass. Instead, she pulled him down with her so they both hit their knees, and Alex felt icy dew spread through his slacks to his kneecaps. Dara made a half-choking, half-screaming sound that was as haunted as it was wretched. "I PUSHED HIM!"

"Shhhh," he said, clutching her, spreading his knees through the grass to keep them both from falling over. Her hair, the layered, fragrant mass of it, was bundled in his hands. His face was lost in it. "Dara, shhhh. Don't!"

"I did! I did!" she said, sobbing so that the words were muffled and incomplete. "I killed our baby! Alex, kill me! I deserve it, I killed him!"

"It wasn't you," he breathed into her ear, through a tangle of hair. "It wasn't you honey, please listen to me. It wasn't you."

"It was!"

"No! No, it wasn't. It was an illness. It was an illness that isn't you at all, sweetheart. It was never you. It could never, ever be you. Please believe me." She continued to sob and formed some words he couldn't make out. In her ear he continued to make his argument, the one he believed as firmly as he believed anything. Mental illness was a monster, he knew this like he knew his own face in the morning mirror. He referred to it not that way to her, but as the "illness." It was the "illness" that had taken over in that one black moment, the illness that had invaded her despite her every wish to be the kind, happy girl she naturally was. Jordan was a handful, God knew, but she still loved him. The illness, though, loved nothing and sought death. That's what pushed Jordan to his death. Not Dara. Never Dara.

"I miss him so much," she said when the sobbing ebbed enough to allow for speech.

"I do too," he breathed, still clutching her, as much for his own support now as hers. He could smell her and for a bright, blinking moment the love he had for her, that pulsing, beckoning thing that started even before his first sexual stirrings, was back, as deep and steady as ever. Dara, with the high, infectious laugh that always seemed to start with her taken by surprise, her eyes popping open like flashbulbs, her mouth forming an adorable "O." Dara, with the lovable pout that knitted her brow and turned her lips outward, making it impossible to be angry with her, no matter what storm raged within her. Dara, the girl he had grown to love as a boy as naturally as he loved anything.

Her head turned, and suddenly his mouth wasn't in her ear. Instead they were nose to nose, her breath in his face. Her lips were parted and glistening. Her tears, salty and warm, mingled with his. His breath caught in his throat. They were coupled again, under the canopy of her hair, the way they had been when they kissed for the first time at thirteen, or when they claimed each other's virginity four years later. Face to face. Heart to heart.

"Not here," she whispered, suddenly and utterly clear. "It's too weird." The breath let go, and Alex thought he was about to cough up a sob himself. But it wasn't crying that was coming forward, it was laughter. Honest, naked laughter, the kind Dara inspired everywhere she went, even when wreckage came with her.

"Oh, for God's sake," he said, when he could finally speak again. She stared at him with a kind of bewildered look for a few seconds, her eyes red rimmed and raw, then smiled herself.

"Don't laugh," she said, turning her head and hugging him. "It's not right."

"No, darling. I think it's exactly what we both needed. Come on." He got to his feet and lifted her up. Both shaking, they held their embrace. For the second time in as many hours, Alex felt an icy but exhilarating clarity, this one inspired not by his father's endless hostility or Danny's wisdom, but instead the almost whispered words of Rolando Garcia. The strange way he once related how his sister described Norman Ruiz: A man who seemed incapable of living, and instead, figuratively at least, existed among the dead.

Alex was, if in a less dishonorable way, guilty of the same thing. It was exactly what he had been doing, he understood at last, since the day his own son had plummeted from the world. It was what Nikki had tried to warn him about, the gentle trap he had stepped into, enshrouding himself in the expanse and tangle of the city and then working with brutal focus, all of that to surround himself under a professional veneer with the fact and details of death, day in and day out. Inside this trap were the machinations he was most comfortable with, the reports and photos, the explanations and theories, the tears and numbness. When he peered out from it, it was only into black memory. In either place, he was among the dead.

It was also what he could see Dara doing, drowning in guilt even he couldn't imagine, enshrining their lost child. She was, in every emotional sense, poised tortuously on a precipice over some bottomless maw. Whether he could save himself with this newfound insight or not, he at least needed to try to pull her back.

"It's time for us to live again, Dara," he said into her hair. "We've been avoiding it for too long. Both of us, in our own way."

"But this *is* my life," she said quietly. "All I have is to be close to him. Here."

"You'll always be close to him," he said, pulling away and looking into her eyes. "And this isn't all you have. Listen to me, okay? It's good sometimes, to come here. To be near him. But you can't live here. You need to walk away from this place and start again. Make your peace and return to the living. You have to, or you'll be consumed by this." They were still for a long moment.

"Do you forgive me, Alex?" she asked finally, looking back at him, her lips trembling. "I can't think about having peace, without that. And it's a lot to ask."

"I forgave you a long time ago," he said. "It was easy, and it's because of what I'm telling you now. It wasn't you. It was a disease. It wasn't you."

"Is that why...why you helped me?" she asked, her eyes searching his face. "With my father?"

"Yes, that's why I helped you."

"Because I know why my father did it. He couldn't help himself; that's who he is. He wasn't being rational, he was being my dad. But you? You were always rational. You were always right."

"Hardly."

"No," she said, shaking her head, "you were, when it came to the big things. You're perfect for the job you have. You see right and wrong, but you see people, too. You understand weakness. You don't make it worse for people when you see it."

"I try, I fail, I try to do better," he said with a shrug. "We all do. But thanks."

"Are you staying at your brother's tonight?"

"No, I'm at the Viceroy in Old Town. I'd love to see a couple of people, but I don't have the energy for visits. I'm starting a trial soon." She looked at him closely for a few seconds, and then kissed him lightly on the cheek.

"Drop me off at my mother's?"

CHAPTER 43

There was a purple envelope slid underneath the windshield wiper of the rental car the next morning when Alex emerged from the hotel. *Dara, of course,* he thought as he drew a little greeting card from it. She still worked in Old Town, at the city archeologist's office where she had been since college. There, in her neat, girlish handwriting, was the message:

Dearest Alex:

I wanted to say 'thanks' for last night. You forgiving me might, in time, allow me to forgive myself. Your little theory about why-the "illness" and not plain old crazy fucking Dara- is sweet and kind. But we both know it's not that simple.

In time, I think I <u>can</u> forgive myself. I think I can promise you that. So I'm grateful to you, because there's no way I could get close to forgiving myself without your permission. Does that sound pathetic? I hope not. Because it's true.

I meant what I said. On the big things, you're

always right. So don't back down when you know you're right, Alex Greco. Because if I'm right about the future, you'll be a powerful man someday. You'll need to rely on your instincts, and you'll need to be true to them to keep being the person you are.
For now, thanks again. I will always love you, my darling Alex.

Dara
P.S. My dad feels the same way- about you being powerful.
P.P.S I know you have a new girlfriend. It was on your face last night. She's a lucky lady. Try not to fuck it up. :)

He read it a second time and smiled. It was a slow, sardonic smile, but not a mirthless one. Two powerful bonds, now broken inside of him at last, had left flailing threads, like live power wires on pavement. He could sense them settling already, knitting slowly into the fabric of his mind. They had broken almost simultaneously. From his father, after a lifetime. From Dara, after nearly three years of anguish.

His phone chimed and he saw a text from Danny. That was reminder enough that, whatever this breakthrough had been, he needed leave it behind for now and get the hell home, and back to work. There was one more thread pulling on him, though. It was a hard and fast one that tethered him to the cemetery of his old life. The thought had been nagging him ever since leaving the graveyard, all through the events with his father and Dara. The thought was that he had acted recklessly by antagonizing Kevin, and through him Steve Paulson. Paulson, who was not only a smug prick but a devious one, happy to get mean over politics. Then the phone chimed again, this time from Raquel. He sighed and forced the nagging to a back corner of his mind. He had a train to catch.

CHAPTER 44

"Early Christmas present," Danny said, and dropped a file on Alex's desk. It was a little after 5:00 on Friday evening. "Your instincts are checkin' out."

"Ryan Isoli? You found something?"

"Something," Danny said. "Not between Isoli and Ruiz, though. I still don't have any evidence they were associated. I got something else, though." He tapped on the file and sat down. Alex opened it. On top was photo of a sealed evidence bag with a smaller bag inside. Inside that were yellow and green, plain looking lollipops.

"Lollipops?"

"Yeah. Laced with fentanyl. Remember what Sean said, about Isoli selling club drugs and pharmaceuticals?"

"Christ," Alex whispered. He hadn't worked narcotics cases in years, but he knew what fentanyl was. A synthetic opioid, it was around fifty times more potent than heroin. Unlike heroin, it was recognized as having a medical application for the treatment of severe pain. It was legal, but only as a highly controlled substance given the possibility of overdose and the serious danger for addiction in the user.

"Isoli had a couple of some-time partners, these black guys who ran a dance club in New Rochelle," Danny said. New Rochelle was a city just northeast of the Bronx, in Westchester County. "The club got raided a couple of weeks ago. These lollipops were found along with a lot of pills and some other stuff. One of the Yonkers detectives was smart enough to ask the two guys about Isoli. They've got an alibi for his murder, but after some squeezing, they also admitted they supplied these lollipops to him."

"I've seen the fentanyl prescription ones," Alex said. "They're shaped like lollipops, but you wouldn't mistake them for candy. They look like medicine on a stick. These look like ones you'd see in a candy store."

"That's how they usually are when it's a club drug, or something sold on a college campus," Danny said. "They draw less attention than the prescription ones. Anyway, if you can synthesize fentanyl or buy it, you can lace a regular lollipop with it in a kitchen lab. So maybe Ruiz knew this guy Isoli and bought some from him. I can't make that out yet, but I'm still working on it."

"So, these were for Hector," Alex said, knowing he was stating the obvious. "To knock him out, or nearly."

"Yep. Once he's out of it, he's easily manipulated, filmed, whatever. You can undress him, re-dress him, all that stuff. Bell said the buyer wants to see him recorded in the tub, remember? If that's the case, Norman has to figure out a way to get him in there. Maybe he offers him a lollipop, if he gets in. And if it's laced with this shit, he's out of it for hours."

"He's also out of pain," Alex said. "Which we know he was probably in, because of his wrist. Norman knew because the staff at HCC told him. So, Hector learns to associate the tub with a lollipop. The rest, he doesn't remember. All he knows is he feels okay for a while. Better than okay, I guess."

"It sounds like this is what Joseliz was getting to," Danny said, and there was a touch of awe in his voice. Alex noticed he was tapping on Sean's notebook, the one Danny had kept since the night Sean was killed. He carried it everywhere. "This is what she told Sean, about how Hector was starting to tell her things. If Norman knew that, then he had a reason to get rid of him."

"Right, but did he know? Everyone thinks Norman was tuned out. Couldn't give a damn about what was happening."

"He's shown he can be clever," Danny said. "We've already seen how he's a different guy in front of a camera, or an audience. So maybe he saw more than he let on. Look, I know I doubted this guy as a killer early on, but I see it now. What we know is, Norman didn't give a damn about this kid. If anything, he resented him. Hector was some far off problem in the goddam DR. Then it's dumped on him. Why not pimp him out if there's some way to do it where the kid won't complain?"

"Two things," Alex said after processing it. "First, I think he'd need a middleman. Norman might be clever, but it doesn't look like he had the tools or the knowledge to access that market. Second, and God knows I may be wrong, but I don't think Norman is the type who would hands-on sexually abuse his own kid. He doesn't strike me that way. Pimping him out? That I could see. Norman has some experience with that, and I agree, he might even do it with his own child. But if there's some asshole on the other end, like this guy in Vermont, who wants to see stuff done to the kid? I don't think it's going to be Norman Ruiz actually doing it."

"I'm with you," Danny said, nodding as if he had done the same processing. "That's the missing link. I suppose it could have been Isoli himself. He was a complete scumbag, and he knew plenty like him. It's a hunch, but it makes sense. If Isoli was connected with the buyer somehow, then maybe he found out the guy got busted. Or he just got spooked. So, then he tells Norman. Then maybe Norman figures Isoli should be gotten rid of in case cops get to him first."

"It still leaves us with the Lido Beach guy," Alex said. "If we think they're all related."

"I thought about that," Danny said. "So, let me ask you this: Has anyone ever run that guy's picture by the ICAC guys? Or with the feds?"

"Huh," Alex said. He smiled at Danny, impressed. "That's an idea, isn't it? I'll call him tomorrow. I'll also ask Margaret to run a tox screen on Hector, specifically for fentanyl. It probably wasn't tested for originally."

"If it comes back positive, how does it affect our case?"

"Honestly, I don't know," Alex said. "I'll give all of this to his attorney. What he'll do with it, I don't know. No judge is going to let us try some sex abuse case within a murder case, like some kind of side show. I guess if all Rick has to do is confuse things, though, this could give him ammunition. Somehow, some way, maybe he can suggest someone else is loading this kid up with poison..."

"Poison what?" Danny asked, watching Alex trail off. Alex went silent for a long moment, staring at nothing in particular. "Lex? You okay over there?"

"*Chupetes*," he said finally.

"Suckers, yeah," Danny said. "Common Spanish word for lollipops."

"The weird uncle. Rolando. He told me he used to bring them to Hector. That and red licorice, I think."

"And he does cell phone and computer repair, right?"

"He fixes screens is what he told me. Still, I'm sure he knows computers a lot better than Norman." He looked over at Danny. "Can you run this down?"

"Sure. I'll take Rolando's picture, show it around Isoli's old places. I'll see if Rolando used a credit card in that neighborhood. That kind of thing."

"Did you get a vibe like that from him, though? At all?"

"What, that Garcia is capable of something like this? He creeps me out a little, but no, not that way. But he had access to the kid, and he doesn't have an alibi. I guess you never know."

"No, you really don't. But at some point, you have to pull the trigger anyway. That's what scares me."

CHAPTER 45

Wednesday, October 19

"Greco," Alex said into his phone. He and Nikki were walking hand in hand along Central Park West, the avenue that ran parallel to the park itself. It was a nearly perfect night, crisp, cool and moonlit just before 8:00.

"Alex it's John Bell, from ICAC. I'm sorry to call so late."

"No worries, John, what's up?" He flashed an apologetic look to Nikki, who just shrugged and smiled. She was used to it.

"The photo you provided us. Of the John Doe found at Lido Beach?"

"Yeah. Anything on him?"

"As a matter of fact, yes. We circulated the photograph among different offices. An investigator in Boston has an informant who was able to identify him for us. The informant traded CP face to face with the dead guy years ago. Nicholas Whelan is his name. We were able to confirm that and get a last known address. He owned a house in Westchester County, Larchmont. We got a search warrant and went through it earlier today. The guy had a pretty sophisticated computer set-up. Forensics is still checking things out, but it looks like he's our New York connection, the guy who was talking to Timmons in Vermont. He's Angel12221."

"Damn," Alex said. "Any connection between him and Ruiz yet? I know you're still sorting through it all."

"We are. And no, nothing yet. But here's something close. Whelan's day job was in IT. He set up computer networks and did some repair. Not too surprising. He was freelance and had several clients from what we can tell. One of them might be significant to you, though. Haven Community Center. Your murder victim received services there, right?"

"Shit," Alex said, stopping in his tracks. "Yeah. You're sure?"

"We've got records. Invoices. You'll probably want to talk to their staff about him. I'm not sure how relevant all this is to your case."

"If I can establish a link between Ruiz and Whelan, it might be," Alex said. "I'd like to run it down. You sure I won't be interfering with your investigation?"

"No, you're clear. We may get around to talking to their staff anyway, but there's no need for you to wait on us. Most of what we need, we've got. Nassau County still has an unsolved murder case, but at least they know who he is."

"Sounds good, John. Thanks," He and Nikki had reached Columbus Circle and were now amidst kids, tourists and different guys hawking souvenirs, tours and carriage rides.

"No," Bell said. "Thank *you*. This was a big hit for us. It looks like this guy might have had several aliases and was doing business in a few different places. We can run a lot of that down now. Good luck with your case."

CHAPTER 46

Thursday, October 20

Bruce looked at the photo Alex handed him of Nicholas Whelan, put his hand to his forehead, and shook his head. Beside him, Connie looked like she wanted to die. Her normally upbeat, pleasant expression was haunted. There was a gray pallor to her face. Underneath that, though, Alex could also see a cold, stubborn look of defiance.

The three were in Alex's office, late on a gray afternoon, and he had just explained the circumstances of where Nicholas Whelan had been found and how. He had also told them about Hector's suspected abuse, and the connection the ICAC team had discovered between Whelan and the buyer, Corey Timmons, in Vermont.

"Of course, we knew Nick Whelan," Bruce said at low volume. "He did some work for us, over time. Different things. We haven't seen him since around the end of March, though. He told me he was going home for a while, like where he was from. I can't even remember where he said that was. Somewhere in Long Island, I think."

"What kind of work did he do?"

"Mostly computer work, wiring, network maintenance,

that sort of thing," Bruce said. "But he wanted to work with the kids also. He helped them with iPads, games, computer assisted learning. That's what drew him to us. That's what he told us anyway."

"We did a background check," Connie said, her voice rising. "We have it on file, I can show it to you!"

"Whelan had no criminal record," Alex said, his voice low and, he hoped, calming. "A background check wouldn't have revealed anything. I used to handle a lot of these cases, Connie. I can tell you most of the guys I prosecuted were working with clean background checks."

"I'm going to be sick," she said, barely above a whisper. Her eyes seemed to plead with Alex. "Do they think he… hurt any of our kids? Is there any evidence, other than Hector?"

"They're still going through his materials," Alex said. "We really don't know yet. It's important to determine what kind of access he had to your facility, and to your clients, if any. What I need to know right now is whether he had any connection to Hector that you saw. Or Norman." The two both looked at each other.

"Norman was only at the facility from time to time," Connie said. "I never really saw him talk to anyone."

"Whelan was around Hector, though," Bruce said, at low volume. "I know that much. That picture game Joseliz used to play with Hector? Nick wanted to create a computerized version of it for her to use." He looked up at Alex. "He took an interest in Hector. I saw it."

"Did you see him interact with Norman?"

"They spoke, yeah. There was an issue of eloping. Hector was just up and walking out of the house, from time to time. It drove Norman crazy."

"I know about it, yes."

"Well, Nick had an idea. He talked to Norman about a GPS tracker he could put on Hector, like a bracelet. Norman never ordered one. We would have known about it if he did. But I saw Nick talking to Norman about it and showing Norman on his cell phone how it would work."

"You mean Norman's phone?"

"Yes, Norman's. So, they could have exchanged information that way. If nothing else, Nick probably had a way to contact him."

"Is there security video we could review?" Alex asked. "Anything archived? It might show them together on the property."

"Possibly," Connie said. "I'll look. I just can't believe this." She turned to Bruce. "He wouldn't have had access to kids by himself, though. Not for long, anyway. We don't work that way."

"Not usually, no. But there were times. I'm sorry, Connie, but it's the truth. We're going to need to investigate this, probably with an outside team." He looked to Alex. "Do you know anyone who does that kind of thing?"

"I do, actually," Alex said, picturing Nikki. "I have a close friend who is very familiar with these kinds of situations. I'll ask her what she thinks."

"Thank you," Connie said. "We should have known better. I am just. . .so sorry."

"Connie, you don't have to be sorry. To anyone, but certainly not me. No one can detect these people, not really. It happens." He paused for a moment. "One thing I have to tell you. All of this information, about Whelan and what we talked about today? Norman's attorney will be made aware of it. He may want to interview you both about Whelan and his involvement here. Whether you're willing to talk to him is up to you, but I can't dissuade you from doing so."

"What will he try to suggest?" Connie asked. "That we're at fault somehow, for putting Norman and Whelan together? Don't they think Norman killed him also, before Hector?"

"Norman's attorney has to protect his legal interests any way he can. That means he has to cast doubt on my theory of the case, whatever it is. My theory is that Norman wanted to get rid of Hector, and either planned it out or snapped on April seventh. Either way, it was a convenient time and he killed Hector in the bathtub. Then he went out and got ready to clean up after himself, but Joseliz got there early and discovered Hector's body. Now, where does that meet this new information? I don't know, and it might not affect my case. You ask if Norman is believed to be Whelan's killer. The answer is that it's possible. Norman might have done it to cover his tracks as part of something bigger. But that would be a totally different case, if it's ever charged at all. The judge on our case won't allow a bunch of theories and accusations to be tossed around without hard evidence behind them, and there's just too much we don't know about this separate situation."

"How is it separate, though?" Bruce asked. "Isn't all of this related?"

"Maybe, maybe not. But from a strict legal standpoint, these other issues can't become a part of Norman's murder trial unless they're admitted as evidence. I'll know more after we're in court again." He looked from Connie to Bruce, both of them looking like the very thing they'd spent their entire lives building was melting beneath their feet. "For now, do what you have to do to protect your clients and your work. I'll be in touch."

Connie and Bruce left Alex's office a little after 5:00 that evening. At almost 10:00, Alex was still at his desk with a collection of Diet Pepsi cans forming a half circle around a pizza box. His cell phone lit up from under a detective's report and he reached for it. It was Bruce.

"I'm sorry to call so late," he said.

"Believe me, I'm working. What's up?"

"I didn't tell you this when Connie and I were over there," he said. His voice sounded pained. "I couldn't bring myself to."

"Tell me what?"

"I saw something between Whelan and Hector. Something Whelan was doing with him."

"Something sexual?"

"Inappropriate, I'd say, looking back. It was only once, but it bothered me then. I didn't say anything, though, I just...pushed it out. I explained it away, I guess. If it was a girl he was doing it to, I'm sure I would have said something. or done something. It's just..."

"I think it's different with boys," Alex said. "It's okay. Listen, it's best not to go into details on the phone. The person most involved here is John Bell, from the Internet Crimes Against Children unit. I'm going to call him. He may ask my office to record your statement. Could you come down if so? Mostly likely tomorrow but let me see what he says."

"Yeah, of course. I'm around all week." He paused. "I'm sorry I didn't say something sooner. And by that I don't mean earlier today. I mean when it happened."

"Don't be," Alex said. "You're not the first or the last guy who has seen something borderline and not reacted."

CHAPTER 47

Friday, October 21

The fourth floor of Alex's office housed the video unit and a small interview room. As Alex suspected, John Bell had asked that he take a statement from Bruce, and they scheduled a video statement for 10:00 that Friday morning. Alex had with him an investigator named Phil Barino, a friendly but stone-faced guy who reminded Alex a lot of Paul Sorvino in *Goodfellas*. Phil was there as a witness. Vince, the same camera tech who had recorded Norman at the Four-Four back in April, was there as well.

"Have a seat," Alex said to Bruce. "This shouldn't take long."

"Take your time," Bruce said, settling into the chair. He lifted his chin to let Vince attach a small microphone to his collar. Vince clicked it into place and then went back to his usual routine, adjusting the camera on the tripod and the lighting. Typical question from Vince, "Mr. Eldrich, you okay with that light? Not too bright is it?"

"No, it's fine," he said. "Ready when you are."

They got started when Alex saw the thumbs-up from Vince. Alex started with preliminary matters and then the easy questions, namely who was being discussed and where things had taken place. The incident Bruce remembered had taken place in December of the previous year, a little before the holidays. He couldn't remember an exact date, but he was pretty sure there were decorations up by then.

Bruce seemed relaxed in front of the camera, but also sheepish as he had seemed before. Alex supposed it was guilt, whether for not intervening somehow or reporting what he had seen, or both. Whatever it was, Alex could relate.

"Do you remember which room at HCC this took place in, Mr. Eldrich?"

"It was in one of the play and activity rooms, down the main hallway," he said. "I can't remember which one. There are three."

"Tell us what you saw."

"Nick always had a computer tablet with him," Bruce said. "There were a ton of games on it. He'd help the kids use it, you know, show them how you opened it by sliding your finger across the bottom. Or how the screen worked. He was doing that with Hector on the day I saw them together. Nick was seated more or less like I am, in a plastic chair. Like a classroom chair, I guess. Hector was on Nick's lap, knees pointed straight ahead. Hector was holding the tablet, but he wasn't doing much with it. His eyes were glued to it, though. Nick had some game on there Hector liked to watch. You could hear the music, and the sound effects.

"Nick had his right index finger on the tablet, playing the game for Hector, I guess. His other hand, his left hand, was resting on Hector's thigh. Well, not resting. It was moving, back to front, like from Hector's waist toward his knee, and then back. At first, I didn't think much of it.

We have kids who respond to that kind of touch. It can be soothing. Sometimes, with a kid, you do what comes natural if you think it's making them more comfortable. That's with trained staff, though, almost always women. Not a man with a kid."

"Did Hector seem to notice, or react?" Alex asked.

"No, not at all. He was fixated on the game. If that was all I saw, I probably would have forgotten it. But eventually, Nick got to the point where he was squeezing Hector's thigh also. Not much, but just like...massaging it almost. And his thumb would kind of dip down, to the inside of Hector's leg. The thumb was...making little circles on the inside of Hector's thigh. Not at his crotch, exactly, but close. He was looking over his shoulder, too, which you'd expect, but he kind of had his chin resting on Hector's shoulder. It was almost like he was nuzzling him."

"Where were you in the room in relation to them while this was happening?"

"I was going in and out of the room, like I said. I was moving some plastic bins, things that held toys, games, art supplies, that kind of thing."

"Was there anyone else in the room?"

"No, just the two of them at that point. It was late in the day."

"Did there come a time when this stopped, the touching you were seeing?"

"I interrupted it," Bruce said. "But, not even on purpose really. I just...kind of reacted. I said something about the game and how Hector seemed to love it. Nick looked up, and there was a look in his eyes. This look, like, 'you got me.' I don't know how else to describe it. He moved his hand off of Hector's thigh, and up to his arm. Then he said something in reply, something like 'yeah, he loves this one,' or something like that. He wouldn't make eye contact with me."

"What happened then?"

"Nothing, really. Nick explained to Hector that it was time for a break. Then he shut the game off, and kind of lifted his lap to let Hector slide off. Hector just popped off onto his feet and went blank."

"Went blank?"

"Yeah, he just switched gears. That was typical. With Hector, it was like an on-off switch usually. Whatever it was he was looking at, if you took it away or turned it off, sometimes he'd make a noise like he was mad about it or wanted it back. Most of the time, though, he just went back to neutral, like the thing had never been there in the first place. That's what he did this time. His eyes went blank and he just walked away. Nick and I followed him out. By that time Joseliz was there."

"Did you and Nick discuss any of this?"

"No," Bruce said, looking down. "Never. I just pretended like nothing happened. I guess he did, too. He had some other task he went to do then. I never mentioned it."

"Not to anyone?"

"No. Not before you, last night."

"Anything to add, Mr. Eldrich?"

"No," he said, and sighed. "That's it."

Alex walked Bruce out to the main elevator lobby of the 4th floor and thanked him again for coming in. Bruce seemed uncomfortable and restless as he zipped up a blue nylon winter jacket.

"I should've done something sooner," he said. "The guy's dead now, I know it's too late."

"It's worth taking a statement on," Alex said. "Sometimes things are revealed that lead them to other stuff, or other people. Anyway, the effort is appreciated. How is Connie?" At this, Bruce's face seemed to tighten, almost into a grimace.

"She's in bad shape," he said. He looked away and shook his head. "We're talking to lawyers, trying to figure out how we tell our clients about this. Then we have to figure out what to do, whether we can stay open. Probably we'll close for a while, at least."

"I hope she doesn't blame herself. It happens, far more than most people would believe."

"She's just...kind of digging her heels in, you know? I mean, this is all that's ever mattered to her. And it's falling apart."

"I'm sure you matter more," Alex said. "What do you mean, digging her heels in?"

"Well, she's fighting for what she built, which is good. But I think she's also in denial, a little bit. Connie is an angel, but no one is perfect, and my angel is as stubborn as a mule. She's just...defensive. Over everything. I know she's trying to keep it together, but it's like everyone is the enemy right now. Even me." He frowned and looked sideways at Alex. "Jesus, I wear my goddam heart on my sleeve don't I? Why the hell am I burdening you with this?"

"You've got to tell someone," Alex said. "Listen, I'll see what I can do about finding you some help. Like I said, my friend Nikki has a lot of experience with these situations. I'll be in touch. In any event, this trial will be over in a few weeks. One less thing you both have to deal with."

CHAPTER 48

Tuesday, November 15

Alphonse Messaria was the "calendar judge" supervising the case of *People of the State of New York vs. Norman* Ruiz. Calendar judges generally supervised the pre-trial process before the case was sent out to a different judge for trial. Quiet and dignified in the classic, old-school Italian way, Messaria was an impeccably neat and fastidious man with thin, snow white hair and a perfectly cropped mustache and goatee.

He rubbed the mustache as he looked over the photographs, reports and discovery letter from Alex to Rick regarding what Bell and the Vermont ICAC team had uncovered. Beside that file was another one, describing the Medical Examiner's finding regarding the possibility of a synthetic opioid called fentanyl in Hector's Ruiz's body. Surprisingly to Alex, though, the test had come up negative. Hector may have been sleeping when he was killed. But he was not intoxicated.

If there was ever a time Alex and Rick were happy to have a judge who wasn't volcanic or easily angered, this was it. He read everything carefully behind the bench with his high, black chair swiveled toward the wall, and then swiveled back toward the attorneys and Norman.

"Mr. Ruiz," he said, with a sad, reserved tone. "Have you discussed these new pieces of evidence fully with your attorney?"

"Yes, your honor," Norman said. "I don't know anything about it. I told the investigators the same. I never gave my son lollipops with drugs on them. Someone else did that."

"You don't have to explain anything to me, sir," the judge said. "I just want to make sure you've had the opportunity to fully discuss these things with Mr. Melendez. They may have grave implications."

"Yes, sir."

"Okay. Gentlemen, this is how I see it: The decedent's body did not contain any intoxicating substances at the time of his death. The photos that appear to be of the decedent child in his home, possibly intoxicated although we cannot say for sure, are not dated, and their age is still undeterminable. Therefore, these other matters do not appear to have a direct impact on the matter at hand. Do you both agree? Mr. Melendez?"

"I do, your honor."

"People?"

"We agree, your honor."

"Mr. Melendez, despite the record I am making, do you wish to take any action based on what the People have provided?"

"Not at the moment, your honor," Rick said. "Mr. Ruiz has spoken with child abuse investigators on this issue, and with my guidance. We have nothing to add. Mr. Ruiz categorically denies any drugging or sexual abuse of his son. It does appear to be a matter separate form this one, barring anything unforeseen. Mr. Greco has a continuing obligation of discovery. I'm confident that he's meeting that so far, and we're appreciative."

"This case was marked for a relatively new rocket docket program, Mr. Melendez," the judge said. "I appreciate your working within that time frame, but are you asking for additional time in light of these revelations?" Alex waited with his breath held. If Rick wanted more time, he'd get it. That wasn't a terrible thing, but it would change very much how the next few weeks or months would go.

"Mr. Ruiz is eager for his day in court, your honor. I've discussed with him the possible implications of this evidence. I have counseled otherwise. But he wishes to proceed on our current schedule."

"Mr. Ruiz?" the judge asked, directing his attention to Norman. "Mr. Melendez is an excellent attorney. I have no doubt he's representing you faithfully and competently. But this case has taken several disturbing and potentially complicating turns. In light of all we've seen, I need to hear from you as well, and directly. Do you wish to go forward with trial on the anticipated date, or do wish to have more time to ask your attorney to investigate these matters?"

"I'd like to get this done, sir," Norman said. "That's all."

"Are you satisfied with the services of your attorney?"

"Yes, sir. He's been good to me. I wish to see the end of this. I think it's time." Messaria nodded and turned to Alex.

"People, what say you?"

"The People are ready, your honor."

"Okay then. Monday November twenty-eighth, be ready for trial. Next case."

"I'll keep you posted on anything I hear," Alex said as he and Rick walked toward the elevators after leaving court. "I hope you know that."

"You've been a class act," Rick said, shaking his hand. "Not all of this stuff was strictly discoverable. Some DA's wouldn't have turned it over, but you did. I won't forget that."

"Likewise, thanks. In terms of who had access to the victim at his house, other than your client, I've given you everything. There were a few school employees and access drivers. There was Joseliz Perez, and Rolando Garcia. There was Conie Morrell, Bruce Eldrich and one or two staffers from HCC."

"I have those names," Rick said. "I put an investigator on the HCC thing, for what it's worth. This guy Whelan? Who the hell knows? We'll see what happens, I guess. Probably a bunch of shit I don't expect. Or want. You can't be a control freak and stay sane as a trial lawyer."

"I agree. And I know he thinks he's ready to go to trial, but I understand if you don't. If you change your mind and want more time, I won't object. It wouldn't make a difference anyway." Rick paused and seemed to search himself.

"It's hard to explain," he said. "In terms of what how I'm trained to think? The rule is, if you have the chance to push a case out, you push it out as far as it'll go. But on this one? Part of me thinks it's better to just get it done. And I shouldn't tell you this, but mostly it's because I don't want to find out anything else about Norman Ruiz."

CHAPTER 49

"Wendy, slow down!" Nikki, smiling nonetheless, called out to her niece who was running ahead toward a pretzel stand in Central Park. It was a gray and damp late morning, leaden with the kind of pre-Christmas New York chill that begged for things like a hot pretzel. She was babysitting for her sister Pam and it was a joy to spend the day with Wendy, who had just turned four. She had a feeling life with Alex, if it continued, would not likely involve children, and that was okay with her. At 38, she felt the option was best left behind her anyway. She loved kids, though, and her only niece most of all. Wendy turned toward Nikki and grinned as if to say, 'catch up.' Then Nikki heard a male voice behind her.

"Nikki Jaynes?"

"Yes?" Her smile faded.

"My name is Ronald Gordon. I'm a private investigator and connected with a possible criminal investigation. I need to speak with you." He handed her a business card. Nikki called Wendy over and briefly examined the card and the man who had handed it to her. He was tall and thin in dark slacks and a leather jacket, with a narrow face and dark eyes shaded by a heavy brow. His accent was mostly neutral, she noticed, but there was nothing local in it either. The card, which couldn't have been simpler with only his name and a phone number below it, confirmed it. He used a 703 area code which matched the one Alex still had for his cell phone. A Northern Virginia exchange.

"First off, would you mind telling me how you found me here?"

"It's my job to find people ma'am," he said. "And I sorry if the circumstances are inconvenient. I do need to speak with you, and there isn't much of a window to do it in. This regards a serious issue."

"Whatever it is, you can contact me at my place of business. I assume you know how, if it's your job to find people."

"Is that your child, ma'am?" he asked, nodding toward Wendy, who had reached Nikki and now wrapped her arms around Nikki's left leg, gazing up at the strange man who was talking to her aunt. Nikki smiled down at her, and then turned, unsmiling, to Gordon.

"She's my niece. And that's the last question of yours I'm prepared to answer for now. Excuse us, please." With that, she took Wendy's hand and began to walk away.

"I'm part of an investigation into the death of a child, Dr. Jaynes." Gordan called out from behind her. It wasn't so loud that people around them would definitely hear it, but it was loud enough to where it was clear Gordon didn't care who heard. "It's one your boyfriend might have been complicit in. You really need to cooperate with me. It's either that or take your chances with what happens next."

"I am with a child," Nikki said, her teeth nearly clenched.

"As you can see, I'm with her alone. Get away from us, or I will scream and you'll be arrested."

"Taking your chances," Gordon continued as if he hadn't heard her, "means you might not see that child or any other for a long time." Wendy, her small face now screwed down into a frown, ducked further behind Nikki who was now glaring at Gordon. Gordon kept a bit of distance but otherwise didn't seem the slightest bit put off by either of their reactions.

"Get away from us," she said, punctuating every word.

"I'm a licensed investigator, doctor," Gordon said, in a lower and somewhat more placating voice. "I'm sorry for how you perceive my tone. I mean no harm to you or your niece, but your boyfriend is in very big trouble. And frankly you might be also." Nikki paused, knowing she was taking his bait and not liking it one bit.

"I'm sorry, my boyfriend?" she asked, and then gently shushed Wendy who was tugging at her coat sleeve.

"Alex Greco. I know the two of you are romantically involved, despite the fact that a man you provided treatment for might be a witness in an upcoming murder trial Greco is prosecuting. That's a separate matter. But it may become related."

"Tell me who sent you," Nikki said, now holding Wendy and patting her back. The child had seemed to absorb the tension and had gone quickly from animated and happy to subdued and nearly upset.

"I work for interested parties, doctor, that's all I can tell you. What you need to know is that they're well-connected with official parties. Like I said, it's likely to become a criminal matter. When can we talk?"

"We have nothing to talk about," Nikki said. She was

continuing an honest tone of disgust, as if Gordon's intrusion was truly offensive, but now her mind was racing and her gut churning. The death of a child? *Alex's child?* She could only assume that's what he meant. She only knew a few details. The child had fallen down some stairs. His mother had been in the same room, or nearby. But Nikki had never sensed there was anything suspicious about it. And then there was this other thing about a witness of Alex's she had treated. He was hinting at that to rattle her, she supposed. But what witness?

"If you say so," Gordon said with a shrug. "You know, I find it interesting you don't have a single question about why I'm here, which I've told you is because of a murdered child. You don't even care to know who it is. You just want to know who sent me. Suit yourself, doc, but next time someone approaches you, it won't be asking for a courtesy. It could be with a subpoena. Or handcuffs."

"I'm not that easily intimidated," she said. Wendy peered over Nikki's shoulder at Gordon. "And if I see you following me, you'll be in handcuffs. And it'll be today." With that, she stuffed Gordon's card into her back pocket and walked off with Wendy bobbing in her arms.

CHAPTER 50

"Alex, talk to me," Nikki said softly. She had returned from her sister's house to her apartment the next day, where she and Alex had plans to spend the evening. Still, she hadn't told him anything about the investigator over the phone. It just seemed like something one needed to be face-to-face to bring up. Now after hearing about the encounter, Alex sat on her gray living room sectional, staring at his hands and silent as a stone. Nikki was at her little kitchen bar where she had just poured a glass of wine.

"I am so sorry," he said at last. He was, she could tell, trying to control his breathing. There had been flashes of anger in his eyes as she related events, but now he just seemed impossibly sad. But it was worse than that. There was something else coming off of him. *Shame.*

"You have nothing to be sorry for."

"I really wish that were true," he said, staring at his hands. She walked over and sat next to him, placing her hand on his back. Just out of the shower, she was wearing nothing but a silk robe and underwear. For a long moment they were both silent. "I left everything when I left Alexandria," he said. "I mean everything."

"Okay."

"I had to get out. For a few reasons."

"You've told me that."

"Well, not exactly. I've told you I *wanted* to leave. I wanted to go somewhere- anywhere- where I would just disappear. Fade into a crowd doing something I know."

"But..." she started.

"But it was more than that. I wanted to leave. But I also *had* to leave. That's where Jonah came in."

"Jonah Schwartz? Dara's father?"

"Yes, Jonah Schwartz. He got me out. He also tied up some loose ends behind me. With the investigation team. A few other people. Then he got me the job here."

"The investigation team," she said. "You mean a child death investigation team."

"Yes. My son." He almost choked on the next word. "Jordan."

"Take a breath. You're safe, here." At this, his eyes welled up, but he seemed to choke down the emotion.

"What I did...I did for Dara. She was...is...not well. I loved her, though. I loved her more than I thought possible, until Jordan's death." He wiped his eyes and grimaced, choking the tears back. Nikki found it vaguely frustrating, this exertion of his to not emote, but she checked her own reaction, which was natural, but also not helpful.

"You don't have to tell me, if you don't want to. Whatever you or Jonah did, I'm sure you believed it was the right thing to do."

"We didn't kill anyone. It was Dara. She...snapped. I told you he fell down the stairs. The truth is, she pushed him.

But Jonah and I buried the truth, and then we buried my life there. I had a duty, above anyone else, to be honest. But I couldn't. It all happened so fast. I just went along."

"She was your wife, and Jonah's daughter," Nikki said, looking into his eyes. "And with your son, gone like that? I can't even imagine the shock, or how you made decisions in the wake of it. No one should judge you for that, Alex. God knows I don't." He drew her little frame closer to him on the couch. She pivoted and laid her legs over the top of his.

"I'm putting it behind me," he said. "Dara, I mean, and what we were. It was better when I visited last, but seeing her has always been like looking in a mirror. There's some longing, for those times, but mostly I see something terrible. Something I was a part of."

"We all have past hurts," she said. "A lot of us also have past horrors. The challenge is remembering them without reliving them."

"And when I say there's a longing," he said, lifting a finger as if he had to make the point, "I don't mean for her. What I long for is another time, I guess..."

"Of course. I get it, and it's okay." Nikki had a decent idea of what Alex was probably going through. She had been there herself. She could see in his gaze sometimes what looked like echoes of a can't-ever-get-back-there feeling he was likely experiencing when Dara and Jordan and the best days floated up into his consciousness. Maybe someday, she figured, he'd tell her more about it. Or maybe not. It was okay either way. She had her own secrets. "What's important now," she said, "is that you know I'm here for you. I don't care about the past other than what it means for us now."

"Yeah, but I feel like I've hidden this from you. It took some asshole in the park accosting you and Wendy to shake it out of me."

"It doesn't matter. Look, let's be practical for a moment. Who is he, and does he pose a danger to you?"

"I don't know. But I've got to find out." Nikki had given him the business card, and a description of the guy. Neither the name nor the description rang a bell from what he had told her, but he was running at full tilt getting prepped for trial. This was, she knew, the last thing he needed to worry about.

"The thing he said about a witness," she said. "I guess he's talking about Rolando Garcia? I did the intake for him on Wards Island."

"That wouldn't make you a goddam witness," he said, disgust in his voice. "I made a note to the file about it, just in case. I also took the names of the other staff members who were present." Nikki nodded. They had both been very careful about keeping their ethical obligations intact once they started dating. Of course, there was some occasional and cursory overlap in terms of who they dealt with, but when that happened it was understood that they'd both note it separately. Neither of them had a problem disclosing to a court what their relationship was if it became necessary. It just hadn't yet.

"I knew why you were asking for those other names back at the psych center," she said. "And we're fine. It sounds like, whoever this guy is, he was trying scare me, maybe into revealing something he figured I knew. Or, he's trying to scare both of us. I know you need to find out why, but you also have a trial to get ready for. Can't you wait and deal with this after?"

"Not if it could affect the case, no. Plus I really want to know who the hell thought it was okay to go after you like that. With a kid."

He wrapped an arm around her waist, and she followed his eyes down across her body to where the robe parted. Beneath it, lacy black underwear with a tiny blue bow in front peeked out. He ran his thumb across the waistband.

"It will all fall into place," she said. "Let it go for right now."

"I won't put you at risk. Trust me on that. Whatever mistakes I've made, I won't compound them by harming you. That goes way beyond this witness nonsense."

"I'll be fine, Alex. We'll both be fine."

"I'm better now, you know," he said, looking finally into her eyes after seeming to avoid them most of the night. I'm better just for knowing you. I'm just sorry for what I brought with me."

Now her heart was beating more forcefully, and for complex reasons she couldn't fully articulate. Most of it was plain horniness, she had to admit. She was turned on, she knew, and in that ancient and silly way that most women are turned on by a man with some air of mystery about him. But it was more than that. Even without this new information, Nikki knew Alex had an edge to him. Not a coldness, really, but a numbness of some sort. He could be playful, and he had a great sexual appetite. He certainly wasn't morose. Quite the opposite, he was usually pretty steady and generally cheerful, if in the sardonic, gallows-humor kind of way that most people in their field were. He was dark, though, and perhaps more than she had bargained for, given whatever had gone on in his old life. With his openness tonight she felt closer to him, but she also saw a red flag pop up in her mind. It was the kind of flag she would have warned a girlfriend about, had she seen it in that friend's boyfriend. Well, that was life, wasn't it?

"Do you know what this city is?" she asked him, running her fingers lightly through his hair. "I mean, in nature?"

"Not really."

"It's an estuary," she said. "One, big estuary with islands and rivers and bays and such. Do know what an estuary does?"

"Again, not really."

"It's a big filter, basically." As she spoke, she pulled the little belt on her robe and drew it open across her body, exposing her breasts and the lovely plane of her torso. "It cleans things. Sea water comes in. Fresh water goes out. On both ends, things get made new again. That's New York, Alex. That's what we are." Now her voice lowered to a husky whisper. His left hand clutched her underwear and she rose to her feet, helping him push it down with her thumb. "This whole island we're on right now. So many of us are here for that same reason. To get clean. It's okay. It's been going on for a really long time." Her panties slid down past her knees, and she lightly kicked them off. Then Nikki looked Alex right in the eye as she planted first one then the other knee to straddle his lap, grabbing his belt buckle as she seated herself. He widened his knees, spreading her legs farther apart.

"I don't want to be clean right now," he breathed into her ear. She smiled inside and went to work on his pants.

CHAPTER 51

Monday, November 28

Karen Angela Moore, the judge who received the Ruiz case for trial, had a smoker's cough and an often terrible disposition. She was almost seventy, tiny and rail thin with slightly frizzy and dyed blond hair. She had been the chief of homicide in the Bronx DA's office in the early 80s, the first woman to hold that job. It was a time when the city was falling apart and crime was sky-rocketing, so she had little patience for the problems of the younger attorneys who appeared before her, what with their Blackberries and such. She could be disarmingly playful, though, and so she was on the cold, gray morning the Ruiz case was first called in her courtroom. It was the week after a quiet Thanksgiving Alex and Nikki had spent together in the city, punctuated mostly by last minute trial preparation for Alex.

"Alex Greco," Judge Moore called out when he entered through the double doors. "Mister Virginia." Alex smiled as he set his files down. She pronounced it like 'Mistah Vah-gen-ya.'

"Good morning, your honor."

"Good morning. And to you, Mr. Melendez." Alex and Rick had just walked over from Judge Messaria's courtroom, where he had officially sent them out, "forthwith," for trial. Once everyone was seated, Judge Moore looked over at the bailiff, who signaled to another court officer. A minute or so later, Norman shuffled out, handcuffed and in bright orange jail attire, a color that signaled he was on trial for a violent offense. He was unshackled and then sat quietly next to Rick. The judge announced the case and presided over the usual greetings.

"I read over the file," she said. "I understand there's been newly discovered evidence in this case, but it appears unrelated to the matter at hand. I know that's probably wishful thinking, but is that right?"

"Correct, your honor," Alex said, choking down the word *ma'am*, which he surely would have used in Virginia. "The People have turned over everything we have on each newly discovered issue. We'll continue to do so. But right now, the other matters seem unrelated." Following this, Rick voiced his agreement for the record.

"The murder of Detective Regan over the summer," she said, frowning. "That's an open investigation still. Any reason to believe- from either of you- that it's relevant in any way to this case at this point?"

"No, your honor," both lawyers said in unison. She looked from one to the other for a few seconds. Both Alex and Rick could tell she was anticipating some kind of unwanted surprise, somehow, to rear its head as the trial unfolded. Surprises were wonderful in courtroom dramas. They were roundly despised by judges.

"Okay. If there is something new you need me to know about, I assume you'll tell me promptly. And I mean promptly. Is that clear, both of you?" Both answered in the affirmative.

"Mr. Melendez, I assume you have a suit for your client to change into?"

"Yes, your honor. The bailiffs have his courtroom clothes."

"Good. Mr. Greco, how long do you anticipate it'll take to present your case? Just an estimate?"

"We have six witnesses, your honor, including the medical examiner. Most witnesses are relatively brief. Depending on cross examinations, I'd estimate a week or so."

"Mr. Melendez, I won't ask you. We'll see what happens." Rick smiled at this. The judge turned to the bailiff. "Call for a venire panel, please."

CHAPTER 52

Outside of court, Rick motioned Alex over to a corner bench. Around them was plenty of ambient noise as people engaged in dozens of overlapping conversations, babies cried, and kids called out to each other. Rick kept his voice low anyway.

"You're a class act, I told you that," he said, looking at Alex with wide eyes through his glasses. "Told you I wouldn't forget it."

"Likewise," Alex said, feeling his bowels clench. "So…"

"I got a call," Rick said. "Some guy from Alexandria. That's where you were before, right?" Alex sighed, and nodded. "Well, he told me he was a retired cop, doing some investigative work."

"I've gotten wind of this," Alex said. "Did he give you a name?"

"Nikki Jaynes," Rick said after a pause.

"Yeah, I know her," Alex said. He looked away, then up at Rick. "I guess you know how well."

"I don't care," Rick said, lifting his hands a little and shaking his head. "She's not on my witness list. But Rolando Garcia might be. Apparently, she did an intake on him at Wards."

"She did," Alex said. "I took note of it, and I have names of other witnesses who were there. I guess if you wanted to, you could still make an issue out of it."

"Listen," Rick said. "Obviously, I gotta do what I gotta do. But first, I don't think it means anything to my case. And second, I didn't like this guy's tone. That's why I'm telling you. I won't sell out a client because I think the DA is a good guy. But I won't throw someone under the bus for nothing. I play a long game. I think you do also."

"I try," Alex said. "I appreciate the heads up. We can put this all on the record, too. I'm not afraid to do that."

"I don't think it's necessary," Rick said, "or wise, for either of us. She's not on my radar. Just watch your back, okay?"

"Believe me, I won't forget this," Alex said, standing up. "Thank you."

"Don't think it means I won't fight you like hell next week," Rick said, giving him a quick wink. "See you soon."

CHAPTER 53

Sunday, December 4

In Alex's office that afternoon, the white board on wheels had only one image on it. He had drawn a simple, four-paned window, and then the numeral "20" inside of it. Alexa studied it as she walked in, grabbing a bag of pretzels off of his desk and plopping down in a chair. She was dressed in knee-high boots, jeans and a tight, black sweater, her hair pulled back into a ponytail.

"So, your trial prep is getting kind of abstract," she said. "What does that represent?"

"That's the window." Alex hadn't yet looked at her. He was in a faded gray Washington Nationals sweatshirt and beat up khakis with his feet on the desk, staring intently at the white board.

"Yes, I see that. With a number 20 inside. And?"

"If you're Rick Melendez," Alex said slowly, "And your job is to stop me from proving Norman Ruiz killed his kid. This is where you live or die."

"Oh," she said. "You mean twenty minutes. Gotcha." She had come from brunch with some girlfriends and was still slightly tipsy, but she remembered now. The timeline.

"Yeah. If he can put someone in there, he wins." He turned to Alexa. "How does he do that?"

"Give me the timeline again."

"Norman says he leaves his house a little after three o'clock," Alex said. He stood up and walked to large map of the Bronx he had posted on the wall behind the white board. "That looks accurate, because he's spotted in a car about five or six minutes away at three-eleven. Joseliz Perez gets there at three twenty-four or three twenty-five. That's accurate, because she bolted and found a cop on the corner of Jerome Avenue within two minutes of finding the kid. Dispatch heard about a body at exactly three twenty-seven."

"So, if it wasn't him," Alexa said, "then it was someone else who wanted Hector dead. And this person either got really lucky and stumbled on the house, unlocked, during that window, or was watching him."

"Right, but the more likely thing is, someone just knew he was going out."

"Yeah, but I thought his plan to go out was a last-minute thing. Didn't he get a message an hour earlier or something, to pick up some money?"

"You're pretty sharp for just having returned from boozy brunch," he said, grinning sideways at her. "Yeah exactly. So, what does that tell us?" Alexa frowned, thinking it over.

"Oh, God. You think Rick will argue someone purposely pulled him away from the house?"

"Bingo," he said. "That's what scares me. Norman got a text from a seven-one-eight number around two o'clock. Danny ran the number back to a burner, so there's no way to know who it was. Norman says he doesn't know but claims that's how it was sometimes. The text told him to pick up some money at three fifteen. So off Norman goes, a little after three."

"And he actually picked money up, right?"

"Yeah, from a used tire place under the cross-Bronx on Jerome. As it turns out, that's also where he reported for work when he was moonlighting with the crew over there. Sean's informant told us that, and it checked out."

"So, Rick could suggest someone drew him out," she said, speaking slowly as it came together in her mind. "It would have to have been someone in his own organization, though, if he actually picked up money from their usual headquarters, right? So, someone in his own circle drew him out of his house to kill his son? So, it was a betrayal or something? He pissed someone off? That's really brutal."

"Well it is a gang, not a book club. And they were pimping out girls escaping from Central America. They play rough. Whatever, Rick doesn't really need a solid motive. He just needs something a couple of stubborn jurors can get stirred up imagining. I can picture two right now who might be amenable."

"But there were no signs of forced entry, right?" Alexa said. "So even if there was some really bad guy waiting to run in and kill a disabled little kid behind Norman. How did they get in?"

"I don't know," Alex said. "That's a good point. But it's an old house, with old locks. Nothing looked disturbed, but it didn't look hard to break into. We verified there were no signs of forced entry that day, but we didn't comb the place either. Norman was a suspect very quickly."

"What about the weird uncle?" she asked. "That's where I'd go, if I was Rick. I thought he didn't have an alibi."

"I'm running that down, actually," Alex said. "I have an idea. I should know more in the morning."

"Okay. What about Connie and Bruce? I know it's crazy, but so are a lot of jurors. Can you cover their timeline?"

"Yeah, they're clear. Connie was at HCC the whole time. Bruce was out, but we know where." He went back over to the map. "He left HCC around two fifteen or two thirty to get their van inspected. The mechanic he goes to is around the corner from the Four-Four, on Cromwell Avenue." He pointed to it on the map. "The shop he goes to is next to a *vivero* near 169th."

"Oh my God, I think I know that place," she said, sitting up and smiling. "I worked a robbery out of there once. They sell live poultry, right?"

"Exactly. So, there are chickens, from the *vivero*, that run up and down the block, and in and out of the garage. For some reason Connie gets a huge kick out of that, so Bruce snapped a couple of pictures and texted them to her at three-oh-one and three-oh-two before he left. Then he saw Norman in his car and got a shot of him up by Mt. Eden at three-eleven. The shop is right around ten minutes from where he saw Norman, so that all works. I doubt it'll even come up, but he's covered if Rick goes there. There's also Joseliz, of course, but I don't think she's in danger of being mistaken for his killer." He went back to his chair and sat down hard. "So, there's just one more thing."

"Now what?"

"These other two guys," he said, and passed the crime scene pictures across the desk to her. "Ryan Isoli, and this guy Nick Whelan. Isoli was selling the kind of laced lollipops we think someone was using on Hector. Whelan, it looks like, was the guy who found a buyer who wanted to see sex acts performed on Hector. Now they're both dead. And in a way similar to how Hector died."

"That whole situation is a giant hornet's nest," Alexa said, waving a hand to make her point. "God, stay away from it."

"I plan to, but what if it's related? If Isoli and this guy Whelan are related, how can it not be?"

"You're still assuming those two are related," she said. "Look, even if they are. That's another case, and it won't be yours. This is your case." She paused and studied him for a moment. "Alex, you're tired. You're under pressure. Don't let it run away with you. I know the feeling."

"Fair point," he said. "I just don't like seeing holes in things."

"Not everything is one-hundred percent knowable, what can I tell you? You call witnesses tomorrow. Get your guns ready, hon."

"No, not everything," he said. She looked him more closely, his hands now locked behind his head in his chair. She was getting to know Alex pretty well. He seemed pre-occupied, but in an almost devious way, like there was something up his sleeve.

"Alex," she asked, drawing his name out. He looked over at her, and his eyes seemed to clear.

"Hmm?"

"What are you thinking about doing?" The question was blunt, typical of Alexa who combined almost eerie instincts with very little guile. He seemed flustered for a moment, then smoothed.

"What? Nothing. Just thinking. Doing a lot of that lately."

"Get some rest tonight, okay? I'm reachable if you need me."

"Thanks. I will, promise." She stood where she was for a moment, studying him. Then she let it go, telling him she'd check in later. But her instincts told her something was up, and as usual she was correct.

CHAPTER 54

Alex had left a message with the pizza shop guy at about 6:00 p.m. that cold Sunday night, asking that Oscar contact him. Now at 11:30 he was at their agreed upon meeting place, the end of 132nd Street at Locust, where it met the East River. Across the black water was Rikers Island, its stout buildings and smokestacks lit up garishly by security lamps. The corner was deep in the Four-O precinct, better now than in the bad old days, but still one of the more dangerous parts of the city after dark.

Alex parked on the street near the fence, stepped out and lit a cigarette. After some rain and sleet it was damp and chilly. The area he was in was heavily industrial and well-lit, as Oscar said it would be, but still. A few minutes later a black, Chevy SUV with tinted windows wheeled down the block toward him. A muffled bass beat thumped from inside the car, amplified, and made clear as the passenger's side door opened. Oscar emerged and walked toward Alex. Then the SUV backed away and angled itself into a parking space, like a sentient guard dog.

"Thank you for meeting me," Alex said, offering his hand. Oscar, in a bulky, black leather jacket, shook it.

"You're welcome. What's this about?" With this, Alex

took out two of the 8 x 10 crime scene photographs of Ryan Isoli and Nicholas Whelan and handed them over to Oscar.

"The one on the bed is Ryan Isoli. The other one is a guy named Nick Whelan." Oscar looked at them one by one before handing them back.

"I don't know either of them."

"You're sure?"

"I say I what I mean."

"They were both killed the same way."

"Yeah, I can see that."

"Well, it's similar to how your cousin was killed, look." Alex leaned in, tapping his finger to the photos. "The cut pattern is smooth across. It indicates no resistance, or struggle, on the part of the victims. Like they were passed out. And both happened within three weeks of Hector's murder."

"I still don't know what this has to do with me."

"Norman doesn't have an alibi for either of these. I can't get into details, but I think it's possible he killed all three people. I'm also trying to rule out the possibility he's been mis-identified. That all of this was the work of someone else."

Oscar lifted his hand and gestured toward the SUV. A younger man Alex hadn't seen before jumped out and walked toward them.

"Don't be alarmed," Oscar said. "But before we talk further, I need to make sure you're not wired. Can he see your phone?"

"Sure," Alex said, handing it over from his slacks pocket. The young man took it, inspected it for a moment, then turned it off and handed it back. "Does he need to pat me down?"

"Very lightly," Oscar said. With that, he said something in Spanish that Alex didn't catch. The young man approached Alex and asked him to lift his arms. Alex did so and was patted down momentarily. With nothing to find, the kid turned to Oscar and shook his head. Oscar nodded and he walked back to the SUV, getting back in without another word.

"You're very polite," Alex said, almost quizzically. Oscar shrugged at this.

"I like to start that way," he said. "You've returned it. To answer your question, I know Norman killed my cousin. But I don't think he did those other two."

"He was in the life," Alex said. "The thug life. You didn't tell me that when you first approached me."

"It wasn't relevant," Oscar said with a shrug. "Yeah, Norman has been an errand boy for a couple of pimps. Ran some whores around the place, lent out his boat for business. But no one would send him out on something like this, killing rivals. He doesn't have the balls unless his victim is a helpless kid."

"What if you're wrong?" Alex asked, looking at him intently. "What if *we're* wrong, biased, maybe, against a bad man, while ignoring something under our noses? It's not really your problem, I know. But it's mine, and so I'm coming to you."

"You're not wrong," Oscar said. "Two other guys showed up dead in a similar way, so what? That method? It works. Quieter than a gun, too, no ballistics left behind."

"The ME doesn't see them very often."

"Not everyone ends up at the morgue."

"Just think about it, that's all I'm asking. Think about whether you know of anyone else who does wet work like this, or who's just brutal, out of control, whatever."

"I don't," Oscar said. "And if I did? Like if I thought it was someone else who cut up my little cousin? You don't think I'd run that down?"

"I think you made up your mind it was Norman," Alex said. "We all did. But his attorney might try to suggest Norman was a victim also, of another guy still out there who came for Hector on someone's orders. I can counter that if it happens, but I'd like to know it's not an actual possibility."

"Do you believe it?"

"I'm trying to keep an open mind."

"You're drinking Norman's Kool-Aid," Oscar said, shaking his head. "Just like so many *zanganos* before you. So, who you been talking to? His lawyer? Your NYPD buddies telling you it's got to be some gang assassin because they can't imagine poor Norman Ruiz murdering his own kid? How stupid are you?"

"Not that stupid or you wouldn't be speaking to me, I don't think."

"Yeah. So why are you acting stupid? You've got your man, Alex. I never went to law school, but I hope I wouldn't wobble on a case the way you are. How is your jury supposed to see this?"

"What they'll see if I'm not thorough is a big goddam hole in this case," Alex said. "Or worse, maybe they'll see nothing, and a guy who's a scumbag but not a murderer goes up for life. That might not mean much to you, but it actually does to me. It's my job."

"Norman didn't generate that kind of heat. He made a few bucks for a crew, that was the extent of it. He wasn't important enough to piss anyone off like that."

"He's got more than just a few bucks," Alex said. "He's

a got a nice boat and a bank account. He's probably paying well over one-fifty for his defense. That came from
somewhere."

"Sure, he's a con artist. I know plenty of people he's
taken money from over the years. Norman always had an
idea. Some new thing that would make him money. He
finds people stupid enough to buy in. Look, I've had deal-
ings with the people Norman worked for. They don't kill
kids. Albanians do that kind of shit. We don't."

"I've heard you don't kill cops either, as a rule," Alex said.
"But someone killed Sean Regan over the summer. It wasn't
Norman. Unless he had it done from Rikers, which I doubt."

"I don't know who killed that cop," Oscar said, his tone
taking on an edge. "You all assume it was gang work, because that's an easy answer. But the fact is the crews up
here know better than to execute a cop. It's a stupid move,
brings heat on everyone. More likely it was personal beef.
Jealous husband, maybe, of some chick he kept down
here, away from his wife and kids in the suburbs. We see
that all the time. They get hero's funerals anyway."

"I don't think he was that type."

"Try your case, Alex," Oscar said, turning and walking
away from him. "Just try your case."

CHAPTER 55

Rick's opening statement, like Alex's, was relatively brief and well delivered. Alex watched the jurors, seven women and five men, closely as Rick talked about the holes he expected to expose in the state's case. A child was dead, he acknowledged. But the task of determining who killed him was the state's responsibility, and they had acted too fast in painting Norman as the villain. A few of the jurors seemed to be studying Norman as Rick and Alex spoke, which was typical in any criminal trial. The guy in the chair, ultimately, was the star of the show. But Alex couldn't get a read on how anyone felt.

After lunch, he called Joseliz and Bruce in quick succession. Joseliz's testimony was almost exactly as she had delivered it in Grand Jury, and as before, she was poised and calm on the stand. The jurors seemed to love her. She described how she came to know Hector, a little about her interaction with him, and finally what she had found at approximately 3:25 p.m. on April 7th. Alex didn't get into the communication exercises she had done with Hector. He couldn't see it as much more than a distraction, and

Rick, who knew about them also, seemed to agree. Rick's cross-examination was brief and gentle, which was smart. She was a sympathetic witness and there wasn't much she could really be crossed on anyway. She had planned to be at Hector's house at 4:00. She had been asked to go earlier, and so she had. His main thrust was about getting her to admit all the things simply impossible for her to know, and she answered without rancor.

Bruce, testifying next, did similarly well. He came off as folksy and friendly on the stand. Alex was happy about this, since sometimes even the most easy-going and seemingly relaxed people could freeze up under the pressure of testimony and look awkward or even unfairly like they were lying. Bruce looked fine, though, and it was obvious he was 'home grown,' meaning a Bronx guy, which the jurors seemed to recognize. He testified to his own timeline that day, and where he was when he saw Norman and snapped a picture of him through the windshield of the van. Alex had him identify an exhibit, a glossy print out of the text messages between him and Connie, including the photo itself. When it came time for cross examination, Bruce, in a simple white shirt, dark blue tie and a Navy blue blazer, shifted easily in his chair toward Rick.

"Mr. Eldrich," Rick started out, "Haven Community Center is not a state-contracted services provider for the disabled, correct?

"Correct," Bruce said.

"You've never applied, right?"

"Correct, we have not."

"So, your facility is really self-governed?"

"It is by my partner, Connie Morrell, mostly. We have an advisory board for oversight, though."

"Right. But really, it's Ms. Morrell's project, isn't it?"

"Not sure what you mean."

"Well, Ms. Morrell, for years, has prided herself on kind of making her own rules, correct?"

"We follow the law," Bruce said, an innocent, almost playful look on his face. "and I pay the insurance premiums. Otherwise, yeah, I guess that's fair." A few of the jurors nodded, and one woman smiled. They liked him.

Alex, so far, was thrilled. Before trial started, Alex and Rick had both agreed, more or less, not to go into the allegations and revelations regarding Nicholas Whelan specifically. Rick reserved the right to revisit the issue, but otherwise agreed not to bring up Whelan's name. Judge Moore, grateful at not having to police that mess, had made a record.

Still, Alex assumed Rick would seek to make points with the fact that HCC was, basically, an island unto itself. Independent, and also not well-regulated. It was inspiring, perhaps, he would insinuate, this grass roots, pioneering place. But did it also have the potential to allow for something reckless? That's where Rick was going, and Alex knew it. He wouldn't bring up Whelan and the pictures of Hector- that was fraught with risk given Norman's own potential culpability- and anyway Whelan was dead before Hector was. But Rick would go to the edges, and in general he would go after HCC. Connie and Bruce prided themselves on doing their own thing, blessed with money and independence. But now Rick would seek to use that against them, suggesting maybe some of their practices allowed for too much risk. Given that possible angle, Alex had told Bruce, the smartest thing he could do as a witness was to be as cool as a cucumber. Short answers, but agreeable. And nothing defensive.

"Joseliz Perez, who testified before you," Rick said. "She accessed Hector and my client's home with a key, correct?"

"She did. It was kept in her work area at HCC."

"Exactly. So, the key to my client's home was at HCC, not something Joseliz kept herself."

"Correct."

"Thank you. Now, there were people, from time to time, who were around Hector, or just at HCC in general, that you hadn't fully vetted, correct?" Alex leaned forward. Rick was cutting it close.

"Again, I'm sorry. Not sure what you mean. Everyone who worked with kids at HCC had to pass a background check."

"Right," Rick said. "In addition to staff members or volunteers, though, there was constant movement in the facility right?"

"Well, sure."

"People coming and going?"

"I guess. Yes."

"I mean, it was really a center of activity, right? People from the community, in and out?"

"Yes. Often."

"Families. Friends. All sorts of people, in and out of the facility. In and out of Hector's life, correct?"

"All of our lives," Bruce said.

"My point is," Rick said, looking at Bruce over his glasses, but in a respectful way, "the idea of HCC is to be more inclusive than exclusive, correct?"

"Yes, I'd say so."

"Right. So more of an open, welcoming atmosphere than a guarded one." He put a tiny, barely noticeable emphasis on the word "guarded."

"I suppose."

Rick asked a few more questions but he had made his point. He had also been smart enough not to push it too far, which so many attorneys did on cross examination, and also to remain respectful and pleasant with Bruce, who the jurors appeared to connect with.

As Alex rose to pack up after that first day, he was cautiously optimistic. The jurors seemed to like his witnesses, and they were paying attention. But tomorrow could be tougher. Connie was up first.

It wasn't that he doubted her ability to be poised and polished on the witness stand, but right now Connie was a wounded bird. In trial preparation, Alex had noticed in Connie some of what Bruce had told him back in October. Bruce had come in with her for prep, but the two didn't seem nearly as comfortable with each other as they had been before. Connie seemed to blame Bruce, however unconsciously, for the presence of Nicholas Whelan at HCC. She felt betrayed, Alex supposed, and helpless in the face of some awful menace she had been unable to guard against. She seemed sincere, wanting to do the right thing, but also defensive and angry. What the jurors might do with that was for tomorrow. Right now, Alex had a detour to take. Jonah was in Manhattan at the Peninsula Hotel. And Jonah needed to see him in person.

CHAPTER 56

Bar at Clement was the sleek, cocktail spot attached to the premier restaurant in the Peninsula at 55th and Fifth Avenue. It felt a little like the inside of a huge and immaculately appointed private plane. Jonah was in a lounge chair with a big martini in front of him when Alex walked in, looking pumped up from court, but also, to Jonah's eye, exhausted. They hugged, and Jonah invited him to sit.

"Should I be worried you wouldn't talk to me unless it was in person?" Alex asked, straightening his tie. "You know I'm in the middle of something."

"Eh, I just wanted to see you. And face it, you needed to get the hell out of there even for an hour. I know you're going back to work." He winked, but Alex couldn't summon a smile to meet it. Jonah reached over and put a hand on his arm. "Alex, relax. It's over."

"Over?"

"This thing, with the investigator. I took care of it."

"Took care of it? Jonah, I hope you didn't..."

"Relax. I didn't threaten him. Didn't need to. I bought him. He was cheap."

"I don't understand, I'm sorry."

"Of course, you don't, you're in the middle of a trial.

The guy who approached Nikki, and who probably called the defense attorney, is an ex-cop. Not from Alexandria, from D.C. He left the force after a shake-up a few years back. He wasn't terminated, but he was forced to quit to keep his pension. The guy's dirty."

"So now he does private detective work in Northern Virginia?"

"Sure," Jonah said. "That's not surprising. The question was for whom. That's what I had to find out. So, I did. You remember Artie Queanan?"

"Artie? Sure. He didn't do a lot of criminal defense, but I knew him. He's a divorce lawyer, mostly."

"Yes, and he's a shark," Jonah said. "He employs all types. Some licensed, some not licensed. This guy Gordon, who approached Nikki, has a license, but he's sleazy. I got to him. I offered him a few bucks. He coughed up some info, and he'll back off for good. Otherwise, I could start poking around into his D.C. past. He knows I can do that. Enough said."

"Okay," Alex said with a deep sigh of relief. "Do we know who sent him?"

"It was Kevin Crane, from your old office. Kevin found him through Artie, I confirmed it with Artie. Kevin, and probably Steve Paulson, sent this asshole up here to see what Nikki might give up about you. And to rattle you, I suppose. Or fuck your case up. I assume that hasn't happened."

"I got lucky," Alex said, shaking his head. "The defense attorney's a decent guy. And Nikki and I really didn't step over a line. But we've been skirting one. We need to work that out."

"She a nice girl?" he asked, again with a wink.

"She is," he said. "I should have told you I met someone. Didn't seem right I guess."

"Life goes on, Alex. I'm glad for you. My driver is out front. He'll take you back to your office. Good luck tomorrow and keep me posted." Alex thought momentarily about insisting he could just take the train back to work, but then thought better of it. The insisting had already been done. He smiled instead as he rose to leave.

"You know I will, Jonah. Thank you."

CHAPTER 57

Tuesday, December 6
11:00 a.m.

Connie looked almost Victorian in court with a long, black skirt suit on, the collar buttoned all the way up. Her hair was put up in a neat bun. She looked positively exhausted and miserable. The victim-witness assistance staff had brought her over to court from the office. Alex was almost alarmed when he saw her, in the hallway just before things were called to order. The day was getting started late due to another case the judge had to hear that morning, so the jury was just getting assembled.

Connie looked edgy, there was no other way to put it. Bruce had stayed behind to tend to some business, she said, but he would be checking in later. Connie assured Alex she was okay, and he sensed she was tougher than he could appreciate. Still, she looked close to something like a breakdown.

He looked over the list of questions for her and trimmed it once again, striking out a few even as she took the witness stand and raised her hand to be sworn in. Her purpose was to give background on Hector, describe

Norman's behavior toward him as she had seen it at HCC, and then provide a few details on the day of his death that would dovetail with Bruce's testimony. These things she handled well, looking calm and answering thoughtfully. She appeared emotional about Hector, but in a measured and believable way. The jurors, much like the ones in the grand jury, seemed to be receptive to her.

Rick's cross started out fairly standard, but as Alex expected, it moved steadily in the same direction as it had with Bruce. His questions were statements really, that Connie more or less had to answer 'yes' to. HCC had some arguably unorthodox practices, correct? HCC had an open-door policy? Hadn't she touted these things in the past as strengths?

Connie handled the first questions decently. Yes, she trusted the community where HCC thrived. She opened her doors and her arms to it, and she was proud to say so. But as she realized Rick was trying to suggest HCC was a kind of unguarded fort in dangerous territory, she began to appear more defensive. She fidgeted in the chair. Rick led her though some uncomfortable questions about Joseliz, how she was acting far outside the scope of a typical volunteer assignment in terms of what she was doing with Hector. There was no denying that Connie had sanctioned a service between Joseliz and Hector that was, however benevolent, not something most agencies would allow. Rick was careful not to make it seem as if Joseliz was the issue, but he was fueling his characterization that Connie sometimes played loose with standards.

"We have not run a perfect program," Connie said at one point. "But you cannot imagine the level of care we provide."

"I understand that, Ms. Morrell," Rick said.

"I don't think you do," she said, and Alex felt his gut tighten. *Please don't, Connie.* Jousting with a lawyer was never a good idea. "My partner and I have very personally cared for every client we've ever known. And Hector? We guarded him with our lives."

"Your partner Mr. Eldrich, you mean."

"Yes," she said. "Just one example, he sensed early on that Hector was in pain, in his arm or his wrist. No one knew that. You may not know autism, sir, but it's far from clear if kids with it are even *in* pain much of the time. Well, we discovered it. With that knowledge, we were able to guide Hector through his tasks and in and out of vehicles without hurting him. We didn't pull him through the street like his father did."

Alex had to remain outwardly neutral in his chair, as if none of this was a surprise, but inside he was brimming with anxiety. There were times when tirades like this from a witness actually worked in one's favor, but not usually. Below that, though, a new thought occurred to him, like a gentle, mental tap on the shoulder. *Bruce knew Hector was in pain before anyone else did.* Well, sure. Connie had mentioned that at their first meeting. She was proud of it. *Okay, so what?*

"I don't understand," Rick said, "is Mr. Eldrich a physician, Ms. Morrell?" It was an almost snarky question, obviously rhetorical. But Rick was adjusting his cross to the attitude of the witness. If she was going to joust, he had more latitude to be confrontational.

"What? Of course not."

"He told this jury yesterday he was basically a jack-of-all trades," Rick said. "So, no medical background?"

"What does this have to do with anything?"

"You. Mr. Eldrich. Your whole staff. You took on tasks you had no formal training in, didn't you, Ms. Morrell?" Connie appeared flabbergasted.

"We...did the best we could. I don't understand..."

"Like Hector's school," Rick said. "You testified on direct you had power of attorney over some of Hector's educational decisions, correct?"

"Yes. Your client asked us to take that role on."

"Because you're an educator," Rick said, again rhetorically.

"Well...no. Not by...not officially."

"And Mr. Eldrich? The jack-of-all trades? Does he have a degree in special education?"

"You know he doesn't."

"Right," Rick said. "Neither does Joseliz Perez, correct?"

"Joseliz was making more progress with Hector than anyone believed was possible," Connie said. Her cheeks were a little flushed now. Alex could not move a muscle, but he felt like burying his head in his hands. Now she was marching into territory they had agreed to avoid. Rick was in a tricky situation. He could go down the road further, but it was a rabbit hole. Then again, it wasn't his job to put pieces together. That was Alex's job. Rick's job was to scatter the pieces until no one could make sense of anything. He seemed to take a middle path.

"Are you referring to the games she played with Hector?" he asked.

"Yes of course. And they were more than games." Connie actually looked at the jury as she continued. "She was teaching Hector to communicate. She was using pictures with him to allow him to express himself. He almost never spoke, but he could use the pictures. He was getting better and better."

"You mean he was getting better in your estimation," Rick said, "even though neither you nor Joseliz had any background..."

"The school never got as far as Joseliz. Believe me, we wanted them to. And that's another thing my partner, the jack-of-all trades, was very prescient about, sir. He told the school what potential Hector had. He wanted to know about what Joseliz was doing, and how it worked. He was very concerned."

Seasoned trial lawyers develop the ability to stew, fret and panic within a body that nevertheless remains still and relaxed in counsel's chair. This is exactly what Alex was doing, but now even the spectacle of Connie going off the rails was being submerged below his new thought string. *Bruce was concerned.* As nonchalantly as he could, he reached for the school records on the prosecution table. Marcie had prepared a series of beautifully arranged folders on them. Wherever Norman's, Bruce's or Connie's name appeared, she highlighted it. And sure enough, there was the notation. Kendra Tucker, the autism educator he had spoken to way back in April, had mentioned it. The note described a meeting between Connie, Bruce, Tucker and a school therapist around the third week of March, a few weeks before Hector died. *Guardians indicate Hector is using communication/learning tools with HCC staff. Request follow up.* He skimmed the rest of the note but had to shift his attention back to the cross examination. Rick asked the judge for a few seconds to look over his notes. In the witness chair, Connie looked proud, almost haughty. Alex suspected she had blown off steam today. Long tamped down steam. How disastrous that would turn out to be was another question, but Alex wasn't as concerned with that now. He was far more concerned with this new thought worm, boring through his brain.

"Nothing further, your honor," Rick said. Alex expected the judge to look to him for redirect, but instead she called the two of them up to the bench.

"We're past one o'clock and I know my staff needs a break," she said, in a loud whisper. "Mr. Greco, do you have redirect?"

"Some, your honor," he said, pushing the new thoughts away for the moment to focus. "Yes."

"Mr. Melendez, if you object, I'll go forward now. Are you opposed to taking a recess before the People's re-direct?"

"No, your honor, that's fine. I need a break also."

Alex rose as recess was called until 2:15. He turned and saw Alexa in the front row, and she gave him a thumbs up. Then behind her, he saw Nikki. She hadn't told him she was coming to watch, but there she was, in one of the spectator rows, between a couple of reporters who were taking notes. She winked at him and smiled. He stared back at her and didn't blink for a long moment, his thoughts racing. He caught himself and smiled back as she rose to leave. He knew she wouldn't wait for him. Their relationship wasn't public and they weren't known as friends, so appearing huddled up together would seem strange. Right now, that was just as well. He had 45 minutes, and he needed to make each one count. From his cell he dialed a number back at the DA's office.

"Vince," he said. *Thank God, he's not at lunch.* "It's Alex. There's a video statement we took back in October. Name is Eldrich. Bruce Eldrich. Can you find it?"

"Yeah, do want me to burn you a copy? I'm headed out to lunch."

"Lunch is on me," Alex said. "But I need you there right now. Can you help me with something?"

CHAPTER 58

The timeline almost blinded me, Alex would think later. And indeed, it almost had. After Vince pulled up the video and Alex saw what he suspected, he went back to his office and shut the door. He thought about trying to reach Alexa, but at that moment it felt like reaching out to anyone else- even someone familiar with the case- would pull him a step away from what he was missing.

And he *was* missing something. If what he believed was true, then his timeline was flawed, somehow. But that didn't seem possible. He had spent weeks absorbing it. Perfecting it. He had mapped each distance between the relevant points against each relevant time. He had driven the damn distances himself with Danny.

On his desk he smoothed out the one exhibit he had moved into evidence through Bruce the day before. It was an enlarged, color copy on legal size paper of the texts Bruce had exchanged with Connie and the photos he had sent between 3:01 at the garage and 3:11 at the Mt. Eden subway stop. The times were printed out neatly in pale gray font above each text and photo. No mystery there. He studied the first two photos, of the chickens on the stained floor of the garage- or roosters, he couldn't be sure.

He forced himself to look slowly from one corner to the next, going around to all four. A detective he had worked with in Virginia years before had taught him that trick for catching detail in crime scene photos. He studied each corner of each photo. There were chickens. An air-hose. The scarred metal of the garage door track. Nothing out of the ordinary.

He moved on to the one Bruce had snapped from his phone in the van, looking out at Hector's car, under the Mt. Eden stop train tracks. At the top of the photo was the bottom edge of the tracks themselves. Then the bright green and black sign of the tire shop, and a garage entrance with old tires stacked everywhere. Then Norman's car, with a figure in it that looked like him. Below that, the photo ended with the interior of the van itself. There was the dark, vinyl strip of the dashboard. The sloping windshield with a few spots and bug smears on it. *Corner by corner.* He started top left. Then top right. Then bottom right. Nothing. He swept his eyes slowly to the left, willing them not to skip over anything. Then his breath caught in his throat. He grabbed for his reading glasses. In the lower left corner of the photo, almost out of sight, was the vehicle inspection sticker. He peered at it for a few seconds, and then raced to Vince's office to get it blown up.

CHAPTER 59

"Ms. Morrell, I only have a few questions," Alex said when the jury was back, and Connie was back on the stand. Connie seemed fused with energy, as if she believed her strike-back at Rick had vindicated her. She nodded.

"Does HCC own the van that Mr. Eldrich took to get inspected on April seventh?"

"We do, yes," she said. "It's the property of the community center."

"Are you certain that Mr. Eldrich left HCC- to your knowledge with the intention of getting the van inspected- on the afternoon of April seventh?"

"Am I certain? Of course. I remember him leaving. He texted me from the garage when he was done."

"Have you seen the van since, and verified that it was inspected?"

"Yes, I saw the certificate. We filed it that day."

"What time did Mr. Eldrich leave the community center?"

"It was about two-twenty or two twenty-five," she said, her brow knitted as if she was confused as to why any of this was being asked. Alex could imagine Rick behind him, wearing the same look.

"Ms. Morrell, are you certain of the dates and times you've just testified to?"

"Yes. I'm certain."

"Are you familiar with how often vehicle inspections are required in New York State?" He almost expected Rick to object on relevance grounds, but then thought better of it. Rick, Alex knew, would be as curious as anyone to see what this was about.

"Excuse me?"

"Do you know, Ms. Morrell? If you don't, that's fine."

"We inspect the van every two years," she said. "I believe that's the law. Please, what does this have to do with anything?" She looked up at Judge Moore, who could only shrug. At the moment, no one was objecting.

"In that case, Ms. Morrell, and if the van was inspected on April seventh of this year, when would you expect it to be due for inspection again, in your experience?"

"Well, I guess two years from April seventh, Mr. Greco." There was an edge again in her voice, almost petulant. Alex walked over to the prosecution table and picked up two items. One was the exhibit he had entered the day before through Bruce, containing the photo taken from the van. The other was an enlarged copy of just the photo itself that Vince had printed for him a few minutes before.

"Your honor may I approach the witness?"

"You may." Alex walked by Rick and Norman, who both stared at him impassively.

"I'm showing you what's been previously admitted as People's Exhibit One, Ms. Morrell," he said. Their eyes met, and Alex saw deep uncertainty in Connie's. He handed her the exhibit. "Do you recognize it?"

"Yes. These are the texts Bruce and I exchanged on April seventh around three o'clock."

"Do you recognize the photo taken from the inside of the van?"

"Yes, of course."

"Ms. Morrell, is this in fact the photo you received via text from Mr. Eldrich on April seventh of this year, at three-eleven p.m.?"

"It is."

"I'm directing your attention to the lower left-hand corner of this photo, Ms. Morrell. Do you see the inspection sticker that's affixed to the windshield in the photo?"

"Inspection sticker? Yes, I guess so."

"Can you read the expiration date on the sticker?"

"I don't think so," Connie said. Again, their eyes met. Connie's were filled with fear.

"This photo," Alex said, "is an enlargement of what is contained in Exhibit One." He handed her the photo, and then walked back to the defense table, handing another glossy copy to Rick, who took it with a look of something like awe on his face. Norman leaned over to look at it.

"Do the two photos look identical, Ms. Morrell?" Connie stared at them both, a look of stunned horror on her face. She didn't answer.

"Ma'am," Alex said, forgetting not to use the term. "Do they look identical?"

"Yes," Connie said, and swallowed audibly.

"Ms. Morrell, can you read the date of expiration on the inspection sticker in the photo? The same one contained in Exhibit One?"

"Yes," she said. It was almost a croak.

"Ms. Morrell, what is that date?"

"April tenth," she said, barely over a whisper. The court was dead silent, though, and the reporter caught it. "April tenth. This year."

"Based on that, Ms. Morrell," Alex said, "the fact that the expiration date in that photo is April tenth of this year, can you testify with confidence as to when exactly this photograph was taken?" Connie stared up at him, unable to speak. She looked at Alex like he had just punched her. Her eyes were filling with tears. Seconds passed.

"Ms. Morrell," Judge Moore asked, and in a surprisingly gentle manner for her, "did you hear the question?"

"I can't," Connie said finally. "I can't say, when this was taken."

CHAPTER 60

"Are you okay?" Alexa asked. She poked her head in Alex's door but didn't walk in. She wasn't sure he wanted to be disturbed. Judge Moore had recessed the case after Connie's testimony, directing everyone to return in the morning. Connie had left the witness stand in tears. The jury, as they filed out, were shaking their heads.

"Yeah, thanks," he said, running a hand through his hair. "Come in, please. Shut that."

"I'm not sure what just happened in there," she said, sitting down. "The picture he sent to her, it wasn't from the seventh?"

"No. I'm positive. Danny sent a guy over to the garage and pulled the inspection record. The car was inspected that day and that time, Bruce testified truthfully to that. He probably left the garage when he said he did. But he wasn't at the Mt. Eden train stop at three-eleven, looking at Norman's car." He handed her a copy of the enlarged photo from inside the car, the one Bruce claimed to have taken on April seventh. "You can see there, the inspection sticker hasn't been changed. That picture was taken some other time. Norman spent a lot of time there, I don't guess it would have been difficult to get a shot like that."

"Oh, dear God," she said, when it finally dawned on her. "So, sending this picture to Connie. It wasn't really meant to prove where Norman was."

"No. Mostly it was meant to prove where *Bruce* was. With this, he could claim to have seen Norman about ten minutes from the house, right in line with minutes after Hector was probably killed. But he could also claim he was in the same place, snapping a picture of him. That way, he's in a spot right at seven or so minutes from the inspection station."

"So then...no one can say he was near the Ruiz house," she said. "In your window."

"Correct. He was keeping himself out of it. Which means he's probably the killer, not that I could ever prove it at this point." He got up and walked over to the map, where he had so meticulously drawn the routes between the established points. "I went in the wrong direction," he said, mostly to himself. "All that time. In the wrong. Damn. Direction."

"I was wondering what you were doing with Connie," Alexa said, shaking her head. "I had no idea why you were hammering her on this. I know she didn't come off well, but I thought she was sincere."

"I think she is," Alex said, turning back to her. "I didn't want to go after her like that, but I had to get this on the record, today. The case is over. It has to be. Whatever else Norman Ruiz did or has done, he shouldn't be in that chair."

"I agree the case is over," she said. "But Alex, really? Are you sure you're right? I mean, this all just happened today." She gestured toward the photograph. "This is bad, yeah. But could it have been a mistake, somehow? Ruiz still had the opportunity. The motive."

"It wasn't him," Alex said. "I'm positive now. It was Bruce Eldrich. The whole goddam time." He walked back to his desk and handed her his iPad. "Look." There was a still of a video on the screen, the video Vince had loaded for Alex during the recess. She hit the 'play' button and saw Bruce, sitting in a chair with a sweatshirt on. He was talking calmly and looking mostly up and to the right of the camera, where Alex had been standing when he took his statement on October 21st. From time to time his eyes would wander to the lens.

"This is his video statement," she said. "From October, I remember. What, did he admit something?"

"No. Just wait." A few seconds later, the video zoomed in on Bruce's face. Vince had done that from the raw footage, and then captured it for Alex. The frame moved around somewhat. It tightened to a small area in the center of his face, then rose slightly.

"What I am looking at?"

"His eyes. He had a light shining in them from the camera. The pupils should be pinpricks. Instead they're dilated." Alexa looked up at him, her face a question mark. "It's a *tell*," he said. "When he was describing the interaction between this guy Whelan and Hector? The contact he was seeing, the touching, the rubbing? His eyes were dilated. That's sexual excitement. What he was describing was turning him on." Alexa went back to the video and turned it to a different angle. Yes, she could see it now.

"Wait. This is an indication he was sexually excited? How do you know this?"

"Nikki knows. She told me a while ago." He paused, shook his head, and then couldn't help smiling. The next thing just slipped out, like he was really thinking it and not saying it. "God, she fucking knows everything."

"Whoa. Nikki? You mean Dr. Jaynes?"

"Yeah, I mean…" he trailed off and felt blood rush to his cheeks as bright recognition flooded Alexa's face.

"Oh my God, you're fucking her!"

"Alexa, please."

"Shit, I'm so sorry," she said, looking mortified. "That's not what I meant I promise."

"It's fine. We're dating, yes."

"Oh my God," she said again, shaking her head. "That is…terrific."

"It was a secret for a while. Not anymore, I guess."

"How did that happen? You two were at each other's throats in court. God, this is hilarious, I'm sorry. It's like TV."

"We saw each other on the D train a few weeks after that trial," he said with a shrug. "We both got off at fifty-ninth."

"What a lovely New York story," she said, putting her hands together over her heart.

"Please stop."

"I'm sorry," she said, trying to bury her grin. "Okay, so… for now, back to this. What did Raquel say?"

"In so many words, she said she'd back me up, but that I'd better be right. The judge will give me tomorrow to figure things out, but I need to make a decision soon. Honestly I'm more worried about where the hell Connie is."

"You haven't talked to her?"

"No. I keep trying but she's not answering, probably because she's furious."

"She's not in danger," Alexa said, "I mean, is she?"

"I have no idea. I can't reach Bruce either, but I'll probably send Danny out to look for him. There's nothing we can arrest him on, but I'd like to talk to him."

CHAPTER 61

6:40 p.m.

Of the many things Connie hated about her childhood, the time she spent on airplanes, jetting between New York, Mexico City, and God knew where else was among the worst. More often than not, her parents would send her and her siblings alone, across continents in the care of nannies or flight attendants. Since then, she had suffered a recurring nightmare of dying in a plane crash and woke up just as the seat in front of her seemed to mushroom into her face. Just as the walls of the fuselage began to crumble inward, the floor buckling and disintegrating. Of course, she woke terrified but painless and alive. The lingering idea of it gripped her though, the thought of what it would feel like, even if it lasted a fraction of a second. The crush of metal and fabric and plastic and flesh. The punch.

In the end, the truth of Bruce Eldrich tore through her in exactly that way.

She had spent the rest of the afternoon driving aimlessly up and down a couple of snowy parkways in Westchester County, avoiding Alex's calls while a sense of mounting dread incubated within her. Alex, who had looked at her on the witness stand with some kind of miserable pity while he dragged her through that nightmare. Bruce didn't try to reach her until around 5:00. She ignored the first call and then a couple of texts. At 6:05 he called again. This time, she picked up.

"Connie, what the hell? Where are you?"

"I'm trying to keep from going crazy. Do you have any idea what happened to me today in court?"

"What? No, why?"

"The picture. The one you texted me, of Norman. Something wasn't right. It was from the wrong day. Jesus, Bruce, how did you do that? What the hell happened?"

"That's impossible. I took it that day."

"You couldn't have. The inspection sticker was still old. The photograph was from another day! He made me admit it, like some. . .fucking criminal!"

"Inspection sticker? What the. . ."

"You took it from inside the van. You can *see* the sticker, and it had an expiration date from the tenth of April, this year. It wasn't taken when you said it was." He was silent for a few seconds.

"Connie, I don't know how this happened. I snap pictures all the time, you know that. Is it possible I. . .screwed something up and sent a different one? I don't know, maybe."

"That's ridiculous."

"You know me with the phone! C'mon, this is me. What the hell do you think I did? Do you think I meant for this to happen?"

"I don't know what to think," she said, barely audible. "I was scared. I was humiliated. Like we don't have enough problems. Has Alex tried to call you?"

"He left a message," Bruce said. "Maybe two. I've been racing around all day. I closed the office early and sent everyone home just to get some work done."

"Are you still there?"

"Yes. For God's sake where are you?" For a split second she considered not answering him, just hanging up and racing for any point on the compass away from him. In the end, the bond they shared won out. He would have an explanation for what had happened to her today. There had to be one, he would have it, and she needed to hear it.

"I'm up around White Plains. Stay there, I'll be there in a half-hour."

CHAPTER 62

She pulled the Land Rover into the alley at the rear of the facility where they sometimes parked after hours. It was fully dark and bitter cold. She fumbled with her keys and went in through the back door, calling for Bruce as she did so. Oddly enough there were no lights on, just the glow from the fire exit signs in a couple of places.

She crossed the threshold of her darkened office and took off her coat, shaking off the cold with it. She reached with her left hand for the light switch next to the door jamb, and then for the briefest moment felt the presence of something behind her, rushing into the doorway. A second later there was an arm around her neck, tightening against her throat. From the other side, a beefy hand gripped her jaw, wrenching her head to the right. The hand gripped a blade of some kind- she saw the reddish flash of it in the glow of the fire exit sign from outside the office. The smell of the man enveloping her was familiar, earthy, and combined with a fabric softener in his shirt.

"Bruce," she said, more of a gasp. He didn't reply, but she could feel his breath against her neck. Her eyes were wide open, and in her field of vision was her favorite material possession in the entire world. She had been tempted to keep it in her own bedroom, but it seemed so at home in the office she had left it here. It was a colorfully painted Mexican wooden rocking horse, a beautiful piece of Oaxacan folk art. The horse had one black eye visible, and a bright orange bit in a curved, smiling mouth. The rocker the horse was balanced on was a shiny red. "Honey, please! What is this?"

"It's who I am," he said, a low, mean growl, as if through clenched teeth. "I'm sorry, Connie."

The folding, straight razor blade he then drew across her throat was not cold, as she strangely expected in her last seconds. It wasn't even painful, really. It felt almost like a finger, harmlessly passing across the folds of her neck. But then she felt herself open, and a glut of blood spilled down her chest. There was suddenly no air, no connection between the back of her tongue and the rest of her. There was no gasping. No screaming. She was incapable of those things. Instead, she stared straight ahead at the still, poised rocking horse, its saddle painted like a rainbow with bright pink, orange, green and red stripes. It seemed to fill her field of vision as shock eventually cradled her into darkness, sliding her feet from under her as if she was weightless. Her last emotion was not fear or anger but utter despair, salved only by bitter resignation and the thin hope that it was temporary. Then blackness overtook her, as if she was falling into the obsidian eye of the rocking horse.

CHAPTER 63

Her body become heavy in Bruce's arms and he let it go, watching her crumble to the floor in the low light. A wave of nausea and disgust, coupled with self-loathing, slid through him. Had he not killed three other people, including a child, with the same folding straight razor, he might have had the urge to vomit all over her. But as it was, his gut was as cold and quiet as a stone. He was miserable, but not sick. He looked down at her and shook his head. *None of this,* he thought. *None of this had to happen. I had it great. I had everything.*

For Bruce, with the perfect cover and an unending stream of trusting victims, getting close to young boys and doing what he wanted with them was laughably easy through HCC. It had gotten even easier over time, and he had reached a point where he could almost completely compartmentalize his activities with the boys, away from his life with Connie, his life as a man who did some really decent things day in and day out. He and Connie were never very passionate anyway. He felt no sexual attraction to her anymore but faking attraction to women in general was something he had learned to do throughout his adult life. He had found a rhythm. The boys came in and out of their lives. He chose the ones he went after carefully. Most were far too limited to express themselves, let alone complain. And anyway, he wasn't hurting them. Not really. He could have gone on indefinitely that way, quiet, occasionally satisfied. And Connie was the goose that laid the golden eggs.

But then he had met Nick Whelan, ambitious, shameless, Nick with his big ideas and keys to a whole new world. Nick had talked him into stepping things up.

Before that, though, Nick had seen right through him. He was the first person Bruce had ever felt exposed to as a someone who liked boys the way he did. Nick figured it out and had let it show, dropping innuendo and making bad jokes at first. That had been disturbing until it became obvious Nick was the same way. He had been drawn to HCC for the same reasons Bruce had. Eventually Nick broke the ice, suggesting some websites they could check out one very drunk night at his house in Larchmont. Then, after a while, Nick was opening up more and more, and challenging Bruce to do the same.

It's okay. You're not alone.

The idea, for Bruce, of confessing who he was- what he wanted- was terrifying. Every cultural and survival instinct he had fought against it. The idea was also liberating, though, and strangely comforting. When you got down to it, no one wanted to feel like a freak. With Nick, and then the world of guys Nick had introduced him to online, he had found something like a community. Even better, it was a community he could approach, mingle within, skirt the edges of, or walk away from altogether if he wanted to.

From there, though, the temptation had increased to start doing some new things. The men he and Nick were getting to know offered some tantalizing material. Picture files, video, even kids you could arrange to meet live. But these men wanted material in return. Giving in to that temptation, the urge to get more, see more, do more, was what destroyed it all.

It had made him a killer also, although curiously that hadn't bothered him as much as he thought it might. The first one, Isoli, was a scumbag anyway, and he'd been passed out on a bed in a shitty motel room. Cutting him was like cutting a doll that bled. There was shock, then an emotional numbness, but it faded quickly. Nick Whelan had been even easier. He and Nick had been drinking all night and Nick ended up passed out on the beach, Lido Beach near where he had grown up. Cutting his throat was as easy as reaching over and drawing the blade across.

As for Hector, Bruce had come upon him asleep in the tub. *And I did that*, he thought in that moment with the razor ready, staring one last time at Hector, beautiful and limp against the smooth surface of the tub. *I conditioned him this way.*

The lollipops had worked. Over a short period of time, Bruce had made Hector as compliant a lapdog on the offer of a simple piece of candy, albeit one that would flood him with a sense of euphoria and relief he had surely never experienced before. First, he had offered the lollipops in the living room. Then with Hector swooning, Bruce had led him into the bathroom and eventually into the tub. He had, as Connie insisted, just the right touch with the boy. He could also lightly accentuate the pain Hector was dealing with as well. A twist of the arm, a yelp from Hector, a string of apologies, and then another lollipop.

It had been tricky, at first, to get the routine started. There was no telling exactly how long he'd be out of it once he fed Hector a laced lollipop, so he had to avoid times when Joseliz was coming over, and those were annoyingly frequent. Norman, though, wasn't much of an impediment at all. Bruce learned this quickly as he and Nick tracked Norman's movements over a few months. Norman would disappear for hours, even overnight, when he was supposed to be watching the kid. And he was almost laughably predictable. When he wasn't at work or at the marina, he was in front of the shitty tire shop on Jerome Avenue, talking trash or just sitting in his car, staring at nothing and waiting for orders. Bruce, if he timed it right, had the run of the place. After a while, he could bring Nick with him. That was the plan, of course. It was also the beginning of the end.

It had occurred to Bruce lately how the entire year had been a series of what looked like points of no return. First there was Corey Timmons, that weasel in Vermont, busted with the pictures and video he and Nick had created with Hector. Timmons would fold like a map and give them up in no time- Bruce knew this even from a distance. His first thought was getting to Timmons, but that would be nearly impossible in jail. But then Nick was swearing they were okay. They were insulated. Timmons didn't know who Nick was, he assured him. Nick was in control of the situation, blah, blah.

And maybe they *were* insulated. Maybe they could have just gone on, or maybe Bruce could have put the brakes on things and gone back to square one. But that wasn't certain, and anyway Nick knew too much. Bruce started to feel an itch. Isoli was the first attempt at scratching it. Isoli had sold him the laced lollipops directly so there was a reason to get rid of him. But mostly? It was an excuse to do it and see how well he tolerated it. Once Bruce realized he tolerated it just fine, Nick was next.

It should have stopped there, after Nick. There should have been no reason to kill Hector-- he was even less able to communicate than most of the kids Bruce went after. But then there was Joseliz Perez and whatever she was drawing out of Hector about the lollipops and the tub and God knew what else. Thanks to her ambitious little experiments, Hector had to go.

Well, that was a kindness, really. The kid was a cursed bag of bones no one gave a fuck about, least of all his miserable father. And Norman, of course, was the guy Bruce would help them pin it on. Norman was an asshole anyway. He deserved it.

That left the decision to try to kill Joseliz herself, which turned out to be the only one he really regretted. In a way he blamed that one on the gun, the .45 he had found in Ryan Isoli's coat. It was beautiful, with a pearl handle carved with Isoli's initials, "RI." Bruce hadn't handled a gun in years, but he got used to the idea quickly. After that, the idea of killing Joseliz, just dropping her out of spite as much as anything else, began to gnaw at him. Then, once she started talking to the law, it felt like an even more justifiable idea. And then that had gotten hopelessly fucked up also. The Irish cop, Regan, turned out to have a quick step and some crazy instinct for bravery.

So here he was, at last, with Connie. Poor little rich girl Connie, whose grandparents hung out with Frida Kahlo and owned whole mountain ranges in Mexico. Connie, to whom his instincts had led him as the perfect fit. It had been so easy to get close to her. He had the ready-made story about the imaginary, retarded kid brother, the same one he had sold to Alex Greco. Alex had lapped it up, like most people did, but at least he had the excuse of not knowing Bruce well. Connie should have seen through it at some point, but she never questioned it. His family was long gone by the time he met her, but still. She never asked where the brother was buried. She never asked for details. But then again, Connie didn't care nearly as much about people as she wanted them to believe. That, Bruce knew, was the dark secret about her. Connie cared about ideas. People were vehicles for her big ideas, like lettuce is for a dressing you really like.

In any event, it was over now. The last, final fuck-up had been the goddam photo he had sent to Connie. He had, somehow, forgotten about the inspection thingy in the window. Who the hell looks for that, anyway? He had taken that picture some other day that week, he couldn't remember now. The lighting was basically the same. Everything was shadowed under the train tracks so it usually looked the same no matter the weather. And God knew Norman always looked the same. He even dressed the same most days.

He looked down at Connie, a blob of hair and bulk with a growing corona of blood spreading outward toward her desk and that stupid rocking horse she kept in the corner. He thanked her silently for what she had at least left him, because he was on the run now, and probably would be forever. Compared to what she had access to, the money he could put his hands on in the office was a pittance. It would get him started, though, and he had to move fast.

In the office safe he found around $85,000. There was more at the house they shared, out on the water near the Whitestone Bridge, but he didn't want to stop there. No one would find her until morning. He could take her car, at least through the night. In a few hours he could get hundreds of miles north, way up into the Adirondacks or Vermont. Then ditch it as remotely as he could manage. A car like that, you could take off-road for a while. Things were yet unplanned after that point, but instincts had carried him this far.

He grabbed her coat and purse from the floor, wiped his hands on the coat and then curled it up under his arm along with the purse. He gently pushed open the back door to the facility with her Land Rover keys in hand and smiled as the big vehicle appeared, like a sentient horse awaiting its rider in the dimly lit alley. He clicked the key fob. The side lights blinked and the interior lit up. He opened the door and threw the coat and the purse in. Then he felt a stunning blow to his head, impossibly heavy and sharp. The world swam out of focus. He hit the pavement a second later, the chiming of the open-door alarm the last thing in his conscious mind.

CHAPTER 64

"So how come he doesn't take the car?" Pascale asked Danny, his breath announcing itself in little clouds in the freezing, early morning air. Like Danny, he was slipping into the present tense as he tried to put together the scene in front of him in his cop's mind. Chris Pascale was another Four-Four detective, just assigned to the precinct's newest murder case, that of Constanza Morrell, the body of whom had been discovered by a cleaning crew about an hour before. Pascale was built like a fireplug, about five-foot-four and bald. He and Danny were watching the crime scene unit guys painstakingly inspect Connie's Range Rover in the cold, morning sunlight. The entire area was marked off and crawling with law enforcement. Already in an evidence bag and carefully sealed was a cell phone, found in the alley under the vehicle itself.

"I don't know," Danny said. "He panics, I guess, at the last minute. Runs instead of taking off in it."

"He throws her shit in first, though," Pascale said. He scratched his neck, a neck so large he owned no dress shirts he could actually button. His tie instead, as always, was sloppily knotted around a stained, open collar. "Her purse and her coat, and shit."

"Okay, so he throws her shit in, but then he hears something. He gives up on the car, slams the door, and runs off with the keys."

"But he drops his phone? And keeps going?"

"Maybe he didn't hear it fall. It's happened to me."

"What the fuck, Lopez?" Pascale said, his face knotted into a comical, unbelieving look. He bent down and rapped his hand on the concrete. "It's got a hard case!"

"Look, this isn't my goddam murder," Danny said. "What the fuck do I know? Maybe he doesn't have time to reach for it."

"Nothin', that's what you know," Pascale said, grinning. He gestured to the Land Rover a few feet away. "Nah, man. There's something else. He gets in the fuckin' car, that's what he does if he's sane. He goes straight down the alley. There's nothing in the way, see?"

"Yeah, well there's still a car here, so. . ." Pascale cut Danny off with a backhanded slap to his stomach.

"What the fuck?"

"Don't move," Pascale said. He called out to the crime scene guys. "Nobody move, okay? Everybody be still for a second." Everyone obeyed, and then Pascale got on his hands and knees. "Shit," he said after a few seconds. "Danny get down here."

"What is it?"

"One-a-you," Pascale said to the crime scene team, "get a camera over here." He pointed triumphantly to what he had seen, sprouting forward from the driver's side door. There were two parallel tracks, faint, but visible, cutting through the dust and detritus of the alley floor.

"Son-of-a-bitch," Danny said, shaking his head. "Good eye, Chris."

"What is it?" a crime scene tech asked, readying the camera.

"He never made it into the car," Pascale said, looking up and smiling. "Fuckin' asshole got slugged, right here. Someone dragged him away."

Alex had all but given up on trying to reach Oscar. He had left a message with the pizza guy on 161st around 3:00 p.m., and then another one around 6:00. Going a back a third time, he figured, would just look weird. Moreover, he was probably starting to make the poor guy in the shop feel nervous. Then around 7:30, still at his desk, he got a call on his direct line.

"Come downstairs," an unfamiliar, young male voice said. "Out front, to the right." The caller hung up and Alex stared at the phone for a few seconds. Then he threw on his overcoat and got moving. He walked out of the building, pulling his coat around him against the cold, and turned to the right. A few seconds later a young, Hispanic male in a hoodie and a down jacket approached him and pressed a non-descript, black flip phone into his hand.

"Answer it when it rings," was all he said, and then continued up the block a few paces, eventually standing still with his hands in his pockets. Alex fished for his cigarettes, walked closer to the building, and lit up. Above him, the sky was clear. A few stars, like tight pinpricks, poked through the yellowish tint of the city lights. A minute or two later the phone rang.

"What do you want?" Oscar asked.

"Bruce Eldrich. Where is he?"

"What makes you think I know?"

"I know it was your people who grabbed him. What I don't know is how you figured it out so fast." There was silence on the other end for several seconds.

"The dead guys you showed me the other night," he said finally. "I checked up on it. I know all about Nicholas Whelan, including how he helped drug and torture my cousin. Which, by the way, you didn't tell me about." For a moment Alex thought about asking Oscar how he knew any of this, what Whelan had done or what had been discovered about Hector, but then thought better of it. There were methods and there were contacts, and Oscar had both.

"I couldn't tell you about that. I wouldn't have wanted to anyway. But if you know, then you know there are other guys Whelan and Eldrich were in touch with. We need Eldrich alive to get to them."

"What makes you think he's still alive?"

"We wouldn't still be talking if he wasn't. And I know it's your decision. Please. He needs to be found and debriefed."

"They've got everything they need. Cops have been at his house all day. We left his phone in the alley for God's sake."

"Did you know about the woman? Connie Morrell?" Alex asked. Again, there was silence on the other end.

"No, we didn't. But we couldn't have helped her anyway. He came out alone, that's all we knew. That's another thing he should be paying for. Let it go, Alex. Your case is over."

"I fought to find your cousin's killer. I fought for Hector's memory. I'm still fighting for it. But it's not just him. There are a million other Hectors out there. Believe me, I know. Please." A few seconds passed, and then the call clicked off. Alex flipped it closed and looked over to the young man who had given it to him. He walked over, took the phone back without a word, and disappeared around the corner.

CHAPTER 65

Thursday, December 8

"Alex, can I have a moment?" he asked, poking his head in the door. Alex looked up from his desk and his eyes grew wide. It was Tony Washington, the District Attorney himself.

"Tony? Of course, come in." He had never been fully comfortable calling the DA by his first name, not in an office of that size and to a man with his gravitas in the community. Tony insisted on it, though. He was a man of deep personal decency and almost curious humility. "I would have come upstairs."

"I need the exercise," Tony said, with a tight, almost mischievous smile. His eyes twinkled above it. Tony Washington was not a large or imposing man. He was maybe five-foot-six, thin, and with a slightly crooked appearance, as if he was favoring one leg over the other, which he actually had been for several years. His skin was dark and his face lined. His hair was tight, curly and mostly white. He was, as always, beautifully but simply dressed in a charcoal gray suit, a light blue shirt and a red tie.

"It's a tragedy about Connie Morrell," he said. His face was placid, his eyes soft. "How are you doing?"

"I'm fine, sir, thank you. I just hope I haven't let you down."

"You've never let me down, Alex," he said. "I've been briefed on what happened. It sounds like you exposed something quite necessary, through Connie. It was unpleasant, to say the least, but necessary."

"I've second-guessed myself quite a bit," Alex said. "I could have given Rick the information. We could have asked the judge to allow the cross-examination to be re-opened. That way it wouldn't have been me, drowning my own case."

"True," Tony said. "But I suspect you felt a duty to uncover what you knew through a witness you originally called. Our job is to do justice, not win cases. It appears you guaranteed that in the moment. It was a little unorthodox, admittedly. But I wouldn't second guess it."

"I'll try not to. Thank you."

"I understand NYPD found a gun in a bag Bruce Eldrich had with him, in Connie's car. And that it likely matches the one that killed Sean Regan."

"It appears so, yes, sir. We've collected quite a bit of evidence against Mr. Eldrich, actually. Unfortunately, he's still at large."

"Indeed" he said, wrinkling his brow. "Possibly abducted from the crime scene, I'm told." He shook his head, then nodded toward the newspaper on Alex's desk. It was the day's *New York Post* dropped off by Alexa earlier and open to the local news section where the headline read '*Courtroom Shocker: DA Tanks Case Of Accused Killer Dad.*' "Well, it's giving the press something to focus on. Always nice when we can help them out, don't you think?"

"Yes, sir."

"They raise you polite down there, don't they?" he said, getting up to leave. "Virginia."

"Oh, you mean the 'sir' thing? Yeah, I guess so. It's an old habit."

"Jonah told me it's how you'd be," Tony said, smiling mischievously again. "It's served you well here. Don't let anyone tell you different." He paused at the door. "Open or closed?"

CHAPTER 66

Alex finally clicked off his wipers once they started dragging across the battered windshield. The rain had tapered off. Now it was just damp, cold and dark on the streets. Oscar had called him a couple of hours before. He had given a time, and the description of an alley, east of a cross street near the 149th street "six" subway stop. That was it.

Alex rolled down the window as he pulled into the alley, making a narrow pass around a couple of city trash bins and a busted pallet on the ground below a fire escape. He slowed to a crawl and then came to a stop about mid-way through the passage, peering ahead for any sign of life. There were a couple of windowless, steel doors on either side, but none opened. The alley smelled like an old, wet blanket.

"Turn your lights off, Alex," Oscar said softly. Alex whipped his head to the left, startled. Oscar stepped out of the shadow of a dumpster and now stood with his hands in the pockets of the same black jacket. For once, he was alone.

"Wasn't expecting you right there," Alex said as he turned his lights off. Oscar said nothing, then slowly produced a folded piece of paper from his jacket pocket. He slipped the paper between two fingers and passed it through the driver's window. Alex looked at it for a second, then took it and unfolded it. It was an address, scrawled in blue ink, and then the words "basement storage room" below it.

"You'll find him there."

"He's there now?"

"I got guys nearby. He's there."

"Okay," Alex said. "I've got to make some calls."

"Listen, I don't want to say this, but I have to. If my name ever comes up, it's not good for you. You have to know that."

"This is an anonymous tip. I'm just passing it on. But you know that already. Or you wouldn't be here."

"Maybe. Just keep that in mind. And there's no need to bring an army. He's tied up. And he's hurt, but not critically. He got a little roughed up."

"Anyone with him?"

"No, he's alone. Have them bust the door down, for good measure."

"Thank you," Alex said quietly after a long pause. He looked over at Oscar, who was looking out the mouth of the alley.

"I didn't do it for you."

"Regardless, I told you I won't forget it. I won't."

"You won't be here long enough for it to matter," Oscar said, almost cracking a smile and looking over at him. "Guys like you eventually go home."

"This is home."

Oscar looked at him for a few seconds longer, then turned and walked back into the shadows. "So long, Alex."

CHAPTER 67

"Ladies and gentleman," Judge Moore said as the jurors sat in their places. The courtroom was packed, many of them reporters. "As you may or may not have detected by this time, the case you were called upon to decide has been resolved. There's no need to tell you how or why, but I suspect you may receive some details from other sources in the near future. For now, I'm dismissing you with the deep thanks of the court. I know I speak for Mr. Greco, Mr. Gonzalez and Mr. Ruiz as well. Good day to you all, and happy holidays."

"All rise as the jury exits," her bailiff called. Once the jurors departed, Judge Moore looked over at Alex.

"Mr. Greco, do the people have a motion?"

"The people move to dismiss the charges, your honor," Alex said simply. He had anticipated the words would sound somehow more august as he spoke them.

"Mr. Melendez, any objection? The dismissal covers the indictment and clearly it's with prejudice."

"No objection, your honor," Rick said. He looked relieved and took off his glass to rub them with a handkerchief.

"Mr. Ruiz, do you understand what's happening here?" she asked him. Norman, who hadn't reacted in any visible way to Alex's motion, gave an insouciant shrug. His borrowed suit was slightly rumpled and a looked a little large on his frame.

"Yeah, I get it," he said. He looked over at Alex with the same, mean, predatory gaze. "The whole time. They were wrong."

"Mr. Ruiz is just anxious to be released, your honor," Rick said. "We thank the court."

"There's no requirement that Mr. Ruiz act graciously, Mr. Melendez," Judge Moore said. "As long as he's basically civil to this court. I will note for the record, though, that I believe you served your client admirably. And in addition, I believe and it should be stated that Mr. Greco, the District Attorney's Office and the NYPD acted with integrity and restraint in this case. A few people worked very hard to ensure the defendant a fair trial, and ultimately, as far as it appears, a just outcome." She looked again at Norman, who stared back at her dispassionately. "You'll be processed for release today at Rikers Island, Mr. Ruiz. I'm sorry for your terrible loss and the resulting circumstances you've endured. Good luck to you. This court is adjourned."

"This," Rick said, gripping Alex's hand after Norman was led out and the judge had disappeared into her robing room, "was one for the books."

"Congratulations," Alex said.

"You deserve it as much as I do. But I'm sorry about Connie Morrell. Really sorry."

"You and me both," Alex said. He looked away for a

moment. "I hate what she had to endure in here, with me, on the last day of her life."

"I know. Still, it was the right thing to do."

"I did it for a mean bastard."

"True, but that doesn't make it any less right. Where's Bruce Eldrich, speaking of mean bastards?"

"NYPD turned him over to US marshals. He was a little banged up when they found him, but he's talking to the ICAC guys. We'll get him back for the prosecution of Sean Regan's murder. After that he'll rot in federal custody I guess." Out of the corner of his eye, Alex saw Rolando Garcia, gathering his coat and scarf, and excused himself. "Mr. Garcia," he called out. Rolando turned and smiled.

"Thank you for everything," he said. "On behalf of my family, such as it is."

"I owe you an apology," Alex said. "Wait here one moment." He dug through a file on the prosecution table and returned with a manila envelope. "I know we talked about why I didn't call you as a witness in this case."

"Of course," he said. "I was afraid it would have been me they suspected. I was going to avoid even watching, because of that."

"You were fine," Alex said. "The fact is, I was being cynical in not calling you, to talk about Hector and to identify him. To bear witness to him. I regret that, and I hope you'll forgive me."

"I understood," he said, looking bewildered that Alex would assume otherwise. "I understood completely."

"Remember I told you, you were still under subpoena?"

"Yes. But I assumed that was because his attorney might have wanted to put me on the stand. I had no alibi. I still don't. There are times I swear, hours pass and I don't know exactly where I've been. I react to my environment. I stop at crosswalks. But I...lose track." Alex smiled warmly and handed him the envelope.

"These are date and time stamped," he said. Rolando gave him a questioning look, and then drew out a series of photographs. They were taken at Woodlawn Cemetery, between 2:30 and 4:00 p.m. on April 7th. In them, pretty clearly, was the figure of Rolando Garcia, a little bent looking and gray from head to feet, walking along the manicured paths between the graves with his hands in his pockets.

"This is me?"

"That's you," Alex said. "There are cameras all over Woodlawn. I had Danny take a look at their security data last week. There you are, Mr. Garcia. Almost four miles from Hector's home, and all through the time of his death."

"But...how did you know? I didn't even know. I didn't remember."

"You told me, back in June. You like to walk around up there. You like the stillness. So, I took a shot, figured maybe that's where you were. I just wish I had done it sooner."

"The stillness," Rolando said, barely above a whisper as if that's all he had heard. He shook his head, then gave a dark little chuckle. "Yes. Among the dead. Isn't that sad?"

"Whatever it is, I know it well," Alex said. "Good luck to you." He turned and saw Alexa and Danny in the back of the courtroom, clapping slowly and quietly.

"Yankee Tavern?" Alex asked as he reached them. It was a bar near the stadium frequented by ADA's and cops. He gave Alexa a hug.

"Not today. We're going to Martinelli's in the city," Danny said. Alex raised his eyebrows. Martinelli's was a classic, wood and brass steak joint on the Upper West Side, definitely a better class of place then he was used to when palling around with cops and fellow prosecutors.

"Pretty fancy for a Bronx crew," he said.

"It was Sean's favorite restaurant," Danny said. "Let's go and raise a glass to him."

"Rick, what are you up to?" Alexa asked him. "We'd love for you to join us, after your media throng is over. They're waiting, by the way."

"Gotta get to know my wife and kid again," Rick said with a tired smile. "Next time I beat you all, I promise, drinks are on me." He slipped into his overcoat, gave Alex one more respectful nod, and walked out to where the press waited.

"You were right," Alex said to Danny. "From the beginning."

"Eh, he's still an asshole," Danny said. He winked at Alexa. "Anyway, I changed my mind. Doesn't count."

"It counted for him," Alex said, gesturing toward the door Norman had left through. He paused for a moment to collect himself, feeling a sudden wave of emotion course through him. Nikki had warned him something like that might happen. It was fatigue, and a major adrenaline release.

"You okay, hon?" Alexa asked. She rubbed his arm. "It's a good day, Alex. You did the right thing."

"Yeah," he said after a few seconds. He wiped his eyes with a thumb and forefinger. "But there's still an innocent kid, a decent woman and a really good cop, dead in the ground. All I did was lose a case in the wake of all that."

"Sometimes that's as good as it gets," she said. "Come on, let's go. And call your girlfriend. We want to hear that story, too."

CHAPTER 68

Monday, December 19
Alexandria, Virginia

Seated across from him at the old coffee shop, Bleekers, below the courthouse, Kevin Crane wasn't sure what to make of Alex's face. It had been the same since Kevin had come down to meet him, a meeting he didn't expect, but didn't mind obliging when Alex called, saying he was in town for the day and needed to talk. Maybe Alex wanted to just say for sure he wasn't going to be an issue in next year's election. He had a lot to hide, after all, and between the dismissal in his big case and whatever rattling he'd experienced from the probing investigator, maybe Alex knew it was time to throw in the towel. That was agreeable to Kevin, but now it wasn't clear at all what was brewing behind Alex's deep-set eyes. He was smiling, sort of. But it was more like a smirk. A satisfied, mean smirk.

"Thanks for coming down," Alex said, in a confident, almost conspiratorial tone. He winked, and Kevin's brow knitted. There was coffee in front of both of them, and Kevin took a sip of his.

"Sure. What's this about?"

"It's about the guy you sent to New York after my girl-friend," Alex said, shaping his hands around his coffee cup with his fingertips touching. "The guy who threatened her while she was caring for a four-year old child." Kevin's eyes grew wide, and inwardly he cursed it. He, like Alex, had worked enough cases to know what a "gotcha" moment looked like, and he had just given Alex one.

"It wasn't what you think it was," he said, abandoning trying to pretend he wasn't involved with sending the guy up there. He cursed inwardly again. He hadn't heard anything from Gordon for a couple of weeks, and had a dim feeling he had sold out. Probably to Jonah Schwartz.

"Of course, it is."

"It's not. Okay, so maybe a guy was sent to ask a couple of well-placed questions. So what? The guy was *supposed* to be obvious, Alex. I knew he wouldn't get anywhere with you, or the psychologist. It was posturing. Look, maybe I've got orders to follow. Believe it or not, I'm still looking out for you."

"Stop scheming, Kevin. Scheming's not what you do well. Sending thugs to scare women and children—that's your strong suit." Kevin froze, then frowned and shook his head.

"You know what? I know you never liked me. I don't really care. You think I've been on an errand, so be it. The point is, you're finished here. It's good you remember it."

"I was finished here the day my son died. And I'm not coming back. I'm catching a train in about an hour."

"So...go, then," Kevin said, his eyes wandering helpless-ly around the table. He was utterly unprepared for this, or most other direct confrontations. Kevin was a back-door kind of a guy.

"Now, when you go back up? Tell Steve I got his message." He set his cup on the next table, then knit his fingers together in front of him. "Tell him he's got what he wants, and his little fiefdom is secure. But not another word to anyone. No more rumors. No more hints or innuendo. And hear me now, Kevin. If I hear anything else about my time here or why I left, you'll pay for it. Both of you, but mostly you."

"You've lost your mind."

"Not yet. There's still a lot in here." Alex tapped his forehead. "I spent ten years with the two of you in that office. We were all there in the beginning, lining up to impress Craig, like dutiful soldiers, day and night. I hated it. I missed my son, and I had no idea how little time I'd have with him. But I saw plenty of things. Things Steve— and you— wouldn't want me to repeat. The receptionist from our first year? Steve was married when he was banging her. You and Tina whats-her-face from Cincinnati? Those pills in the evidence bag that went missing..."

"This is all garbage," Kevin said, shaking his head. "A bunch of rumors. No one would even care."

"Take your chances with that," Alex said. Then he shrugged. "Or, maybe that won't be what I do. Maybe I'll just come to you, personally. I've met friends in my new life I can bring with me. Or send your way." At this, Kevin physically reacted, gripping his cup as if he was hiding behind it. Then he licked his lips and looked around the coffee shop, quiet in the post-docket call rush. There were a couple of students on laptops, and one or two bored looking lawyers going over files. He looked back at Alex, who hadn't moved and still wore that excruciating, dangerous grin.

"Seriously. Are you crazy?"

"I said my life here ended when my kid died on a concrete floor. That's true. A part of me died too, Kevin. The part that gives a shit, mostly. Don't test me. You'll find I have fewer limits nowadays." Kevin stared at him for a few seconds, then nodded slowly, as if something was at last making sense.

"The Bronx," he said finally, almost spitting it out. He shook his head in mock disgust. "You belong there, you know that?"

"I do. And I'm goddam proud of it." With that, he swatted Kevin's cup with the flick of three fingers, sending it skipping forward and splashing coffee, with Kevin recoiling behind it. "So long, Kevin."

ABOUT THE AUTHOR

Roger Canaff is a widely known child protection and anti-violence against women advocate, legal expert, author, and public speaker. He has devoted his legal career to the eradication of violence against women and children, first as a prosecutor in historic Alexandria, Virginia, then as a Special Victims ADA in the Bronx, and as Deputy Chief of the New York State Attorney General's Office Sex Offender Management Unit. Most recently, he was employed as a U.S. Army civilian, serving as a Highly Qualified Expert training and advising military prosecutors on sexual assault and other special victims cases. With over 20 years' experience, he has prosecuted and consulted on cases involving sexual and physical abuse of children and adolescents, sexual assault against adults, and crimes against the elderly and persons with disabilities.

Mr. Canaff continues to provide training to attorneys, medical experts, law enforcement officers, victim advocates and the general public on all issues related to the investigation and prosecution of child abuse and sexual assault. He teaches law, comments on special victims issues for major networks, and is the author of three novels. He lives and works in New York City.